D0469354

Skin Deep

NO LONGER PROPERTY OF
ANYTHINK LIBRARIES/
RANGEVIEW LIBRARY DISTRICT

Skin Deep

A SIOBHAN O'BRIEN MYSTERY

SUNG J. WOO

The following is a work of fiction. Names, characters, places, events and incidents are either the product of the author's imagination or used in an entirely fictitious manner. Any resemblance to actual persons, living or dead, is entirely coincidental.

Copyright © 2020 by Sung J. Woo
Cover and jacket design by Mimi Bark

ISBN 978-1-947993-95-2
eISBN: 978-1-951709-13-6
Library of Congress Control Number: 2020937779

First trade paperback edition July 2020 by Agora Books
An imprint of Polis Books, LLC
www.PolisBooks.com

For Dianne, Heather, and Sarah
three sisters who welcomed me into the fold
and Dawn
who showed me what it means to serve with a full heart

When *you are old and grey and full of sleep,*
And nodding by the fire, take down this book,
And slowly read, and dream of the soft look
Your eyes had once, and of their shadows deep

—William Butler Yeats, "When You Are Old"

1

My assignment this morning was Dr. Henry Michaelson, who was getting out of his white BMW with a box of donuts and two cups of coffee in a paper tray—treats for his girlfriend and son. He walked across the courtyard of the apartment complex with a faint smile.

Crouched behind a prickly bush, I trained my 300mm zoom on his unsuspecting face.

Click. Click.

Taking photographs of people in secret is capturing a kind of innocence. Which is ironic, because more often than not, the images serve as confirmation of guilt.

As Michaelson disappeared through the building's entrance, I caught a whiff of eggs and bacon. My stomach growled. Surveillance makes the tummy grow fonder—for food, that is. I slipped the camera into my backpack and made my way to the shiny diner on the corner. Autumn chill had firmly descended here in upstate New York. It's the time of the year when I feel like I'm either wearing too many layers or not enough, there's no in between. Today, I was a wool scarf away from being comfortable.

On the weekends he had his son, Michaelson wasn't supposed to have overnight female company, yet here he was, thinking he was being smart by hiding out at his girlfriend's apartment instead. Michaelson might lose custody of his boy, and I felt bad about that. In the three days Ed and I had been casing him, he took good care of his son, taking him to the movies, the park, the mall. But he wasn't paying us; his pissed-off ex-wife was.

A bell on a string rang when I opened the door of the Tick-Tock Diner. A rush of warm air and the buzz of eaters greeted me. I'd passed by this place a few times since their grand opening last month but hadn't had the occasion to stop in. It didn't look all that different from its former incarnation, Time to Eat Diner. Like before, a gigantic round clock behind the counter grinned at me with oversized googly eyes. The new owner didn't want to spend money to redecorate so they kept the same temporal theme.

"Just you, miss?" the host asked. He was fat and jolly and was wearing a pretty obvious hairpiece that made his head resemble a Brazilian nut.

"Just me," I said.

He led me to a cozy two-seater booth by the windows. The faux leather upholstery was cracked along the edges and taped at one corner with black duct tape, but it was still cushy and comfortable. Coffee, two eggs over easy, rye toast, home fries. If I could eat breakfast every meal, I would. I cleaned my plate before the waitress had a chance to refill my cup.

"Hungry, were we?" she said.

"Very," I said, and handed her my credit card.

She took it and was about to step away but stopped.

"See-ohb-haan?" she asked, reading my name off the card.

"That's what it looks like, but it actually sounds like Show-vahn. It's Irish."

"Like your last name, O'Brien," the waitress said. "You're Irish?"

"Why wouldn't I be?" I asked.

The waitress laughed.

"I'll be back with your receipt, lassie."

2

Nestled in the valley between the Catskill Mountains, the city of Athena is a picture of fall perfection from the second week in October until Election Day. Some people prefer the flowers of spring, full of promise and warmth, but I've always been attracted to the quiet fires of fall, the final burst of color before winter.

On Buffalo Street, a bearded crooner busked by the water fountain. I threw five dollars into his guitar case and clapped when he finished his song about getting stung by a bee ("Bee, bee, why, why?"). At the end of the block, I entered the white-brick building and rode the elevator to the third floor.

I was already excited for my plan to come in later in the week and surprise my boss Ed with a fresh coat of paint on the door of our office. Ed was not a fan of surprises, but I figured this was not a bad one, since I didn't plan on changing the color or anything. It was a heavy wooden door with a large translucent square window, the name of the firm stenciled on the glass: ED BAKER INVESTIGATIVE AGENCY. The door was painted black with dark gold trim, a reassuring combination of professionalism and class. Friday was my second anniversary. Ed probably didn't even remember—or care if he did—but I wanted to express my gratitude. Instead of hiring someone with more experience (any, truth be told), he'd taken a chance on me, a laid-off newspaper reporter who wrote restaurant and movie reviews and occasional human interest pieces, neither Woodward nor

Bernstein.

Our office wasn't much, a Keurig sitting on a wide filing cabinet in the back and three desks, one for Ed, one for me, and one for Stacy, our part-time bookkeeper. Ed had the biggest one, with two wooden armchairs in front of it for clients. Behind him was the only window, and he often stared out at the city below and the verdant landscape beyond when he thought through a case.

I placed my purse on my desk.

"Good with Michaelson," I said, removing my jacket. "Got the photos."

Ed's chair was, as usual, facing the window, and his head was tilted in an angle that suggested he'd nodded off.

"Ed?"

I walked over to his desk. Slumped in his chair, he clenched his left arm with his right hand. I placed my fingers on his wrist, but I already knew I wouldn't feel a pulse. His skin was cold. The expression that remained frozen on his face was somewhere between a grimace and a smile, but only for the next thirty-six hours. Everyone knows about rigor mortis, but few realize that the body goes slack a day or so later.

The way Ed had grabbed his arm suggested heart attack. He was on medication for high blood pressure, and for type 2 diabetes, too. He was not the healthiest person I knew. A few crumbs of his half-eaten glazed donut were embedded in his mustache, so I brushed them off. Now that my assessment of the scene was complete, I stood next to him with my hand on his shoulder. I saw what he saw last, the bronzed beauty of the mountains in the distance, and I wept.

3

One of the more popular stories I'd written when I used to be journalist with the *Athena Times* was a profile of the funeral home in town, and in the week I spent with the Lesters, I saw a dozen bodies rolled into the basement and sat through three services. I witnessed cremation, embalming, and of course, the preparation for an open casket viewing, which meant dressing the body and applying makeup. You'd be surprised at the amount of primping the men receive—in many cases, it's more than women because women tend to take better care of themselves and look fairly fabulous even dead.

They'd done a nice job with Ed, even shaped his unruly eyebrows. In black suit and red tie, surrounded by folds of white silk, he looked at peace. I'd never seen Ed in any kind of formalwear, as his dress code for work was a button-down shirt and a pair of faded jeans, so it was odd to see him so prim and proper. It was almost like it wasn't him at all, but of course, it was.

The Lester family owned both Athena Funeral Home and Athena Ambulance Service. The oldest joke in town was that maybe they took their time to get to an emergency so both of their businesses would benefit. I must've heard that joke a dozen times during my visits for my newspaper piece, and yet each and every time, Gwen Lester smiled, shrugged, and said, "We're here to serve the citizens of Athena during their greatest times of need." I was glad she was taking care of Ed, because there was no one else. Ed had a brother in Akron, but he was blind and couldn't be convinced to travel for the funeral. That was it for his family—his parents were long gone and so were an uncle and an aunt, and he'd never married.

Including me, only six people attended Ed's service. I knew them all, as three were recent clients and the other two were Keeler, an Athena cop who sometimes helped us with our cases, and our bookkeeper, Stacy.

"I kept telling him to stop eating those Cinnabons for breakfast," Stacy said.

"But they're so good," I said, and that got her do a half chuckle, half cry.

"Gonna miss the big guy," Keeler said.

"I miss him already," I said.

The service took less than fifteen minutes, and that was including me going up to the podium and muttering a few words of remembrance. I hadn't prepared anything, just said the usual things—a fine man, a great boss, etc. I'd only known him for a couple of years, but I'd spent more time with him than anyone else in the room, probably combined, and arriving at that fact made me sadder than anything.

Stacy, Keeler, and I went out for drinks afterwards, but my mind drifted after a couple of rum and cokes. What the hell was I going to do now? I'd spent a couple of years as an apprentice to a private detective. I just got my license, the guy at the bureau had let me take the exam early thanks to a favor he owed Ed, but there was so much to this business that I knew nothing about. I could find another job with another agency, but which? I remembered a friend from a long time ago telling me that a shitty job with a good boss was better than a good job with a shitty boss. For the last two years, I had it great on both fronts, and now I was about to have neither.

Did I mention I turned forty a week ago? I don't care what they say, forty is not the new thirty. Forty is two drinks maximum, a balky knee, and lower back pain.

4

When I arrived at the office next morning, a man in a suit was waiting outside the door.

"Robert Schafer." He handed me his card. "I was Ed's attorney. My condolences."

He took a seat in one of the client chairs, so I sat behind Ed's desk. It was weird to see the office from this vantage point. My eyes kept drifting to my own empty desk. Ed's was just enormous, one of these steel jobs from the fifties. It'd probably taken a team of weight-lifters to move it in.

"Ms. O'Brien?" Schafer said. "Did you hear what I said?"

I apologized. Schafer said he understood my distractedness, but that didn't temper his impatience. He now spoke louder and slower than necessary, making me feel slightly stupid.

"Ed left the firm to you. Not *you* specifically, but to whomever was his partner, or if not a partner, then an assistant. You qualify as the latter."

"I *own* this agency?"

"Yes, but I'm afraid it isn't much of an inheritance. The only asset Ed had was his car, worth about four thousand at book value. There are presently no sizable debts, so the business is not leveraged in any way, but there isn't much left in the operating bank account. Looking at the average rate of outflows, there's enough for the agency to run for three months if there was no new business coming in.

I brought some paperwork with me, but please don't sign anything now. Hire your own lawyer and have them review it."

I didn't know what to say. It'd been just three days since Ed's passing and this was the last thing I expected. Schafer must've noticed my bewildered expression, because his voice softened a notch.

"You can also close up and liquidate. I estimate you may net somewhere around twenty thousand dollars. It'd be like a severance."

I nodded. Schafer rose, shook my hand, handed me a paper-clipped sheaf of papers, left.

I turned around and stared out the window. It was an overcast day, everything muted and gray. The phone rang. By reflex, I answered it like I always did.

"Ed Baker Investigative Agency. Siobhan O'Brien speaking."

"Kim Shee-Bong?" the voice asked.

It took me a second to realize that the caller was not announcing her name, but my own.

5

I can't say exactly when I realized my parents were not related to me by blood. As strange as this may sound, it was a gradual realization rather than a sudden epiphany.

People have trouble believing me when they meet my freckle-faced, red-headed Irish father and my blonde, six-foot Nordic mother. Didn't I ever look into a mirror? They'd asked. I certainly had. I was a beanpole Asian girl with thick, straight black hair. Let's say the Heavens parted and Jesus came surfing down a cascade of cumulus clouds. That'd be surprising, right? My eyes would be wide open, but they'd still be narrower than the calm pair of blue glow-dishes my mom has in her sockets.

But truth is truth. They were Dad and Mom, and I had no reason to think differently until other people's questions forced me to think. Like the time I got lost in the mall and the security guard wouldn't turn me over to my parents because she was convinced they were kooky kidnappers, or the old lady at the grocery store who refused to believe me when I told her I was an American. "But where are you *really* from?" was the question people eventually asked, and I did not have an answer.

Adolescent years are difficult for everyone, but they were especially hard for me. The prime objective of a teenager is to be like everyone else, and I had been like no one else. There were just a handful of Asian kids in my upstate New York hometown of Lyle, and of course they all had parents who looked like them. The technical name for a person in my situation was "transracial adoptee," but I was what I felt: a freak.

When I turned fifteen, my parents sent me to St. Paul, Minnesota for two weeks. My mother had grown up across the river in Minneapolis, so she knew there was a large population of Korean adoptees and a camp where kids like me got together to learn about their heritage. Since I was a hormonal, bratty teenager, I didn't want to go and thought the whole thing was "stupid," "a waste of time," and most likely "completely lame," but as soon as I got there, I started a journey to find myself. At Camp Wooram, I learned the Korean alphabet, I sang "Arirang" with my new friends, and made kimchi (my fingers stayed red for a day). For the first time, in an auditorium packed with Korean adoptees, I didn't feel alone. I went for three more years, then after college, I flew to South Korea to visit the motherland.

Mother. Land. Literally the land of my birth mother, whom the adoption agency was able to track down after six months of searching. We all went to South Korea, including my brother Sven. (Obviously, my dad got to name me while my mom got to name little bro. Sven is black, by the way. Nothing is simple in the O'Brien household.) Sven was eight then, sweet as anything and amazed at how, in this city, everybody looked like me.

"All the babies, too!" Sven said in the subway. They all stared at us, of course, a sea of black-haired and yellow-skinned people, my people.

We hired a translator to come with us for the meeting with my birth mother, but there was almost no need, as my story was the default template of so many like me. My birth mother got knocked up after a one-night stand, the deadbeat took off, and since single mothers were shunned like lepers (still are to a large degree—Korea, you really need to step up to the 21st century) and she had no support from her family, she had little choice but to give me away. I enjoyed meeting her. We shared the same high forehead, which, for some reason, didn't surprise me. What did completely disarm me was her laugh, because it sounded exactly like mine. I guess I thought my laugh was something I'd created, but as it turned out, it was more like my forehead.

I don't know what I'd expected from meeting my birth mother. Catharsis? Revelation? I'd felt neither. Satisfaction, yes. Not like eating a good meal, but more like finishing a crossword puzzle. It was a thing I'd started, and I was glad to have done it. Maybe it was as simple as this: I'd found my answer, so now I could move onto the next question.

A year after graduating from college, I went to work at Camp Wooram as a counselor, where I became close friends with Marlene Sykes. Like me, she was also adopted by a pair of well-meaning white folks, but unlike me, she had a younger non-adopted sister, Josie. Marlene's mom was told she couldn't get pregnant, which is why they adopted, but then it turned out that the doctor was wrong.

And that was who was on the phone now, little Josie. It didn't take me much time at all to identify her, the way she called me by my Korean name, something she used to do back when we all lived together in Rochester: me, Marlene, Josie, and an elusive fourth housemate whom we had to scramble to replace a half a dozen times in the three years we shared that big old house on Waring Road.

Marlene was like the sister I never had, my bestie. She was killed in a head-on collision with a sleep-deprived truck driver, just two days after we'd all celebrated her twenty-fifth birthday. It still hurt to think about her, which is probably why I rarely did.

"Josie?" I said into the phone.

Her sigh of relief came through the receiver like a blast of white noise.

"I thought you wouldn't remember me," she said.

"That's ridiculous," I said.

11

"Is it?"

Holy shit, that tone, needy and accusatory at once; I hadn't heard that unsavory combination in years, but it stung with startling familiarity.

6

"It's been a while," I said. I switched the handset from my right hand to my left when I noticed how tightly I was holding it.

"Time goes by."

Silence.

Was she going to tell me why she was calling, or was she going to make me ask her?

Considering who I was talking to, it'd probably be the latter. Josie had a way of involving you this way, quietly, furtively, passive-aggressively. She'd decided against college and worked at the Wegmans across the bay, manning the register and stocking the shelves of the grocery store, though what she really wanted to do, at least from my vantage point, was to get high and date the worst kind of men. Sometimes dangerous men—like I still remembered Rudy, who had a devil tattooed around his neck, its body bright red and elongated like a snake. One time Marlene and I had to restrain him—literally throw our bodies on top of him—because he and Josie had taken mushrooms and his trip was not working out. I doubt I'll ever be able to forget Josie's crazy cackles while her sister and I struggled to keep Rudy pinned on the floor.

"In that old house we shared back in Rochester, do you remember the lock breaking on the downstairs closet?" she asked.

This was a strange tack, but I figured I'd go with it.

"Not really."

"Must've been from the 1800's. You took it off the door and we all took turns holding it. It was so heavy, made out of cast iron. We figured out that the spring was broken, but no locksmith around town had the right part. You drove that lock all the way to Buffalo. In the three years we lived together, I never saw you give up on anything. You never stopped watching a movie, no matter how bad it was. I once saw you make the same cake recipe seven times in a row because you wanted to get it right. You never broke up with a guy—the guy had to break up with you."

"Either you're paying me a compliment or telling me I have a mental disorder."

"I'm outside your building right now," Josie said. "In the lobby."

I was about to ask, *All the way from Rochester?* but that was stupid because who knew where she was living nowadays.

"I'll be down," I said.

Four years my junior, I remembered Josie being kind of trampy-looking, never leaving the house without some serious red lipstick and her long bleach blonde hair in a wild, sexy wave. I guess it was foolish of me to expect her to look the same, because she did not. Her attire was all business, a dark blue suit jacket and skirt outfit that gave off a lawyer-like vibe. Her shoulder-length blonde hair curled inward in a way that only hair stylists have been able to do on mine. She'd gotten heavier around the middle, but then again, so had I.

As soon as I stepped off the elevator, I thrust out my arm to shake her hand, but I hadn't counted on her coming towards me to give me a hug. So her belly ran into my hand; I kind of stiff-armed her like a running back fending off a tackler.

"Oops," I said.

An awkward gesture fortuitously became an impromptu ice breaker: she smiled, I smiled, and now we hugged for real. We moved away from the elevator and stood next to the wall of mailboxes.

"You look so much the same," Josie said.

"You look...not the same. But in all the right ways."

"I was just a girl when you knew me."

"That's true."

"That's not who I am now."

Almost defiant, the way she said this.

"What are you doing here?"

"I just started my new job at Lenrock. As a marketing associate."

That was Lenrock University, whose sprawling campus was within walking distance of where I lived.

"Congrats, but I figure you didn't drop by just to tell me that."

"My daughter," Josie said. "I don't know where she is."

7

I couldn't see myself sitting behind Ed's desk again, or moving those client chairs over to my desk. I knew it would be weird to be in the office without him, but I didn't realize just how weird. So Josie and I walked over to Elkwood, the world-famous vegetarian restaurant on the Commons. It was the quiet hours between lunch and dinner. We sat at the bar and watched the workers set up the dinner tables while we talked.

"Penelope Hae Jun Sykes," Josie said. "Penny."

She handed me a photograph. Her daughter stared back at me with a smile as promising as tomorrow. In a one-piece yellow bathing suit, she sat cross-legged at the bed of a stream, one foot dipped in the water, a cascading waterfall flowing down in the background.

"Her twelfth birthday," Josie said. "That was a great day."

It's next to impossible for girls not to be beautiful at that age, and Penny was no exception. She held a red tambourine in her right hand, and I could almost hear all the sounds frozen in this picture: falling water, the laughter of youth, a festive shake of the musical instrument.

The girl in the photograph was Asian, Korean, I presumed from her name, which meant Josie had adopted her. I suppose it made logical sense, since Marlene was an adoptee like me, so this was like a form of honoring the memory of her sister, but something felt off. On the back of the photograph was the print date, and a quick calculation told me that she'd adopted Penny two years after Marlene's death. Which meant at twenty-five—the age when her sister had died—Josie had become a mother.

Was it possible that Marlene's death straightened her out, turned her into a responsible adult? Absolutely. But it was equally possible this was an impassioned gesture by a callow person.

"Oh my god, your face," Josie said.

"Excuse me?"

"You're making that face you used to make. Like you're smelling something rotten."

"I don't think I'm making any kind of a face," I said.

"Of course you don't, because it's your face. You're not looking at it."

I'd forgotten just how much Josie and I used to argue.

"You said you have some documents for me to see?"

I scanned the police report she'd brought. It stated Penny's last seen location as Llewellyn College, an hour northwest of Athena. Scars/marks/tattoos, last seen health condition, all standard questions and answers. There were no signs of a kidnap or a struggle. She'd packed a suitcase and was gone, so this was more like a runaway situation, but not technically even that, because I noticed her birthday was two months ago.

"She just turned eighteen," I said.

"That's right."

"She's no longer a minor."

"So she can just take off without telling me, her own mother?"

The answer was yes, but saying it out loud wasn't going to help matters.

"Do you have any other photos, something more recent?"

Josie took out her phone and swiped the screen until she found one, looking like it'd been taken in her dorm room on move-in day, boxes on the unmade twin bed, a cluster of clothes on hangers thrown over the desk. Somebody else, perhaps Penny's roommate, had snapped the picture, as Josie was standing next to her daughter. Outside of looking slightly taller and older, Penny didn't seem much different than the bathing suit picture, except for that forced smile on her face.

"Maybe you can fill me in a little bit, how you guys got along," I said.

"We love each other," Josie said. "She's my baby. It's us against the world."

Us against the world. That phrase took me back. Josie used to say it a lot, mostly in jest. Now, it sounded like a threat.

"Just you two? I thought adoption as a single parent was almost impossible."

"Andrew and I were married for eleven years. The year Penny turned ten, he died. Brain cancer."

I looked up from the photo on the phone and met her eyes. They were her best asset, as green as dewy grass, but the sparkle that I re-membered —devilish, trouble-making glints—that was long gone.

"I'm sorry," I said.

"Hasn't been easy raising her by myself, but I've made it this far."

"The last guy of yours I remember is Rudy."

Josie laughed. "With the neck tattoo." I laughed, too. "A real winner. Like I said, Siobhan, I'm all grown up now. With grown-up problems."

I hailed the bartender and we ordered gin and tonics. He brought us a bowl of pretzels with the drinks.

"Penny had her troubles with self-identity, as I'm sure you'd un-derstand. I stayed in Rochester after Marlene's passing. Not many venues for Penny to connect with her heritage there, so I sent her to Camp Wooram, just like you. She was fourteen then. Didn't want to go, so I kind of forced her. When she returned, she didn't speak to me for a month. And when I say 'didn't speak to me,' that's exactly what I mean, complete and utter silence." She stared at the photograph. "But we got through it, together. When I lost my job last year, Penny was so sweet—she asked if we could delay her college enrollment, you know, so we could save money…."

Josie closed her eyes and turned away from me, then fished out a packet of tissues and dabbed at her eyes.

One of the many things Ed taught me was the importance of keeping clients talking, so I thought it might be a good time to lament over our career choices for the moment. As it turned out, we'd both gone into industries that had been ravaged by technology. Josie had been working for Kodak until it went bankrupt. I told her about the *Athena Times'* slow demise, the newsroom shrinking every year until we were running a skeleton crew.

"They folded the *Times* into the *Binghamton Bulletin*," I said. "The satellite office in Cortland is now covering Athena, supposedly."

"I used to read your movie reviews. They were funny, especially if you didn't like the films. Almost emailed you once."

But she hadn't, because, well, I'd run out of her life, hadn't I? Back when we were living together, we'd had a flexible lease so we could vacate any time with a month's notice, so I paid in full and got the hell out of there and never spoke to Josie again after Marlene died. I had every right to do this, but it sort of made me a heel, or at least feel like one now.

"When I looked up private investigators in the area and saw your picture next to your boss on the website, I had to admit, I was surprised. But then I thought of that lock in our Buffalo house. Your tenacity."

"I don't even know what's going to happen now that Ed just passed away," I said.

I gave her the *Reader's Digest* version of my past week: the death

19

of my boss, the inheritance of the investigative agency, my uncertain future.

"Well," Josie said, "all I know is that my daughter is missing. I don't care if you're unsure because I know who you are. So will you help me find her, Siobhan? Kim Shee-Bong? For old time's sake if nothing else?"

Josie no longer looked like a mother with a lost daughter; she looked like Marlene's little sister, in trouble, in need.

"Yes," I said.

After the gin and tonics were empty, we switched to soda. Time to get down to business.

"When's the last time you heard from Penny?" I asked.

"A month ago. I dropped her off at Llewellyn in July. They have a six-week summer program for incoming freshmen, and because Penny's very shy, I thought it a nice way to get her better situated. Of course she didn't agree, we fought, she didn't call for two weeks, but by the time the school year started at the end of August, she was so happy, Siobhan. I drove down to see her when the rest of the students moved in, and I got to meet her roommate. We all went out to dinner…"

Josie paused to take a sip from her cup. She shook her head, as if to clear it.

"Sometimes I wake up and I think I'm in someone else's life. How can she just…"

"You're doing something about it now."

"It's that school, Siobhan, that fucking school. It seemed like the right place for her. Tiny, just five hundred students altogether, smaller than most of the survey courses at Lenrock University. I didn't want Penny to get lost in a huge school like that, and she didn't, either. We picked it together."

I'd driven by Llewellyn a number of times, a small women's college in the quiet hamlet of Selene. A few years back, I wrote a glossy interview of the new president, an alumni of the school who became a successful high-fashion model and an even more successful businesswoman. Overlooking Lake Selene, it always seemed like an idyllic way to spend your undergraduate years.

"For the first month, Penny and I talked every day…"

"Every day?"

"We're best friends. It's not unusual for best friends to talk, sometimes even more than once a day."

I smiled and nodded and kept my opinions to myself.

"But then by the end of September, she told me not to call anymore, saying she needed some time by herself. She stopped returning my calls and her voicemail message box got full. I got nervous and called the school. I talked to one of her professors, and he said Penny was still attending class. But obviously something wasn't right, so I drove down to see what was going on. So I get to her dorm room, and on the door there's a sign that says to call this phone number if you want to see Penny. I dial and wait, and two girls come sauntering in. One had dyed her hair green like a clown, and the other had so many earrings that she would've set off a metal detector. They said they were expecting me because this is what the abuser does after the victim makes her stand."

"Abuser?"

"That's what they called me. At this point I was beside myself, and maybe I got a little dramatic, because they called security to escort me away."

"You never saw Penny?"

"Once I calmed down and explained the situation, the guard took me back to those two girls, who led us to a different dorm, the one overlooking the lake. The guard explained they were headed up to TLC, Tender Llewellyn Care, the emotional support group on campus where they work with students who have issues with sexual or physical abuse. They called it their safe house."

"And that's where Penny was, kept safe, from you."

"Her own mother."

"Did she have anything to say?"

"She read from a note card. It was like a press release. Penny said she felt manipulated, how co-dependent we were with each other. I don't like remembering it, Siobhan. I ran out of there, so embarrassed. Those two girls stood by her, all pious and supportive, but I swear it was all for show. That bitch with the green hair, that smile of hers—she was enjoying it."

"But then Penny must've left the school without telling you."

"The dean called me two weeks ago to tell me she took a leave of absence. I drove back there, but she'd already moved out of TLC. I found those two girls, but they told me Penny is working things out and that I had to stop hounding her. I called the police, but all they did was fill out this stupid form. The way the officer was dealing with it, it felt like he was just going through the motions."

We finished our drinks. Waiters and waitresses clad in white shirts and black pants visited each table to light up a votive candle and drop a single yellow rose into a tiny vase. Early diners stood by the hostess's station; four college-aged kids looked like they were on a double date. The joy they exuded was in stark contrast to the sadness and disappointment of Josie. Her relationship with Penny might have been the stifling kind, but it didn't seem unreasonable for a mother to know where her daughter was.

"Before you lost touch with her, did Penny mention anything that seemed strange or unusual to you?"

Josie considered the question for a bit. "No, not a thing. I thought you looked surprised when I told you that we talked every day, but our chats were nothing more than just two girls prattling on about a whole lot of nothing. What we ate, what we wore, that sort of thing. She hates it when I ask her about her meds, but I have to stay on top of her."

"Meds?"

"She's got Graves' Disease. Her thyroid goes into overdrive. It's manageable, as long as she takes her methimazole. Wherever she is, I hope she's remembering to take it."

"Did Penny sound different when you talked to her last? Stressed out, maybe angry? Think back."

"What the hell do you think I've been doing since? Our conversations are on permanent repeat in my mind. Nothing. She was my happy little girl, and then…gone."

"Living away from home, in college, this is usually when kids break away from their parents," I said.

"Breaking away is one thing, but just up and leaving completely? It's ridiculous. It's ungrateful. After all I've done for her. After all we've been to each other."

Josie insisted on paying the bill, which was actually the perfect moment to bring up the issue of money.

"I do need a retainer to do my work," I said.

"Right, of course," Josie said. "How much?"

"A thousand is what Ed went with, but five hundred would be enough for me to get started."

"I just started a new job at Lenrock last week, so I won't get paid until next Friday. I had some moving expenses, too, so money's kinda tight. Could I postdate it?"

My first client, and she wasn't even going to pay me. Not the best way to usher in my new firm, but she was a friend and in a bind, so I told her it was fine. I asked her to email me the photo of Penny from her phone, which she did as we waited for the waitress to return with the credit card slip.

"Is it any wonder Kodak went bankrupt?" Josie said.

"I feel old just holding this thing," I said. "I still remember what a big deal it was when we got the extra long cord for the only phone in my house, so I could drag it to my room to talk privately."

We rose from our stools. When Josie slung her purse on her shoulder by pulling on the strap with her thumb and middle finger, I flashed on the young woman I used to know before she became a mother. Many a Saturday, we four girls line-danced to Garth Brooks at our local bar, going a little crazy when the jukebox landed on our favorite, "I Got Friends in Low Places." We leaned over the pool table with our low-cut tops and skin-tight skirts, catching the eyes of the geeks from RIT and the jocks from U of R. What simple times they were.

Outside, the clouds were back with a vengeance, making an earlier arrival of nightfall.

"I'll give you an update when I find out anything," I said. "No matter what, I'll call you in a week to see how you're doing."

"Okay," Josie said.

We waited for a second, watching each other. I thought she was going to offer another hug, but she didn't; maybe she was waiting for me to do it.

I watched her walk away until she turned the corner and disappeared.

9

I opened the door to my apartment and was greeted by silence, sweet silence. It'd been a long day, and I looked forward to being alone with my thoughts. I like people, but I like being by myself more, though I would never take the Thoreau route and live in the middle of nowhere. What makes me feel best is to be here in my one-bedroom apartment, with strangers above me, below me, and beside me. It's like every moment I spend alone here, I'm choosing to do so, and that makes me feel better about myself. No doubt this makes me some kind of a weirdo, but that's fine. We're all weirdos in our own way.

I stood in the kitchen and watched my Lean Cuisine meal carousel inside the microwave. I imagined what it would've been like if Josie had talked to Ed instead of me today. Ed had been a big guy, six-two and two-fifty, with a baritone that rivaled Barry White's. Everyone who came into our office left feeling like they'd be taken care of. I was five-three, a hundred and ten after a big dinner, and the only reason why Josie wanted me on this case was because of our personal connection. Would strangers who came to Siobhan O'Brien Detective Agency really hire *me*?

The microwave dinged. I carried my sad excuse for a dinner to the couch and turned on the television, and wouldn't you know it, there was black and white Humphrey Bogart in a trench coat and a fedora.

"You won't get into trouble?" a woman asked him.

"I don't mind a reasonable amount of trouble," he said.

I turned the TV off and set aside my meal. Okay, so I didn't look like Sam Spade. But that could be a plus. In my fifteen years of writing for the *Athena Times*, the only quasi-investigative journalism I'd done was a story between two rival hair salons. I faked my way as a shampoo girl and accidentally stumbled upon a state assemblyman's torrid affair with one of the hairdressers. As awesome as Ed was at what he did, he couldn't have worked at a hair salon. Though the idea of him with a curling iron and chatting up the ladies kind of cheered me up.

On my first day of work, Ed and I had sat in his Buick, watching the front porch of a house whose mail kept getting stolen. *Any time you're confused about anything,* he'd said, *make a list.*

I got up from my couch, went to my desk, and found my yellow pad and pen.

David Girard, missing persons reporting officer
Green haired girl
Pierced girl
Tender Llewellyn Care

Every case started with a few names and a place. We ran a skiptrace for a client this past summer in an effort to find her long-lost brother, and it had been a doozy, connecting through seven states and more than a dozen cities. I'd taken notes. The notes were in the office. My dinner was now cold, but it wasn't frozen, so I ate it. Then I drove back to the office.

10

It was eight thirty and there were plenty of lights still on in the building. On our floor, we had a civil engineer and a lawyer, and they were both still working away. Whatever happened to the eight-hour workday?

I flipped on the lights in the office. I opened the filing cabinet for my notes and found a hanging folder pushed all the way to the back. Inside the well was a thin white box with a bow on it.

It was a very beautiful white pen inside a black case lined with felt, like jewelry. I couldn't figure out what the pen was made out of—it didn't look or feel plastic. Maybe bone, because there were slight variations in the color and it had a certain heft. A small white card was taped onto the bottom of the case. "You made it to year number two, Siobhan," Ed had written in his tiny handwriting—for a guy who looked like a linebacker, his personal font was six-point. "The pen is mightier than the sword, and even the gun."

So he'd remembered.

I'd be lying if I said I hadn't considered what Schafer, Ed's lawyer, had told me this morning, that I could walk away from this with 20K in my pocket. Heading my own shop with just two years of apprenticeship was sheer folly. But Ed did leave his agency, his only real possession, to me. And I did have a case.

On my desk was the stack of papers Schafer had given me. I sat down, uncapped my brand-new pen, and signed my name on nine different pages. Congratulations to me. I already knew the best way to celebrate.

I walked over to the supply closet and dragged out an open box pushed against the wall. A gallon of black paint, a pint of gold paint, brushes and trays. I was in my sweats, so already in uniform. I covered the floor around the door with yesterday's edition of the *Binghamton Bulletin* and got down to work.

Another one of Ed's pieces of advice to me was to think about the case while doing something rote, like washing the dishes or painting a door. *Airs out the brain,* he always said. The window pane now fully blue-taped, I dipped my brush into the tray and applied the first stroke like my dad showed me years ago, going over it just once, top to bottom.

The girl with the green hair knew where Penny was. If she didn't tell Josie, she probably wasn't going to tell me. So I'd do a lot of sitting and watching. It's pretty amazing how much information just being in one place and paying attention can reveal.

Josie had said that the reporting officer seemed like he was just going through the motions. Was that because it'd been a long day or because this was a fairly common occurrence at Llewellyn?

"And I thought I had it rough today."

Behind me was Craig, the lawyer who was two doors down. No matter the time of day, Craig always looked like he could use a strong cup of coffee. It was mostly his watery blue eyes that made me want to yawn, which I just did.

"I'm sorry about Ed," he said. "I was in Syracuse on a case all last week and just heard about it."

"Thanks," I said. "Hey, can I ask you to look something over?"

Craig nodded and I brought him the document Schafer gave me. He flipped through it like a pro. "You already signed it."

"But I haven't handed it in. Ed's lawyer said I should have my own guy look it over, so if you have the time? I'll pay you for your trouble."

"No trouble," Craig said. "This is a template contract you can download off a website, I see these once a week. It won't take an hour for me to read it."

"I appreciate it," I said.

He pointed at the glass panel of my door. "So you gonna change the name?"

"I don't know. I only decided to keep the place running half an hour ago."

Craig chuckled. He loosened his tie and hitched up his pants. This suit, like all the others he owned, didn't quite fit him, the sleeves slightly long, the waist too wide.

"Well," he said. "Good luck with the painting. I'll have this for you tomorrow afternoon."

"Okay."

I was halfway done with the front part when I heard him lock up for the night.

"Hey," he said. "You're gonna do fine."

I plucked off a loose paintbrush bristle before it stuck onto the door forever.

"With this door or with my brand-new agency?"

"A little of both," Craig said.

I watched him walk down the hallway. He never took the elevator, always the stairs. There's a vending machine at the end of the hall, and I've never seen him feed it a dollar bill. Private eye Siobhan was having an a-ha moment: Craig used to be fat.

He looked back and waved before leaving me to my job, and that's when I realized that I sort of liked Craig. Which is strange because usually I know I like a guy right away. I've bumped into Craig at least a hundred times since I started working here because his office is on the way to the bathroom, and all that time, nothing, and now this.

Life. I'll never understand it.

11

It'd been a few years since I'd been on Llewellyn's serene campus by the lake, but colleges don't change all that much. They may add a building or two, a new statue or a sculpture might grace the garden— but there was something very obviously different about this place, and you didn't have to be a detective to notice: male students.

After parking my black Honda Accord in one of the designated visitor spaces, I stood in the visitors parking lot and saw my first, a guy in a Buffalo Sabres jersey. Then a pair of dudes, with white ear-buds and eyes glued to their phones. Now that I was thinking about it, I did vaguely recall hearing rumblings about the college possibly going co-ed a few years ago, but that was right around when the *Times* was being gutted and my mind was on other, more pressing things, like how I was gonna keep my apartment and buy food.

No question, women's colleges were a dying breed. Vassar, Skidmore, Bennington, these had all once been female-only institutions of higher learning, but they eventually brought in men; Radcliffe used to be the top women's college until it was absorbed by Harvard. When I'd interviewed the new president here five years ago, Vera Wheeler, there hadn't been an inkling of this. In fact, I remembered her specifically declaring her single-most important agenda was to continue Llewellyn's traditions.

Another change was the security guard posted at the entrance of the parking lot. I walked over to her and we met at her glassed station. Vasquez, according to the name tag on her navy blue uniform.

"Good morning," she said. "What brings you to Lewie?"

She was a short Latina with a big smile, but there was something else there. Concern. Weariness? She didn't trust me, and I didn't understand. These people made their living by being nice to prospective students and parents. So my gut told me to lie.

"Is WILL still a thing?" I asked.

Vasquez smiled again, and this one was genuine. "Of course. We may have opened our doors to men, but that doesn't change who we are."

"Broadhurst, right?"

She nodded. "Just follow this path from here to the red building over there, but it sounds like you know your way."

"I do, thanks," I said. WILL stood for Women in Lifelong Learning, a program for older students. It was one of the items Wheeler had highlighted during our interview, something I wouldn't have remembered had I not read over my piece before coming here. Preparation was, as always, half the battle.

The ivy growing over Broadhurst Hall had turned crimson like the rest of the trees, the red bricks harmonizing with nature into a ready-made postcard. A clock tower rose from the center, its gray peak tiled with oval-shaped slate like the scales of a dragon. Now half past ten, the bells above rang throughout the campus with their reverent resonance, a simple ding-dong as if someone was at the door. Having attended a large institution for my undergraduate years (SUNY Buffalo), I've always been envious of schools like Llewellyn. Well, maybe now I'd get my wish. It actually made sense to register as a student; I'd have full access to the campus without raising any alarms.

I walked up to the massive white doors of Broadhurst, big enough for a horse-drawn carriage. That's what the building used to be, the carriage house of Horace Llewellyn himself back in the day. The sunflower-shaped brass handles were polished to a shine, and so was the rest of the lobby inside. A set of ruby red Victorian sofas and chaises were arranged in an inviting semi-circle in the center of the room, and a receptionist sat primly behind an ornate antique wooden desk, its feet shaped like lion's paws. I didn't remember seeing the enormous chandelier shining above, either, the last time I was here, but it was hard to miss its gaudy gleam now.

"Pretty bright, isn't it?" the receptionist said. Her name was embossed on a transparent prism, Gloria Reedy. She had on enough makeup to be an opera singer. "I've gotten used to it, but almost everyone has your initial reaction."

"When did all this happen?"

"The couches were reupholstered at the beginning of the semester. Believe it or not, the chandelier has always been there. We just had every crystal resurfaced and the metal buffed. I imagine it looked like this a hundred and fifty years ago, except back then it'd have been candles instead of light bulbs."

"Must've cost something to restore it like that."

"Students! The more the merrier. This is my tenth year here, and we've never had it so good."

"When did you start registering male students?"

"Just this year—you're seeing the inaugural class, the Neil Armstrongs."

"Quite a change," I said. A pair of students walked by, heading for the open double doors to the right that led to the administrative offices. Boy and girl, they held hands as they disappeared through the doorway.

"I suppose. Like in the past, that would've been two girls holding hands," Gloria said with a wink. "We'll survive. We're tough. Anyhoo, I've talked your ear off and I don't even know your name or why you're here."

I told her I wanted to register for WILL, and she held up her hand for a high-five.

"You go, girl! I celebrate every lady who comes in here to keep on learning. I applaud you, Siobhan!"

And then she did actually applaud. I took a small bow, which delighted her to no end. Gloria wrote up a visitor's sticker for me to apply on my jacket then told me to go up to the second floor to sign up.

12

Climbing the stairs, I saw that not all parts of Broadhurst got the facelift. The white paint on the walls was chipped along the baseboard, revealing an unsavory sky blue hiding underneath, and when I arrived at the registration office, I sat in an orange plastic thrift-shop-reject of a chair to fill out a web form on an old desktop computer. The keyboard and mouse had once been white, but now they'd both aged to the color of coffee-stained teeth.

So the place wasn't overflowing with cash. Back when I wrote the story, I learned that schools like Llewellyn depend heavily on student tuition to survive, unlike, say, Lenrock, their gigantic counterpart on the other side of the lake. Lenrock has six billion dollars in their endowment, which means that if they generated a five percent return through investments, they had $300 million a year. Llewellyn's endowment was eight million, total. As usual, the rich got richer while the poor struggled to make ends meet. The infusion of male students probably did mean a fair amount of financial relief.

After filling out some non-virtual paperwork (i.e., pen on paper) and paying my processing fee, the registrar instructed me to go downstairs for my photo ID. I was about to take the stairs when I saw a man off to the side pressing the button for the elevator.

The man was a cop. He wasn't wearing his uniform, but it was as plain as the beard on his face. It's the way cops stand that always outs them, the way they hold themselves, a confident rigidity that I think half of them don't even know they're doing.

When he turned to press B on the panel, I saw the ID dangling from his belt: DAVID GIRARD. That was the name of the officer who'd filled out the missing persons report on Penny, but that had been from the Selene Police Department. What was the likelihood that there was another David Girard around here? This had to be the same guy. But then what was he doing with a Llewellyn ID?

The elevator dinged, signaling its descent. Girard smelled of a fairly strong cologne, and I felt a sneeze coming on. I tried to stifle it, but it still sort of half-assedly came out.

"God bless you…?" Girard said.

"I didn't want to fill the elevator with my germs."

He laughed. "Thank you."

"Aren't you an officer with the town's police department?"

"That's right," he said. Only in movies are cops stupid and in-competent. In my own experience, they rarely miss a thing. And they never tell you more than what they want you to know.

"I just signed up as a WILL student. Getting my photo ID."

The elevator opened and Girard gestured for me to exit first. It was all very utilitarian down here in the basement, beige concrete walls and industrial pipes by the ceiling running along the wide corridor.

"That's where I'm going, so you can follow me," he said.

"So are you guys, like, providing security for Llewellyn?"

"Yes."

It was like pulling teeth with this guy. "How long?"

"Just started this semester."

"Why would a college want police protection?"

"What's with all the questions, miss?"

"I'm sorry," I said. "Maybe it's just being back in college, getting ready to be intellectually inquisitive, academically eager, that sort of thing. It's been twenty years since I had homework."

That seemed to soften Girard a bit. "It's a cost-saving shared-services initiative that the mayor of Selene and the president of Llewellyn came up with. I supervise the rookies who are getting their feet wet. I hope that satisfies all of your curiosities."

It sounded reasonable enough, and maybe that's why I didn't buy it.

We arrived at the windowless office where one of Girard's rookies sat behind his desk, nose buried in a paperback.

"Keeping busy, Russ?"

Russ almost fell over in his haste to look like he was being attentive.

"Yes, sir," he said. Unlike Girard, Russ looked like a guy in a play dressed to look like a police officer.

"This lady here—I'm sorry, I didn't get your name."

"Siobhan O'Brien," I said.

Girard did a double-take. "Not what I expected."

"I'm one of those rare Irish Korean-Americans you've never heard of," I said.

Girard, unimpressed with my attempt at humor, disappeared into an adjoining office and shut the door behind him.

13

"Follow me, miss," Russ said, as he walked over to the wall and pulled down a white screen. He carried over a stool and had me sit on it, then took meticulous care in setting me up, asking me to look straight, then straighter. Still not happy with the way I was positioned, he took both of his hands and tilted my head just so.

"Now just a little smile, not a big one. That's it, perfect!" he said, then snapped three pictures with the digital camera on a tripod.

"You should be a portrait photographer, Russ," I said.

He shrugged and blushed. "Just doing my job, ma'am."

Russ opened up Photoshop and messed around with a slider control that made my skin glow. And then he used a lasso tool to just slightly lower my bangs. I've never looked so good in real life.

"I can't believe you don't do this for a living."

"You should see what the pros can do," he said, but the pride in his voice was unmistakable.

"How long have you been with the force?"

"Just a month out of the academy."

"A nice quiet way to start your career, I'd imagine," I said.

Russ copied my photo onto the ID and clicked the print button. He rolled his chair over to the other side, where the little printer slowly stuck out the laminated card like a tongue.

"You'd think that, right? It's actually been kinda crazy around here," he said. "Some student unrest."

"Let me guess—having men on campus."

He took an X-Acto knife and delicately trimmed the excess plastic. I could watch his brand of precision all day.

"The female students were notified last year. President Wheeler sent out the memo, but I guess there was some confusion with the wording and the women thought they had another year. Some of the hardcore feminists transferred out immediately, but the ones on the fence stayed, and they're not happy. A couple of buildings were spray-painted, the statue of Horace Llewellyn defaced…"

He was talking real easy now, so it was the perfect time to sneak in. "…and that girl who went missing, what's her name, Penny something…"

"Penny Sykes, what a pain that was."

"Is that right."

Russ buffed my ID with a lint-free cloth. "David had me talk to her roommate, but that was a waste of time because she didn't even live with her."

I was pushing my luck, but Russ was in the groove and we were chewing the fat. "Then who did she live with?"

"Grace Park. Park Industries? She's like a celebrity around here."

Park Industries was one of the largest corporate conglomerates out of South Korea. Not as big as Samsung or Hyundai, but not far behind. They were known for manufacturing heavy machinery, but they had their fingers in a lot of pies. Like I remember buying an ice cream scooper from Wal-Mart and seeing their logo, the "i" inside the empty wedge of the "P" on the label. So a daughter of one of the wealthiest companies in the world had become besties with Penny.

I thanked Russ for his awesome job and walked up a floor and back to Gloria.

"Is Vera Wheeler still on the fourth floor of this building?" I asked.

"She is, but she's not in. You can check with her executive assistant, but President Wheeler is away for the week."

I thanked Gloria and walked down the steps back to the quad when a girl with tats from her arms to her neck stepped in front of my path.

"You're WILLing?" she asked. I didn't know what she meant, until she pointed to the red folder I was carrying, the acronym WILL on its cover.

"Ah yes, that is I, WILLing."

She removed a flyer from her backpack and handed it to me. "As an experienced woman who's been out in the real world, we'd totes appreciate your point of view."

Experienced woman. At least she didn't say "older" or "mature" or "almost dead."

THE WOMYN OF LLEWELLYN
"Hell hath no fury like a womyn scorned!"
Time to talk tofurkey about the manvasion.
Eldred Hall - Douglas Theatre

It was for tonight at 8 p.m..

"Manvasion," I said. "*Man* and *invasion* put together."

She adjusted the straps of her backpack, and white and yellow lily tattoos peeked from the root of her neck.

"A portmanteau," she said.

"You mean a port-women-teau," I said. I was kinda getting into this female power thing.

14

Stacy, our part-time bookkeeper, was sitting at her desk when I returned to the office. I always knew what day of the week it was whenever I saw her—Thursday. I'd liked our office best when we were all there—Ed behind his big old desk, his chair turned around toward the window overlooking the mountains, ruminating on a case. Stacy with her laptop and her extra monitor, her eyes darting from one screen to next, two fingers punching numbers into the keyboard with machine-gun rapidity. Me at my desk, writing up a report or scouring through a stack of old phone books, from which a surprising amount of information could be gleaned. We were a team, now missing its captain.

"Hey, Stacy," I said.

"Hey, you," she said.

Our eyes met, and we flitted between uncertainty and sadness. Ed was the one who talked to her about business, not me. But now this was my job.

"Ed's lawyer paid me a visit yesterday," I said.

"Schafer and Associates. I just paid their bill."

I summarized the situation, and she listened and nodded. Stacy was a numbers gal, so when I told her Schafer estimated there were three months left for the agency without new business coming in, she cracked her knuckles and bounced from one Excel spreadsheet to another to verify that conclusion.

"Sounds about right. Maybe another month, since A1 Insurance is on an installment plan and they still have two more payments to make, but better to err on the side of caution."

"Ed had a good reputation, and referrals mean a lot in this business, so I think I'll still get cases, but then I'd need to create my own history of success to keep the machine going. Like this."

I presented the check I received from Josie.

"Hey, look at you!" she said, but then furrowed her eyebrows when she looked at it more closely. "Half the usual amount and a postdate to boot."

"Thanks, Debbie Downer."

"Sorry, but you *are* talking to your accountant."

"Better than nothing, though, right?"

"True, it's a start," Stacy said. "I'll deposit it at the end of the week. So instead of cashing out, you're going all in."

"Dumb move?"

Stacy twirled a lock of her hair absentmindedly. I've always envied her strawberry-blonde hair, a natural perm that she complained about all the time, especially on humid days.

"Nine out of ten small businesses fail, so the odds are against you. But I think it's cool that you're gonna try. *Don't be too timid or squeamish about your actions. All life is an experiment. The more experiments you make, the better.*"

"Who said that?"

"Ralph Waldo Emerson," she said.

"*I became a transparent eyeball. I am nothing, I see all.*"

"Now you've made him sound like a pervert."

While Stacy finished up balancing various numbers on her spreadsheets, I thought about what I'd learned from my brief visit to Llewellyn. There were male students there now. Penny had roomed with Grace Park, who was loaded like a Rockefeller. How did that come about? And what about the school hiring Selene cops to provide security? Russ, the young officer who made my ID, had mentioned

42

"student unrest," but what did that really mean? A single string may have led me to Llewellyn, but I left with a dozen different knots. I probably needed to create another list, though first I needed to find that list I'd started earlier. So the first thing on this new list would be, "Find the old list." Sad.

"Knock, knock."

"Why is it that some people say 'knock, knock' instead of actually knocking?" Stacy asked.

"It's less intrusive," Craig said. "You can do it with a regular knock, but the force and the cadence both need to be perfect."

Stacy snapped her laptop shut and slid it inside her bag. "Lawyers. They have an explanation for everything." She turned to me. "See you in a week."

"As always," I said. We watched her bouncy mop of hair as it floated away and out the door.

15

Craig's hands were full. In his left was the contract Ed's lawyer had left, a few yellow Post-Its sticking out like tabs. In his right was a plain white paper bag.

He sat down on the client chair that I now had dragged in front of my desk. "Just a couple of suggestions regarding the language," he said, and slid the contract to me. "Nothing huge, clarifications, that's all."

"Thank you. I'll have Stacy cut you a check—just send us an invoice?"

He waved me off. "I've always thought we should have a working relationship. Our businesses can feed off of one another, you know?"

I nodded. "Makes sense."

"And speaking of feeding…"

He pushed the white bag toward me. Inside were two giant weird-looking croissants. One had a dab of chocolate at an end. They smelled fat and delicious.

"Cronuts—they're all the rage. A donut made like a croissant."

"Thank you, Craig. That's very sweet of you."

I tore both of them in half so we could each have a taste. Croissants were pretty good as is, but fried like a donut? This thing was insane. The center was still warm, and I devoured my halves while Craig ate his slowly, pinching one small bite at a time. He comps the contract review, he brings me food—maybe I should just marry the guy.

"How come you never came around when Ed was here?" I asked.

"I asked myself the same question this morning," he said. "And I don't know if I have an answer. It's not like we weren't friendly—he and I chatted whenever we rode the elevator together, which was at least once a week."

He did like to talk, but then again, he was an attorney. He had a smooth, easy voice, almost radio-worthy. I imagined him in court, gesturing with his hands, swaying doubtful jurors over to his side. He was probably pretty good at it.

And he had nice hands. His ring finger was bare, but I had a strong feeling he was a divorcé. You can just tell, a certain gist of weariness that's worn like a jacket, which was fine. At this point in my life, I preferred divorced men over the never married. They handled disappointment better.

"Going back to college?" he asked, pointing at the Llewellyn folder on my desk.

"Did you know that Llewellyn is now co-ed?"

"To tell you the truth, I kind of forgot that Llewellyn even existed, since we live in Lenrock country around here. Regardless, it must be quite a switch. But then again, it was probably a concept whose time had run out. Colleges are businesses, and I can't imagine shutting out half of the population is good for the bottom line. With women 'leaning in' and attending colleges more than men now, I'd think the necessity for an all-female college is not what it used to be."

"I suppose," I said. "It's still a man's world, though. Harvey Weinstein, Louis C.K., Bill Cosby…"

"Good point—if nothing else, colleges should teach a course on how to kick oversexed men in the nuts. *Park Industries*? Why did you write that on the folder?"

"You got a good pair of eyes there. I can hardly read my tiny handwriting."

"20/20," Craig said. "Plus it's a skill I've developed. Stealing a few lines of a prosecutor's notes can be very handy in a trial."

"The daughter goes there. Grace Park."

Craig nodded, then narrowed his eyes, thinking back to something.

"I tried to sue them once, six, seven years ago. They make *everything*, you know that, right? Including hydraulic lifts that auto mechanics use. A couple of garage owners in town got pissed off because there was a defect with a relay switch and Park Industries wouldn't fix it. So I suggested we all get together and threaten them with the possibility of a class action suit. Everyone was on board, until an army of lawyers shocked and awed us. That's not a figure of speech—I'm being literal. All six of Park's lawyers on retainer had graduated from West Point, and these guys, five men and one woman, were not to be trifled with."

"What happened with the case?"

"Settled out of court, like 99% of all civil cases. They swapped out the old lifts with newer ones for free, as long as all the garage owners agreed to sign a non-disclosure agreement. No bitching and moaning to newspapers or the internet, that type of thing."

There was a knock, and unlike Craig's, this was a real one, two hard raps against the glass.

"That's probably my client," I said.

Craig popped the last morsel of the cronut into his mouth and wiped his fingers on a napkin. He swept the desk clean of crumbs, neatly catching them into the now empty paper bag.

"Thank you for lunch," I said.

"There'll be more." I liked the way he said that, a promise that had some oomph behind it, a friendly threat.

He opened the door and greeted Marie Michaelson on his way out, who was looking sexy and sharp in a red body-hugging above-the-knees dress. She shuffled right up in her high heels and hugged me. A few strands of her big hair got in my mouth, but I didn't mind because they sort of tasted like cherries.

"Oh, Siobhan!" she squealed. "Those pictures were just what my lawyer needed. Thank you, thank you, thank you!" She rooted through her Louis Vuitton purse and handed me an envelope. "The rest of the payment. I wanted to hand deliver it and give you the good news myself."

Taking the envelope, I said, "I'm glad you're satisfied."

"Oh yeah," she said. "My lawyer says this was worth at least another grand a month."

So it was just a ploy for more alimony. I was actually relieved, because I had a feeling, even with Henry Michaelson violating the custody agreement, that he was the better parent for their son.

"I'm here if you need anything else," I said.

"I've already told a bunch of my girlfriends about you, so don't be surprised if you get a call or two."

I put on my best fake smile. "I look forward to it."

Marie hugged me once more, then she was gone, leaving me with her cherry hair aftertaste. I opened the envelope and stared at the check for $1000. I stared at the empty chair where Ed used to sit.

Even in the shittiest of cases, as long as you get paid at the end, that's what matters.

I could still hear his voice in my head if I wanted to, and I wanted to.

16

Like the blinding chandelier in Broadhurst Hall's lobby, the refurbished cafeteria ushered in the new and improved Llewellyn. One of the perks I'd discovered in the WILL welcome packet was a comp meal ticket, which I now handed to the girl behind the podium, a round-faced smiling machine.

She held my ticket up to a scanner, and it dinged me in.

All the old wooden tables and chairs had been refinished, sanded and varnished to look like new. This probably cost more than replacing it with newer furniture, but Wheeler had promised to honor the Llewellyn traditions, so perhaps it wasn't all bullshit. In one corner of the room, a server with a toque hat cut slices of prime rib kept warm under a heat lamp. Next to her was a dessert bar that offered eight different treats, including crème brûlée, finished on the spot with the gal wielding a tiny blowtorch over the sugary surface to brown it.

I picked up a tray and got in line and slopped a nice portion of sirloin beef tips in gravy and a scoopful of Yukon gold mashed potatoes onto my dish, probably more than I should have, but it was supper time and my stomach was calling the shots.

"Doesn't it smell wonderful?"

Right behind me was a tiny old lady, cotton-haired and with thick glasses that turned her hazel eyes into pins.

"I want to start eating it right here," I said.

She giggled. "I'm guessing you're a WILL like us? Sit with me and my pals, why don't you. We're over in the back, the table underneath the school insignia. I'm Betty."

"Siobhan."

"Siobhan! I wish I had an exotic name like that."

"It's never too late to change," I said, and she giggled again.

"You're funny. You should take the humor class they offer here, it's very popular. *Make 'em Laugh: From Aristophanes to Zero Mostel.* My class schedule is pretty full, but there's always next year."

At the fountain, we filled our glasses, apple juice for her and iced tea for me, then she led me over to her table, where two other ladies of identical hair color and sunny dispositions greeted me with such naked enthusiasm that I felt like I should do cartwheels or break out in song.

Their names were Joan and Margo, and from where I sat, one table across, I saw the back of another head that was hard to miss. Josie had told me the girl who had brainwashed Penny had hair that was "green like a clown," so unless dyeing one's hair the color of spring leaves had become a fashion statement at Llewellyn, she was the one who might know of Penny's whereabouts.

"So what do you do, Siobhan?" Joan asked me. Or was it Margo? I couldn't remember, but it didn't matter. As I told them about my job as a private investigator, I kept an eye on Green Hair's table. She'd been the first to arrive, but now other girls were taking their seats, and it was definitely the assemblage of the alternative lifestyles. Twin girls with very short spiky hair, a Latina with a lip ring that looked like it could double as a door knocker, a black girl whose ears were infested by earrings. And a familiar face, the girl who'd handed me the "manvasion" flyer in front of Broadhurst. I had a feeling I was looking at the core members of the Womyn of Llewellyn, chowing down before their meeting.

"Did you watch *Murder, She Wrote* when it was on TV?" Betty asked me.

Coming from anyone else, I would've thought they were being sarcastic, but no, Betty was quite sincere.

"Not when it aired originally, but I have caught a few episodes in reruns," I said. "I wouldn't want to mess with Angela Lansbury."

"She did run into a lot of dead bodies. Every week, in fact."

"In the last episode," Joan or Margo said, "I thought they'd reveal that she'd been a serial killer."

While the ladies discussed their Bizarro takes on television's favorite gumshoe Jessica Fletcher, I watched Green Hair preside over her table. Whoever was talking stopped immediately whenever Green Hair decided to chime in. And even when she was listening, it was she whom everyone was watching.

"You guys were WILL students before Lewie became co-ed, right? What was the campus like then?"

Betty sipped her coffee and weighed her answer. "More than anything, there are kids on campus all the time now. Not that I frequent this place at night, but sometimes I come for a play or a concert, and Lewie used to be as quiet as a graveyard on Friday and Saturday nights. The girls left because there were no men. Mostly they'd either drive themselves or take the school van to Lenrock."

"All those fraternities and parties at Lenrock," Joan or Margo said.

Green Hair rose, and all the girls at her table rose with her. Green Hair then started clapping rhythmically on her way out of the dining hall, and the rest of the Womyn clapped, too, as they filed out.

"And of course, those girls weren't as vocal as they are now," Betty said.

"A security guy said there have been incidents?"

She laughed. "They put Horace Llewellyn in a dress, the statue on the quad. A blonde wig, lipstick, I thought it was hilarious. But the president was not amused, as you can imagine."

"They also dropped red dye into all the toilets one day," Joan or Margo said. "At noon a banner unfurled in front of Broadhurst: *Lewie menstruates for her daughters!*"

"Somebody must've gotten expelled or something?"

Betty shook her head. "They're smart and sneaky. Even with the Selene police officers here, nobody has been caught yet."

I pulled out the "manvasion" flyer and presented it to the table. "One of the Womyn invited me to the meeting."

Betty, Joan, and Margo each brought out their own flyers.

"Did they feed you a line about being an experienced woman? Real world, we appreciate your worldly point of view, etc.?" Betty asked.

"I think they left out *worldly*," I said.

"Well," Betty said, "maybe you have to be of a certain age to be awarded that adjective."

17

The walk from the dining hall to Eldred Hall would've taken me maybe a minute if I'd been going by myself, but traveling with three octogenarian ladies turned my pace a bit more leisurely. It was fine—lovely, even—because slowing down let me take in the gorgeous surroundings that I otherwise would've ignored. When we crossed under the gigantic sycamore, I stepped over hand-sized brown leaves on the ground, enjoying every crispy crinkle underneath my feet.

Betty glanced up at the tree. "Glad there are still things older than me."

As we made our way to Eldred, we passed by a foursome of boys kicking a soccer ball around, then a circle of girls practicing dance moves while singing a cappella, then a boy and a girl sitting on a bench making out. Such a mellow collegiate scene, and now this one in stark contrast, the Womym of Llewellyn standing straight ahead through the doorway, nine girls in a line on the stage, holding hands and singing:

> *Lovely Llewellyn, thy daughters sing for thee,*
> *Dear Llewellyn, hear our hearts beat free,*
> *Our Alma Mater, dear Alma Mater,*
> *Thy daughters praise thee, Llewellyn!*

The meeting room was in a theater where the walls and ceiling were painted jet black and the stage was located in the middle, with folding chairs along all four sides looking in, like ringside seats. I'd been dragged to one of these "black box" experimental spaces when I lived with Marlene and Josie, a play where all the actors wore paper bags over their heads, except for one who wore a plastic one. It was titled "Paper or Plastic," and it was supposed to be a comedy, but the joke had definitely been on the audience, since it was us who'd paid five bucks at the door.

I counted about seventy-five people here, a pretty impressive number, considering the school itself only had five hundred kids total. Betty and the rest of the golden girls led me to the front row, since their hearing aids worked better closer to the sound source.

"Welcome, fellow females of Llewellyn," Green Hair announced. There was a mike stand to her left, but she didn't need one. If there was a part for a female god voiceover on TV, hers would be it: booming, authoritative, with a hint of condescension. "I'm so glad to see so many sisters here tonight. We've got a full agenda here, so let's get right to it. This is our fourth meeting this semester, and I see a lot of familiar faces, but I also see some new ones. So for those newbies, you'll find our meetings short and to the point. They never run for more than half an hour, and afterwards, we'll break out Jackie's famous brownies and mingle." The Womyn sat down on a long cafeteria table, with Green Hair in the center.

For the next fifteen minutes, I couldn't quite reconcile what I was seeing and hearing. I don't know what I'd been expecting when I received the invite from the lily-tattooed girl, but hearing about "old business" and "new business" and phrases like "I move to postpone" and "I refer to amend the motion," right out of Roberta's Rule of Order, was definitely not it. I mean I wasn't thinking we'd be throwing our bras into a bonfire, but this was as sleep-inducing as C-SPAN.

"Sister Faith," the black girl with the mass of earrings said, "I move to divide the motion on the table into two separate motions."

So that was Green Hair's name—Faith.

"Is there a second?" Faith asked.

"Second," one of the spiky-haired twins said.

"Let us take a vote. All in favor, say aye," Faith said.

The theater was filled with an unequivocal, "Aye."

"The motion passes," Faith said with a tap of her gavel, which meant that they now had separated the budget for snacks and drinks. Riveting.

They moved onto flyer postings, a bake sale, then some other stuff that I zoned out of, and finally, the other twin said, "I move to adjourn," and thankfully the meeting came to an end. Faith smacked her gavel twice, and as the Womyn rose, I caught her smiling at the doorway of the theater, and now I knew what Josie meant during our initial meeting, when she'd said Faith had enjoyed it while Penny read from her note card.

Outside of her green hair, Faith was an ordinary-looking young woman, about five-six with brown eyes, but that smile of hers had dimensions beyond pleasantness or good humor; it had menace. I turned around and saw a man in a business suit staring back at her, then leaving in a huff. I recognized him from the WILL brochure; he was the Dean of Students.

And now it all made sense. This meeting was a sham, a front put on by the Womyn for the administration to pretend they were nothing more than an organization that schedules bake sales and charity 5Ks. How appropriate that it was held in a theater.

"Reading my Medicare statement might have been more entertaining," Betty said. She and her girls had seen enough and were ready to head home. I told them I'd hang for a bit, so I wished them good night.

Most of the audience was still here. From the refreshments table I snagged a marbled brownie and sat down on one of the stools by the sound board in the corner. It was elevated and gave me a nice view into the mingling that was now going on. All but two of the Womyn were in conversation, and they were all talking one-on-one with interested students, not in groups, so the girls formed lines and waited their turn. Meanwhile, Faith scoured the floor intently, and the lily-tattooed girl waited with her phone at the ready to transcribe whatever it was that Faith was telling her. I was too far from them to hear what Faith was saying, but I'd bet a dollar that she was naming names. Potential candidates, perhaps. One common thing about student-run organizations was that they were perpetually turning over. Seniors graduated and freshmen came in, so bringing in new blood was always a priority.

It was just a matter of time until Faith saw me. She stared at me, so I stared back. She muttered something to the lily-tattooed girl, who took her eyes away from her phone to stare at me, too. And now she was walking over.

"Enjoy your brownie?" she asked me.

"Ungodly good. Siobhan O'Brien," I said, and we shook hands.

"Sister Molly. Is there a reason why you don't want to get in line like everybody else?"

"I'd like to talk to Faith."

She crossed her arms and stood straighter. "And why is that?"

"Penny Sykes," I said.

Molly's face was like a door slowly closing shut. When I can, I prefer to go with Plan A, which is by way of honesty, but I had an inkling that wasn't going to work here. So onto Plan B.

"I'm an investigator for K-1 Adoption Services. We operate out of St. Paul, Minnesota, which was Penny's entry point from South Korea. Her birth mother wants to communicate with her. I've spoken with Penny's mother, Josie Sykes, and she gave me the rundown. I was about to approach Faith myself after this meeting was over, but you beat me to it."

And just like that, the door swung wide open. Molly touched my shoulder and said, "Let me talk to Sister Faith."

She scurried back, and now she had to wait because Faith was in deep conversation with a girl with dreadlocks. There were a lot of interesting-looking people here, not unlike the cantina scene in *Star*

Wars: a little person wearing farmer's overalls, a black girl in a skin-tight bodysuit whose shaved head looked as smooth as stone in water, an Asian gal wearing a pink tutu. Perhaps she was a dance major and had come rushing after a class. Or more likely, this was collegiate fashion now and I was hopelessly out of step with the times.

Faith and the dreadlocked girl exchanged a heartfelt hug, and now Molly was talking into her ear. And once again, across the open space of this black box theater, Faith and I locked eyes. Lucky for me, she didn't smile. Molly listened to her, nodded, and made her way back to me.

"She can see you at headquarters at ten tonight. Can you come then?"

This day was growing longer by the minute, but it was fine. Well, no, it wasn't fine, but killing time is often part of the job.

18

In the basement of Fordham Hall, I stood in front of a vending machine that looked like it'd been here since Nixon was President. I pressed a green button that had almost turned black from use, and a dark stream of liquid coughed and sputtered into a Styrofoam cup. It resembled a pool of dirty mop water and tasted like burned toast. I drowned two spoonfuls of powdered creamer plus three packets of sugar, but that hardly made it better.

Regardless, I leaned against the kitchenette counter and drank it down, because I needed the caffeine. It was now five before ten. To keep awake, I crossed the empty room, which was some sad sort of a recreational space. Against a wall was a stack of Hula hoops, a few coils of jump ropes, and what I deciphered to be a limbo dance kit, comprised of a long bamboo stick and two stands with multiple tiers. It was all rather dated, but then again, this entire room felt that way, from the fake wood paneling to the large oil portrait of the donor that hung by the door: HUBERT AND MARGERY BETHUNE (Class of 1942). Hubert was forever frozen in his fifties buzz cut and Margery wore lacey white gloves. He was standing with one hand on her shoulder while she sat daintily on an equally dainty high-backed chair with her legs crossed.

Click.

The door had just closed.

"Hello?" I said.

I walked over and reached for the knob. I turned it, but it didn't budge. And on the other side of the door, I heard the footsteps of the person leaving.

"Hey!" I yelled out, but the footsteps got fainter until they disappeared altogether.

And then the lights went out.

19

This basement room had no windows, so without the fluorescents above, it was pitch black. It was one thing to be plunged in total darkness in the comfort of my own bedroom, but in this unfamiliar space, every little sound was heightened, especially my own heartbeat, which thumped against my chest like a wild animal ramming itself against its cage.

If somebody was trying to scare me, it was working.

Breathe, Siobhan, breathe. Deep breaths, not little tiny shallow ones like you're doing now.

I was close to the door, that much I remembered. I reached out with my left hand until I felt the reassuring wood against my fingertips. I leaned against it for support and turned around. That helped a little but not a lot.

I had to get control of my mind, because it was thinking a lot of nasty thoughts. Like how easy it would be for someone to stab me right now, the blade coming from nowhere, the cold metal sinking into my body with a *squish.*

Better thoughts. Think better thoughts.

I thought of Ed, sitting at a bench in Athena Park, his body as still as a statue. This was a couple of months ago, when we were on a vandalism case that pushed the limits of our patience. Somebody kept defacing the flower garden at night and it was driving the city nuts, and us, too, because after two weeks, the culprit hadn't shown.

You're it, Ed had said.

I sat down for my shift.

You would never think waiting is a skill, but it is.

On the seventeenth night, I found the guy, a disgruntled employee of the grounds department. I out-waited him. I survived that trial. I would survive this one, too, if I was patient, if I was calm, if I kept my wits about me.

Somewhere in the basement, there was a squeak of another door opening. That wasn't possible—I'd seen no other entryway—so I must've missed it. So much for my detecting skills. Fordham used to be Horace Llewellyn's home, which meant it was old and most likely had doors made to look like the wall, the ones servants would use. If only I'd paid closer attention instead of fiddling with the bad cup of coffee.

I felt movement about me. Something grazed my cheek and I stifled a scream. An idea: I thrust my hand into my purse and found my phone. But before I could unlock it, somebody ripped it out of my hand. *Fuck!*

Only someone who could see in the dark, like someone wearing night-vision goggles, could do that.

"Ever see *Silence of the Lambs?*" the voice said, a voice I recognized: Faith.

"I reviewed it for my school paper, actually," I said, doing my best to keep my voice from shaking. I didn't like remembering the creepfest of an ending, where the serial killer stalks Jodie Foster in the dark, everything in that alien green. "Gave it a B. I still don't quite understand how that movie won Best Picture."

Bugsy, JFK, The Prince of Tides—there was one more. *Beauty and the Beast*, that's it, the best picture nominees that year. I would've given the Oscar to any of those others. Robert De Niro, Warren Beatty, Nick Nolte, Anthony Hopkins, and one more leading actor I couldn't remember, but that was okay. Like counting from one to a hundred, this kind of rote recall was a good way to bring the blood pressure down.

Feeling a little more serene, I thought of something else that might further bring the good juju and maybe also telegraph to my captor some confidence: I slowly sat down Indian-style. With my back against the wall and my hands on my knees, I felt more grounded.

"Make yourself at home," Faith said. "Because we're gonna be here a while."

I said nothing, and she said nothing. The silence was broken when I began to hear other sounds—a clatter of metallic objects as a cart was wheeled over the linoleum, a liquid poured from one container to another, fabric ripping, chain links clinking on the ground as it was dragged.

I laughed.

"Glad you're finding your situation so hilarious," Faith said.

Unfortunately for Faith, instead of frightening me, the sound effects had the opposite effect. Because what I now thought of was Garrison Keillor and his show, the *Prairie Home Companion*, his troupe performing all their little honks and gongs for sonic verisimilitude on his radio show. And the longer I sat here, the more time I had to think about the situation at hand. These were not hardened criminals, they were kids. Of course it was possible they were deranged and violent, but it was more likely that the majority of the Womyn of Llewellyn were theater majors. Which was probably the real reason they'd held their meeting in the black box in the first place.

"Siobhan. O'Brien." Faith tsk-tsked, as if she were admonishing a child. "No more games. Tell us who you really are."

I cleared my throat. "Believe it or not, that is my name. I was adopted by an American couple when I was a baby."

"Investigator for an adoption service? You really want us to believe that?"

There was no reason for me to keep up the front because it wasn't going to get me anywhere.

"I am a private investigator who was hired by Josie Sykes, Penny Sykes's mother, to find her. I lied so I'd get to talk to you, Faith, because it seemed like the fastest way for us to communicate."

After a pause, Faith screamed, "Lies!"

"If you flip the lights back on, I'll show you my PI license. I'll also show you the copy of the contract I drew up for Josie."

After a long moment, someone else spoke as quietly as possible, which I heard as clear as broadcast news because the room was silent.

"Maybe we should turn the…"

"Damn it, Raven!" Faith said.

"Sorry," Raven said. "It's just that I don't think she's playing us and I still have to cram for my chemistry exam."

"I haven't even started my bio report," someone else said, which opened the floodgates.

"…on page 4 of *War and Peace*…"

"…Dr. Polansky is such a hardass…"

"…if I don't pull a C, I'm gonna friggin fail macro…"

I heard a deep and disappointed sigh, shuffling footsteps, then had to shield my eyes from the lights above. Faith stood over me, the night-vision goggles hanging off her neck. There was probably more duct tape on that thing than any original part. A small gray patch was still stuck on her cheek, so I pointed to my own face.

"Thanks," Faith said.

"So can I go?" said the black girl with the oversized earrings. In the darkness, Faith had referred to her as Raven.

"Yes, yes," Faith said, "whoever needs to go, go." Then she pointed to me. "Not you."

20

It was just me, Faith, and the lily-tattooed girl Molly now left in this very large room. Molly was very happy about this. In fact, it wouldn't have been an understatement to say that she reminded me of my childhood dog Ginny any time she got near a Frisbee.

"How about if I get us some chairs, Sister Faith?" she chirped.

"Sure," Faith said, who was perhaps one percent as happy as Molly. Their relationship was as obvious as the nose on my face. Molly, the underclasswoman, looked up to Faith the upperclasswoman with great reverence. Faith didn't strike me as someone who didn't enjoy being worshipped, but then again, everyone had their limits. Molly ran over to the closet and brought over a trio of folding chairs, then wiped the one for Faith free of dust with the sleeve of her shirt.

"Do you plan to resell my phone on eBay?" I asked Faith once we were all sitting.

She tossed the phone back to me, which I thankfully caught. It may be in vogue for every kid to have a phone with a broken screen, but I was too old to have to peer past a spiderweb of cracks.

"What are you doing?" Faith asked Molly, who had silently, magically produced a pen and a notepad.

"As the recording secretary of the Womyn of Llewellyn, shouldn't I be taking notes?"

Faith closed her eyes and rubbed her temples. "Does this look like a meeting to you?"

"I don't know, Sister. We've had Ex-Com sessions with just three sisters, too. You call this a meeting, and I'll do my job. You say it's not, and I'll wait for you to give me your next command."

"It's not a meeting."

"Yes, Sister," Molly said. Shot down pretty hard, but her smile was wider than ever as she put away her notepad and pen and sat with her hands on her lap.

"You know what you could bring me? My iPad. It's in my…"

She was already up and on her way. "I know where it is, Sister Faith." Molly ran over to the wall and pushed, and there it was, the hidden door I'd missed. There was a bookcase right where the seam would be, smartly concealed.

"Driving you a little insane?" I asked.

"Is it that obvious?"

"Molly's quite the whirlwind."

"Like the Tasmanian Devil. Sometimes she leaves little whorls of air behind her. But she's a good girl. There aren't many of us left."

"And what do you exactly mean by that?"

Faith looked at me and said nothing. I found the copy of Josie's contract in my purse and handed it and my New York State Private Investigator's License to her.

"All I want to know is where Penny is."

Faith raked her fingers through her hair and tied it up into a tight ponytail. Her bright green hair no longer framing her face, she looked like any normal girl of her age. She'd have to dye that hair back to a non-nutty color if she wanted to work in the real world. College is so short, too short.

"What's in it for me?" Faith asked.

I laughed. "How about satisfying your innate human desire to do good?"

"Her mother fucked her up, you know."

"Don't all mothers fuck up their children?"

"Some more than others. Which is why we have TLC, to take care of girls like Penny."

"I've only heard Josie's side. What did Penny tell you?"

"That's between me and her," Faith said. She handed the contract and ID back to me. "You could've just made all this up with a laminator and a laser printer."

I handed her my business card. "If you change your mind and want to help, get in touch."

I got up and headed for the hidden door.

"That's it?" Faith said. "I thought real detectives were tenacious."

"Real detectives find other, less time-consuming ways to get information," I said. "If you still think I'm lying, then I'm wasting my time."

"Wait."

I turned around and saw her sitting there. I don't know what it was—maybe the two empty chairs that flanked her, or just the vastness of the room itself, but from where I was standing, she seemed quite alone.

"Please, sit," she said. I walked back and sat. Faith rose and paced as she spoke, her sneakers squeaking lightly against the floor.

"I assume you went to college," she said. I nodded. "So you know what it's like. This is my fourth and final year, and even though I don't expect my alma mater to never change, you have to admit, this is a special case. The Llewellyn I fell in love with is not the Llewellyn I'm leaving."

"The boys," I said.

Her shoes squealed sharply as she came to a sudden halt. "See, she's fooled you, too. And you are someone who is professionally difficult to fool. The boys are just a distraction. A good distraction, I'll give her that, the sneaky bitch. Oh no, there's a long con going on, and nobody else is seeing it. God, how can everyone be so fucking blind?"

"The sneaky bitch being your president, Vera Wheeler?"

Faith spoke with a passion that rivaled any evangelical Sunday sermon. Outsized hand gestures, flailing arms, her whole body expressing every word: Faith was either going to become a Broadway actress or a dictator of a small nation. If she had a lectern, she would've slammed it as she told me about all the evil Wheeler had done. Some of it went over my head because it was too Llewellyn-centric, acronyms like FOS and SDM whizzed by me in her impassioned speech, but in the end, I wanted to apologize to my brain for working to piece together this ridiculous ramble.

"So what you're claiming," I said, "is that Wheeler is in the process of turning Llewellyn into a breeding ground for…fashion models?"

Faith stuck out her arms akimbo and stared me down. "You think I'm batshit crazy."

"Batshit might be a little harsh. Maybe duck poop?"

"And now you turn me into a joke."

"You have to admit…" I said, but I was interrupted by Molly's flourished reentry. She sprinted to Faith with her iPad in hand, and once she caught her breath, asked, "I hope I didn't miss too much."

"You did good," Faith said. "Perfect timing, Sister Molly."

"I'm here for you, Sister Faith," she said. "Always and forever."

If Faith's eyeballs could roll back any further, they'd be on the back of her head.

"So," Faith said to me. "Here's some duck poop for you."

21

Faith swiped at her iPad until she got to what she wanted to show me. "Look through these photos. There's two on each page. On the left is a freshwoman from the class four years ago. On the right is the incoming freshwoman class. There are a total of eighty-four comparisons, and I'll be more than happy to wait as you go through each and every one."

The photos on the left from four years ago looked like yearbook portraits, while the ones on the right were selfies. So if anything, the older ones had the advantage of being taken by a professional under proper lighting, coiffed hair, etc.—and yet as I swiped from one picture to another, there was no comparison here. Much of the incoming freshman class was a collection of striking young women. Not necessarily beautiful in a traditional way, but almost every time, my eyeballs were drawn to the right for some specific feature: brilliant blue eyes flecked with gold, lips as thick as pincushions, a nose as sharp as a blade. Runways models, I thought. Magazine covers. There were three or four that I had to stop and stare for a good ten seconds, because they were every bit as gorgeous as any Hollywood starlet. And these were just cell phone pics.

"How did Wheeler get all the incoming freshwomen to send photos of themselves?" I asked.

Molly chimed in. "We were strongly recommended to interview with Llewellyn alumni, and at the end of each interview, the interviewer suggested we take a selfie together."

"You see? This is how noxious Wheeler is. She used our alums to do her bidding."

As much as I found it to be an insane notion, the evidence before me made her assertions harder to ignore. But still, this was outlandish. As if she felt my lingering doubts, Molly jumped in.

"Can I see the iPad again?" she asked.

Molly swiped and moved things on the iPad with such speed and confidence that only comes from being born in a world that had always had the internet. A few more deft strokes of her fingers later, she held up the screen and showed me the same two-photo output like before, except this one had the faces aligned and split into four quadrants by way of two perpendicular green lines.

"Symmetry is one of the keys to facial attractiveness," Molly said. "There's an app that'll calculate your beauty quotient."

"As if girls don't have enough reasons to feel bad about themselves," I said.

Molly touched a button and all the faces blazed by me while two numbers floated on the top left and top right part of the screen. A pleasant ding later, the slideshow stopped and the numbers held fast. 6.835 on the left, 9.129 on the right.

"This is just the beginning, I'm certain of it. There's a building…" Faith said, then trailed off as another thought took her over. "Okay. You want to find Penny, right?"

I knew where this was going. "What do you want?"

"Have you seen Travers Hall?"

I had not. Faith signaled to Molly, and the wizard was back at it, and in a moment she had a photograph of a white shoebox of a building with scaffolding around it and a big yellow sign, UNDER CONSTRUCTION – NO ADMITTANCE. When Molly expanded a corner of the screen, I recognized the sundial near the side of Broadhurst Hall.

"So this Travers Hall is behind and to the right of Broadhurst," I said, seeing the campus layout in my mind. "But I don't remember this, and it's hard to miss because it's so white."

"It's behind three rows of huge evergreens to separate it from the rest of campus. And the building is strictly off limits," Molly said.

"It is being built, so there are probably hazards," I said.

"True," Faith said. "But look here, and here. Why are the windows covered? And why is there a security guy posted at the entrance? Not to mention that there's an active alarm system at night."

"And how would you know that?" I asked.

"That's not the point. Why would you install an alarm system when the building isn't even completed yet?"

I didn't know, but I was getting kind of curious myself.

"So here's the deal. I'll tell you everything I know about Penny," Faith said.

"But you don't know where she is."

"No. But I probably know more than anybody else outside of Grace Park, and good luck talking with her."

"What, is she involved with too many clubs to make time for me?"

"She's got bodyguards," Molly said.

"Bodyguards?"

Faith corrected her. "'Special security' is what the meatheads call themselves. It's like when the President's daughter goes to school, spooks keep eyes on her. Look, I'll grant you full access to Penny's room, too. You can spend the night there, even, since it's pretty late and this way, you can look all you want. I just want you to find out all you can about Travers Hall."

"Breaking and entering."

"We have the alarm code. None of us Womyn can go near that building because campus security is keeping tabs on us, but you, you're a WILL. They won't suspect you."

"Because I'm old and feeble."

"Exactly," Molly said, oblivious to my sarcasm.

"I have a contact in the media, and if the story is juicy enough, I can nail Wheeler for the fake that she is," Faith said. "There is something going on here. Right? You think so, too. I can see it in your face, Siobhan."

"I agree there is *something*, but I doubt it's what you think."

"This will take like an hour of your time, tops," Faith said. "A few photos, just a quick peek, that's all."

I didn't glance at my watch but it felt like it was well past midnight. I took a good look at Faith, and then at Molly. They seemed like silly girls with their weird hair and tattoos, but their passion for their school was as real and as deep as any devotion. And who knew, maybe digging around Travers would get me closer to finding Penny. Getting to the end of a case was never a straight line.

"Okay," I said. "Let's help each other."

Faith and Molly slid from their chairs and onto the floor. They held hands and knelt.

"You too," Faith said. "By our bylaws, two Womyn of Llewellyn can consecrate another."

Consecrate? Lordy. But when in Rome…I knelt, and we formed a circle. Faith and Molly spoke together.

"By the power vested in us, we Womyn of Llewellyn bring you, Siobhan O'Brien, and your everlasting feminine spirit inside our inner circle and declare you our dear Sister."

I wanted to ask if this honor was temporary or forever and ever and ever, but kept my mouth shut.

22

As we climbed the stairs to the second floor of Fordham, Faith told me about Penny.

"Some quiet girls, when they leave home, they get even quieter. And some blast off in the opposite direction. I don't know what her mom told you, but Penny was pretty out of control. She was already here for a couple of months for the pre-frosh summer program, which is where she made friends with Grace Park, so I'm not sure exactly what was going on between the two of them, but the first night I met Penny, she got drunk and passed out.

"At that point she was living with Grace—you know the school bent over backwards to get that girl here, right? They converted a part of an admin building into a dorm just for her. Only a few girls have been invited inside, and from what I hear, it's like a fancy hotel suite. Nobody has any pictures because there's always a goon posted at her door who collects the phones before you can enter. It's nuts."

We were now at the double doors that led to Tender Llewellyn Care. Sitting behind a small desk was one of the twin girls with spiky hair I'd seen at Faith's table in the dining hall.

"Glad you finally showed up, Faith," she said. "You and Molly are the last ones, so everyone's in now."

"Excellent," Faith said. She turned to me. "Since you're WILL-ing, you can just show Katie here your Lewie ID." Katie used her phone and scanned the barcode on the back. Then she pressed a button under the desk and released the electronic lock. Faith held the door open, and we all went inside.

"I'm here," Molly said, stopping at the first room on the right. "It's great to bring you into the fold, Sister Siobhan." She opened up her arms for a hug, so I hugged her, and then she was gone.

The hallways were bathed in red light.

"Some of the girls have trouble sleeping," Faith said. "Red light doesn't interfere with melatonin production. And you might have noticed a bit of white noise in the background."

I hadn't, but now that I was listening, I did hear it, like a running fan. "Soothing," I said.

"That's the idea."

The hallway ran down the middle of the floor, then branched off at the center to the left and right. From a bird's eye view, the layout would resemble a giant cross.

Penny's room was at the far end. It was a basic college dorm room, a twin bed, a desk and chair, a dresser. Outside of some books on the desk, there was nothing else that suggested someone lived here.

"Where's her stuff?" I asked.

"That's it. She had a fridge but gave it away. Gave away just about everything before she left. And threw away the rest, like she had a few photos in frames of her and her mom, her and her high school friends, that sort of thing."

"When did she leave?"

"About a week ago. Right after the fight in her writing class."

"A fight?"

"A literal fight. Sorry, I don't mean a literary fight, but like hair pulled, punches thrown. Who knew Creative Writing 201 could be so interesting? I should've taken it when I had the chance."

"You must've heard what happened? From her classmates?"

"It happened after class, when it was just Penny, the girl, and the professor. The girl she fought with—Henrietta something—she's gone, too. She was very Mormon and just didn't fit in here, so she went back home. I can find out her last name and you can track her down, I suppose. You can also talk to Professor Marks, though he's funny about CW201. He considers it therapy and himself a thera-pist, so you might get stonewalled with doctor-patient privacy type of bullshit."

"Did you and Penny talk about it? Or are you going to stonewall me, too, with doctor-patient privacy type of bullshit?"

Faith smiled. "The whole point of TLC is to be a safe house. We want our girls to get better, but on their own terms. Unless they want to change, nothing's going to work. I asked her if she wanted to talk about what happened, and she didn't, so I just held her for a while. She cried, then fell asleep."

"So Penny didn't tell you where she was going."

"No, but I know that Wheeler personally came to see her in her room."

"Is that something that normally happens, the president of the college making house calls?"

"Wheeler makes it sound like she's all hands-on, but she's hardly around. In the four years I've been here, I never heard of her visiting any student in her dorm room."

"And the next day, Penny was gone."

Faith nodded. "I went to see Wheeler when I found out, but of course, she wasn't available. And the registrar's office told me Penny took a voluntary leave of absence."

"Why did you give Josie such a hard time? She said Penny read from a note card, listing all her grievances."

"It's part of the healing process. You have to confront your fears, and there's no greater source of fear than from those who love you. Her mother was way too involved in her daughter's life. You know she tracked Penny's periods in a ledger?"

"Excuse me?"

"You heard me. Jesus, I thought she was gonna kill me when she came here, looking for her daughter. Thank goodness security showed up."

"When did Penny come to TLC?"

"Right after she and Grace had a falling out. Mid-September, so she was here for about a month. It was supposed to be temporary, but then she realized how much she wanted to stay. How much she needed it."

I glanced at my watch. One thirty. No wonder I felt like a zombie.

From the bottom desk drawer, Faith brought out a Hello Kitty bag and a bath towel and handed them to me.

"Just what I always wanted," I said.

"Basic toiletries, so you don't have to go to bed all gross." She handed me the key to the room then bid me good night.

After she left, I trudged to the bathroom down the weird red-lit hall. The bathroom was bathed in red, too, and I was reminded of the darkroom I used to frequent way back when, during my high school photography class. That was about how old Penny was, myself back then. Who was that girl? I could hardly remember. Not that different than who I was now, though I was probably wrong. I bet I would hardly recognize my younger self if I ran into me now.

These were some strange thoughts I was having. Late night thoughts. Penny's bed was made, but it'd probably been weeks since the sheets were changed, so I stayed in my t-shirt and jeans and got under the blanket. As I fell asleep, I hoped to absorb whatever remained of her identity here, because it looked like I was going to need all the help I could get.

23

With my mind awake and clear in the morning, I searched Penny's room again, the kind of searching that involved turning over the mattress, checking its seams, and moving furniture. There weren't many pieces to move, and the only thing I found was a packet of gum that possibly predated even me: JUICY FRUIT written in a blocky font that I remembered from my childhood.

All that remained in the closet were a handful of wire hangers and a white belt from a terry cloth bathrobe. The only objects that saved this room from complete anonymity were the four books on the desk: *The Collected Stories of Richard Yates*, Stewart O'Nan's *Last Night at the Lobster*, *The Riverside Shakespeare*, and a plastic spiral-bound packet that looked like it came from a print shop. CREATIVE WRITING 201, it said on the cover, Professor Lawrence Marks. On the first page were his office location and hours: Grover 212, Tue 9-11am. Since I hadn't overslept too badly, I could head over there after breakfast with time to spare. The spiral-bound packet itself seemed brand new, with no notes on the margins or food stains. According to the second page of the syllabus, the class was supposed to have read a third of its contents by now.

TLC looked much more inviting in the morning, the sun filling the hallways with natural light instead of the eerie bloody red. I could've used a shower, but I didn't have any clean clothes with me, so didn't see the point. Besides, from the way the girls here were dressed, I'd fit right in with my frumpy, lived-in look. I brushed my teeth and washed my face in the bathroom then made my way out.

"Hello, Katie," I said to the spiky-haired girl at the front desk.

"I'm Carson," she said. And to make matters as clear as possible, right behind me was Katie herself.

When I got to the dining hall, they were already closing up. I grabbed a bagel and slapped a hunk of cream cheese in between and made my way over to Grover, one of the uglier buildings on campus, a squat, flat-roofed thing that looked like it was built in the seventies. How could anyone think this garish orange and bright yellow trim on the windows was ever a good idea?

Marks's office was on the second floor, and there were two students waiting in line, sitting on the floor outside the closed door. Earbuds in ears, eyes on the phone: this was the default mode for just about every kid I saw here at Lewie.

I didn't have earbuds, but I did have a phone, so I sat next to a boy and unlocked it. The campus had wifi everywhere, but for some reason, I couldn't connect to it.

The door opened and a girl came out hitching her backpack, and the next student went in.

"You need the Lewie app if you want to connect to the five gigahertz access points," the boy said. He then looked up at me and correctly assumed I was in the techno-neophyte age group. I offered him my phone and a few magical swipes and taps later, I was online.

"Thanks," I said.

"Which class of Lare's are you in?" he asked.

"Lare?"

"That's what we call him, Professor Marks. Or, more accurately, what he wants us to call him."

The boy was Rob Lowe cute. But remembering that I was a professional gumshoe, I cleared my throat and managed to respond calmly.

"I wanted to talk to him about Creative Writing 201," I said.

"Ah, the class everybody wants to get into," the boy said. "You have to submit a writing sample. Three poems or a story at least fifteen pages long, double spaced. I tried with my poems but he wasn't feeling them."

"Sounds like freshmen would not have an easy time getting into the class."

"Just one this year, from what I heard," the boy said.

Penny, who must've submitted something that really caught Marks's eye.

"I'm trying again next semester, for CW202. I still have seven more chances, so I'll just keep at it. Lare wrote me a very nice letter why he didn't let me in, though. He's like the fairest guy around."

"Even fairer than Judge Judy?"

The boy laughed at my terrible joke, and it sort of made my day that I got him to laugh. Oh, Siobhan, you really need to get a grip. Or maybe just get laid. And preferably with someone who wasn't young enough to be your son.

"The way he runs his workshop, he makes sure that students have something good to say before they can start criticizing."

"Because positivity is the source of all that is good," a voice interrupted.

24

Lawrence Marks stood over us like a gentle giant. He could've served as the model for the lumberjack on front of Brawny paper towels, with his full beard and flannel shirt.

"Hey Lare," the boy said, and got up. I did, too, because I felt awkward to be the only one sitting.

"Ricky, my man," Marks said, and they exchanged an orchestrated flurry of slaps and bumps with their hands that ended with a manly half-hug.

"Your John Hancock, please," Ricky said. He produced a sheet and handed Marks a pen. Marks looked it over and nodded, then signed.

"Much luck with it," Marks said.

"Thanks, Lare." Ricky then turned to me. "See you around," he said, and for a second, I thought to myself, *Did he really mean that?* Then I had another thought: *You're an idiot.*

"I don't know you," Marks said. "I assume you are a WILL student?"

His hand was as soft as a pillow when I shook it.

"I am," I said. "Siobhan O'Brien."

"That's an interesting name," he said. "A novel-worthy name, I bet."

He led me into his office, which was messily academic, with books and journals crammed into every possible space. On the floor were pillars of books that reminded me of several Jenga puzzles leaning on each other.

I sat and showed him my PI license. "I was hired by Penny Sykes's mother to find her."

"I didn't know she was missing," Marks said. "The registrar informed me she took a leave of absence."

I gave him the rundown. He was an intense listener, focused on every single one of my words.

"Sounds like she left on her own volition," Marks said.

"I don't know. That's why I'm here, asking questions. So can you tell me what happened between Penny and Henrietta?"

"No," Marks said.

"I thought you were there."

"I ran in to break up the fight after it had started. The class had ended, I had a department meeting to attend and was halfway down the corridor when I heard the screaming. Henrietta had Penny in a headlock of sorts, and Penny was punching her in the stomach. Like professional wrestling."

Marks didn't seem fazed recounting this story. In fact, if anything, he sounded a little proud.

"I take it this is not the first time something like this happened," I said.

"Fiction is a rough mistress," he said. "Sometimes truth reveals itself best through a veil of make-believe. No, it's not the first time in my career that two students went at it, but it is rare for them to have a physical altercation. I don't promote their violence, but I support their passion."

"So the fight had to do with something one of them wrote."

Marks put up both hands like a traffic cop. "We abide by the Vegas code."

"What happens in CW201 stays in CW201."

"It's a safe zone for my students to express themselves without repercussions. If I can't provide that protection, what good am I?"

"Would you allow me to sit in class, then?"

"And what would that accomplish, outside of you procuring a list of kids to interrogate later?"

The fairest, Ricky had said. I had to appeal to that side of him.

"Would you be willing to tell your students who I am and why I need their help, then put it to a vote to determine the fate of my visit?"

He stroked his beard thoughtfully, a practiced pose if I ever saw one. But he did look like he was actually considering it.

"I like the way you think," he said. "I'll email my students today and let you know what they say. It'll have to be unanimous. One dissenting voice…"

"Of course."

We shook hands and that was that. Two more students had queued after me, so Marks's office hour parade continued on. Popular guy.

25

As I descended the stairs of Grover Hall and was about to head back out, I felt like I had enough at this point to hit up the source. Now that I had access to the Lewie network on my phone thanks to my new boyfriend Ricky, I got on the student directory's website and looked up Grace Park. I'd half expected her to be unlisted, but there she was, Hawkes 204. I consulted my pocket campus map and found Hawkes, a two-story colonial situated on a hill. It was labeled as an administrative building and not a dorm, which matched what Faith had told me last night about Grace's special living arrangement.

The day had turned dark, a heavy gray curtain of clouds moving in from the west. With most kids in classes, the walking paths were almost deserted, fall leaves turning in the wind. I was twenty feet from the main entrance of Hawkes, a bright red door with gold trim, when a man came to walk beside me.

"Good morning," he said.

He was an Asian male about six feet tall with a military-style crew cut. He didn't have the thick neck or the thigh-like biceps of a bodybuilder, but I felt an undeniable sense of strength coiled beneath his white turtleneck and black slacks. People might say he looked like an athlete, but there was a sharpness there that went beyond tossing a ball around.

"Hello," I said.

"Brent Kim, Special Campus Security." He spoke with a slight accent but enunciated each word extra clearly, like somebody who was taught formal English back in Korea. When he extended his hand, I caught a glimpse of a circle of black stars on the inner part of his wrist.

"Nice to meet you," I said.

"May I ask the nature of your business in Hawkes?"

Time to play stupid.

"I thought Hawkes was an admin building." I took out my pocket map and read off the directory on the back. "Here it is, Student Services."

When I looked up at him, he had his phone out and snapped a photo of me.

"It's rather rude to take pictures of people without asking their permission."

"Apologies," he said, then his phone dinged. "Ms. Siobhan O'Brien?"

So it was a face recognition thing, hooked up to the school's ID database. "Special" indeed.

"Yes. Now that you know who I am, can I go into the building?"

"Of course. But I'll accompany you."

"So everybody who comes here is escorted by you?"

"Myself or one of my associates," Kim said. "Shall we go?"

I didn't see a reason to mince words with Mr. No-Nonsense.

"I'd like to ask Grace Park a few questions," I said. I showed him my PI license.

"May I take a picture of this document?" he said.

"Yes."

A click later, he handed it back to me. "May I ask the nature of your business with Ms. Park?"

"I've come to understand that Grace was friends with Penny Sykes. I've been hired by Sykes's mother to find her."

"What if I capture your information and your purpose and present it to Ms. Park?" Kim said. "If she agrees to speak with you, then a meeting will be arranged. Does that sound satisfactory to you?"

It certainly did not, because I had serious doubts my request would even get to Grace. But before I could reply, Llewellyn's bell tower began to ring. Which was odd, because my watch told me it was 11:38. After ten rings, the bells stopped—and then they began again.

Simultaneously, both Kim's and my phones chirped. The text message read:

```
    *** A BOMB THREAT HAS BEEN RECEIVED AT
             LLEWELLYN COLLEGE ***
Please  follow  your  instructors  or  Llewellyn
personnel  to  exit  the  building  in  an  orderly
fashion.
```

"Does this sort of thing happen often around here?" I asked Kim.

He jogged away from me without an answer.

All around us, students and professors alike were filing out of their classrooms. My phone chirped again with a text from a different number.

```
guard just left travers. disarm code 62031.
go through hedges right of hawkes and you are
there.
```

The number was 111-111-1111. Probably from Faith or Molly, since they had my phone last night, and Molly seemed the techie type to mask the Caller ID. I looked around to see if they were watching me, but good luck with that. Five hundred students may not sound like many, but having all of them outside at the same time, plus all the professors and the employees, walking about on the grass—it looked like Times Square on New Year's Eve.

At first glance I couldn't see how I could go through the thicket of hedges on the right side of Hawkes, but as I skulked toward the back, I found a space between two bushes that I could slip through sideways. I closed my eyes and got a few light scratches on my cheeks, but I made like a crab and squeezed through to the other side.

Travers Hall, in its brand-new whiteness, stood in front of me. Even with the clouds, the building was almost too bright to look at. I walked up to the front doors, two large panes of glass which were the only ones not covered up by white paper. Initially, I thought I was seeing nothing at all, but then my eyes adjusted and saw a black desk and black chair in the lobby where the guard would've been, camouflaged by the blackness of the rest of the space. I punched in the five digits into the keypad to the right of me, and the blinking red light turned green. The door unlocked with a thud.

26

Inside Travers Hall, the black theme was relentless. Literally everything was black: the walls, the doors, the floor, even the pens in the cup sitting on the guard's desk. The smell of new materials was pervasive—fresh paint on drywall, little piles of sawdust by the trims and molding, a slight burned scent of warm forced air pushing through galvanized steel metal ducts that snaked around the ceiling.

White on the outside, black on the inside; whoever put up the cash for this building was in no mood for fifty shades of gray, or even one.

A corridor wide enough for a truck to drive through ran left and right. Each hallway was terminated by an impressively large circular window, covered over with white paper. I took a left and walked down, passing by a staircase and an elevator to my right. I pressed the UP button on the elevator. Nothing lit up, so there probably wasn't power going to it yet.

I kept walking until I stopped in front of the first door, the number 1 embossed on its obsidian surface. All the doors looked identical, a porthole-sized window placed about normal height, which meant it was a little too high for me; all I could see was the ceiling, which was, you guessed it, black. I tried the doorknob and it opened right up.

There were four rows and four columns of oblong stainless steel desks, each of them with two chairs. A small circular sink was installed in the middle of each desk. On the left and back walls were oval-shaped cabinets and shelves, and six large circular windows lined the right wall, each one with a smaller circular window embedded inside on the bottom that opened on an axis.

The color black and the geometric shape of a circle—whoever

designed this was in love with both. Maybe a little too much.

Faith thought there was some nefarious goings on here, but as far as I could see, it was an ordinary classroom, with a dry-erase board hanging in the front and a pull-down screen above it for projections of PowerPoint slides and whatnot. I took snapshots with my phone.

I exited Room 1 and entered Room 2, which looked like a mirror image, the dry-erase board and the cabinets reversed. Rooms 3 and 4 were also the same. On my phone I searched "Travers Hall" and found it on Llewellyn's website: a science building that was set to open next year. The information was scant; usually on these types of pages, they say why the building was being built, who the donator was, the progress so far, etc., but there was nothing.

And then I entered Room 8, and it was filled with body parts.

Not human body parts, but the mannequin equivalent. Half of the room was taken up with what looked like the rolling industrial laundry baskets that hotels use, and these baskets were organized and overflowing with limbs and heads and torsos. Perfectly shapely legs, with heel-ready feet pointing to the ceiling. Arms both straight and akimbo, some ending with a hole instead of a hand. The most striking of the baskets were the two heaping with heads. Many didn't have actual faces, but some did, and these kind of freaked me out. Peeking out from the pile of bald plastic heads were eyes, blue and green and brown, some staring right at me.

The mannequins were not new, their bodies scuffed, hands with fingers broken off. On a few of them, I found price tags from department stores taped on the bottoms of their feet—Macy's, Victoria's Secret, Sears, K-Mart, the usual suspects of retailers. I tried to think of why a science building would house mannequins. Chemical experiments with a certain kind of plastic? A study of physics requiring human-sized dummies? I knew I was wrong, so I kept looking.

Room 9 was a normal boring classroom. Next.

Room 10 had desks like others, but there were no sinks. And

instead of cabinets in the back, there were brown boxes. Smallish, about the size of a liquor box, stacked about six feet high. They were labeled BRU, BLO, BRO. I slid a box down, and behind it was another one labeled RED.

It felt about twenty pounds. I used my car keys to cut along the tape. Individually vacuum sealed in clear plastic bags, it looked like a box full of minks or otters or some exotic tubular animal pelt (chinchilla?). But then I saw what they really were: wigs. The box I'd opened was BLO, blond, packed to the hilt with glossy golden hair. Mannequins in one room, wigs in another. Interesting.

When I entered Room 12, my phone chirped.

```
*** A MESSAGE FROM LLEWELLYN COLLEGE ***
It is safe to return to your classes and build-
ings now. We apologize for the inconvenience.
If you have any questions, please dial Public
Safety at x1000.
```

From the hallway, I heard footsteps and voices. Sounded like two people. They somehow must've gotten the message earlier than me. I hadn't shut the door all the way and I wasn't about to do so now. Like Room 10, 12 also had boxes stacked high, and in one place there was a gap between the boxes and the wall. It was the only place where I could hide, and the voices were getting louder. I walked as quickly and as quietly as possible and crammed myself in the empty space, my arms stuck close to my side so I would fit. Standing motionless behind the boxes, I couldn't see what was going on, but I could hear, and it was a good thing I did make myself scarce because they entered here, in this very room.

The door slammed shut behind them.

27

"Didn't I tell you to close the door when we left?"

It was a woman's voice, almost as a deep as a man's.

"Don't yell at me, Val. You were the last to leave."

A man's voice, almost as light as a woman's. It was like something out of a *Saturday Night Live* skit, the man playing a woman and the woman playing a man. If this wasn't actually happening, I'd think it was a joke.

"Shit. You're right. Sorry."

"It's okay. This bomb thing just threw us for a loop."

A set of footsteps came closer. If they pulled away any of the boxes near me, there was nothing I could do. The footsteps stopped, and I could hear the person breathing. I opened my mouth so they wouldn't hear mine. A box at the height of my stomach was being pulled out. There were four boxes above that one, still enough to cover me, as long as they didn't topple.

"Jesus, can't you see I need help here?" Val said.

The other set of footsteps hurried over. The box was pulled fast, and the boxes above teetered, but luckily, my face was there to keep them from falling down. I stood cheek to cardboard until somebody pulled the box and stabilized the rest of the stack.

"I finished the first draft of the syllabus last night," the man who sounded like a woman said.

I heard a blade cut through the box tape.

"You have the abstract for the course catalog?" Val said.

"What do you take me for, an amateur?"

"Let's hear it."

"Hands-on experience creating and evaluating hair and skin

products. Emulsions including creams and lotions; surfactant systems including shampoos and gels."

Val chuckled. "That actually doesn't sound half bad."

"I broke down the fourteen weeks into three sections, the face, the body, and the…"

A pause.

"Come here," Val said.

They were hugging—I could feel it and hear it. Comforting one another.

"Twenty years of researching polymers…and this is what it has come to, skin creams and shampoos."

"I thought we were done talking about this, Roberto."

"I don't understand how you can just be…"

"A professional?"

A few footsteps, Roberto walking away from Val? Crinkling sounds—maybe Roberto digging his hands into the box. Frustrated and angry.

"Look at this shit! A million false eyelashes for us to, what, run fucking experiments?"

So that was what was in these boxes. And now I had a pretty good guess at what this building was about—cosmetics research. Was Faith not so far off after all? Because if this were true, it certainly seemed like Travers Hall would turn Llewellyn into an institution of higher Barbie learning. There were already trade schools that taught makeup, hair styling, that sort of thing. Offering a major in it seemed like a dangerous move to make, potentially disastrous for the reputation of an accredited college.

More crinkling sounds, and then an empty thud hitting the floor. Then a heavy, forlorn sigh.

"You're just gonna have to pick all that up," Val said.

Feet shuffled around.

"You don't have to clean up my mess," Roberto said.

I got the feeling these two were more than just colleagues. There was an aged, comfortable vibe to them, either by marriage or a long-term relationship.

"Why did this happen to us?" Roberto said.

"Why does anything happen to anyone. Things were good when Fairchild was around, and now with Wheeler, they're not. It's a cycle. Things will…"

"Come on. You don't really believe that, do you? This is different. This isn't just a regime change. There's a reason why Collins is going with Wheeler."

"Collins is going because she'll do what it takes, which is more than I can say for you. Or for me, for that matter," Val said.

Footsteps moved toward me, and then darkness, as the box flew over the stack in front of me. On pure instinct, my arms shot up, and now I was holding up that thrown box up over my head. It wasn't heavy, but I hoped I didn't have to hold it up for long.

"Did you see what she's going to present?"

"She emailed me her PowerPoint slides, too," Val said.

"We wouldn't last two seconds up on the podium."

"I don't know how she's gonna keep a straight face."

"Probably by thinking about her fast track to tenure," Roberto said.

Now the footsteps were moving away, which was good because my arms were starting to shake.

"We still have to configure the two labs upstairs before the end of the week," Val said.

"My meeting's at three, so I can spare a couple of hours."

Door opened, lights off, door closed.

28

I waited a few more seconds before I put the box down on the floor. I opened up the box Roberto and Val had tossed and pocketed a pack of false eyelashes for Faith. Pasted onto a white cardboard and wrapped in clear plastic, they were a pair of happy, hairy eyes. Crazy what some women went through to feel pretty.

So the mission was a success, except now I was inside Travers and didn't know how I was going to get out without alerting the guards. I didn't have Faith's or Molly's number, so I looked up TLC and dialed it.

"Hello," the voice said.

"Carson," I said.

"Katie."

"You know what's going on?" I said.

"I do," she said. "Give me five minutes and you'll hear back." Click.

I felt like I was in a spy movie. Another text from 111-111-1111 vibrated my phone.

```
take stairs to basement
emergency door not hooked up to alarm
```

But to get to the staircase meant I had to sneak out of this room, sneak out to the hallway, and open the door to the staircase, sneakily, without alerting the guard at the door, not to mention other professors who might be roaming the halls. How did the Womyn know the layout of Travers, anyway? They probably broke in at some point. Or maybe they had the blueprints of the building. The other option was to wait it out —at some point, the guards had to leave for the day —but was I really going to stay here for the next four to five hours? I had to remember that this was a college, not Fort Knox. Except it was littered with private security people like Brent Kim, plus actual cops from town. I had to be careful here, because these weren't rent-a-cops.

I made my way to the door. I opened it as if I were in slow motion, as if any sudden movement would set off a bomb. Because everything was new, nothing made noise, not the turning of the knob, not the languid swing of the door. I hazarded a peek and it took every ounce of my self control to stifle a scream, because there was a guard right here, his back to me. Close enough that I could see the fabric of his navy blue uniform. Again, I opened my mouth to silence my breathing. In the tiniest of increments, I pulled the door back toward me, but before I could shut it completely, white noise screamed out of his walkie-talkie.

"The fuck," the guard said. He yanked the walkie-talkie from his belt buckle. "Yeah, whaddya want?"

"There's something going on with all the sinks here in 28." It was Val.

"I ain't a plumber."

"Please, just get up here. We'll need your approval anyway for maintenance to come over."

"Fine," he said. I listened to him opening and closing the door to the stairwell, and waited until I heard the fainter sound of the same door opening and closing upstairs until I made my move to the stairwell.

I pushed open the beige steel door to the basement just a crack, in case there were more guards posted down here. I didn't see anyone, but then again, I probably couldn't, as the lights weren't on. I slipped through the stairwell door, gently closed it, and waited for my eyes to adjust. Outside of an occasional rush of water running through pipes, it was noiseless here in the basement of Travers. From where I was standing, I noticed tiny blue blinking LEDs, embedded where the ceiling met the wall. I took a left and a few steps until I was standing below the LED. I was just about to turn on the flashlight on my phone to examine it when I heard the walkie-talkie static again, entirely too loud for it to be coming from anywhere but here in the basement. I flattened myself against the cool wall.

"Why do you want *me* to look at it?" the male voice said, far down the hallway but moving closer. A beam of flashlight swayed as he walked toward me. More static, and words I couldn't make out. "No, the protocol is that you come down first, then I go up there."

Now the guard was close enough that I could hear the walkie-talkie.

"Can't. It's like a game of Twister here. I got both hands on this pipe and if I let go, it's gonna spray all over the fucking place."

"Jesus. All right, but this is on you if we hear about it," the guard said.

The outer beam of the flashlight grazed my shoes, but the guard was too distracted to notice. He opened the door wide open and sprinted up the stairs. I let out a large breath of relief; my body felt almost numb from the tension.

I turned on my phone flashlight, shined it on the blue LED —it was a status indicator for backup lighting, the kind that turned on during a power failure —and hurried to the far side. Along the way, I maneuvered around clusters of empty office chairs and student desk-chair combos.

At the end of the hallway was an emergency door, as my mysterious texter had promised. There was a metal bar that clearly stated opening this door would cause an alarm to ring. I pushed. Silence. Even though it was overcast, the light blinded me. I pulled out my sunglasses from my pocket and put them on. The hedges were ahead of me, and there was no one around. I closed the door, walked away at a leisurely pace, and passed through the thicket once more.

29

Even though I'd only spent one night at Llewellyn, it felt like I'd been away for a week. The mailbox at my office agreed with me, as there were sixteen envelopes piled inside the mail bin, way more than normal. Three of them were credit card offers for Ed Baker. How long until the snail-mail spam lists found out about your demise and let you go? There's that theory that as long as someone remembered you in this world, you weren't allowed to move on. Perhaps the unsolicited mailing lists were keeping a legion of the dead from ascending to the next plane of existence, which I suppose was a bad deal for the spirits. But as a flesh and blood creature of this plane, I was glad for these envelopes with Ed's name on them. I wished he were here so I could tell him about all the nutty things I found out about this case so far.

Scanning my notes, I came upon something Faith told me: "Josie tracked Penny's period in a ledger." What the fuck was that all about? I probably should call her, if for no other reason to give her an update. But now I just needed a little bit of time to myself.

My office phone rang. Jesus Christ, what now?

"Kim Shee-Bong." Déjà vu all over again.

"Josie. Maybe I should mention that nobody calls me that anymore. In fact, I don't think anybody ever did, not even my own birth mother the one time I met her, so maybe you should just cool it with calling me by my Korean name, okay?"

Silence.

Was that a tad on the bitchy side? Maybe. It was just after one, but it felt like five o'clock. Yakking with Professor Marks, all that sneaking around in Travers Hall, I was hungry and stressed and I guess taking it out on Josie, who was now…crying?

"Josie?"

"Fuck you, Siobhan, fuck fuck fuck you!"

Click.

Holy shit.

As soon as I placed the handset back in its cradle, it rang again.

"Hello?" I said.

"Siobhan, it's your friendly neighborhood officer of the law."

"Keeler. How are you?"

"Fine, until I had to walk down from my desk to deal with your agitated friend here."

"Friend?"

"The one who just called you. Josephine Sykes."

"I don't understand."

"She's here. In custody. I suggest you get here because she just burned her one phone call on you, and from what it sounded like, it didn't go so hot."

The Athena Police Station wasn't far, not even a five-minute drive from my office, but before I rose from my desk, I paused. I got a bad feeling I'd fucked up.

Once you get a client, check up on them. To make sure they are who they say they are.

Thanks, Ed. Maybe next time, you come into my head a little earlier?

I opened up my browser and went to TLOxp, TransUnion's background checking service. There was no easier way to look into someone, which is why I felt even dumber for not doing it until now. I punched in "Josephine Sykes" into the search box and chose the state of New York.

Josie said her husband had died when Penny turned ten, so that would've been eight years ago. Except according to TLOxp, that was when they'd divorced, and Andrew Ulster, 39, was doing just peachy, living in Albany with a new wife. Okay, so she lied about her husband. What else?

Employment: she wasn't working for Lenrock. She was working for a temp company. Not exactly a lie.

Address: she wasn't living in Athena but rather Slaterville, which is the sketchier, uglier, trailer-park-ish neighboring town. Definitely a lie.

Rap sheet: pot possession. Disturbing the peace. Simple assault. The kind of shit she was pulling when I knew her when.

Except these arrests were from the last two years.

Like I said, Siobhan, I'm all grown up now.

I put my head down on my desk and closed my eyes.

30

The words above the door of the Athena Police Station read HALL OF JUSTICE. Being a sleepy upstate New York town, Athena could probably get away with VESTIBULE OF JUSTICE, but that doesn't sound as impressive.

I'd devoured a convenience store hot dog on the way over here, so my mouth still tasted of greasy mystery meat as I walked through the double doors. I identified myself to the officer manning the front counter and told him I was here to see Keeler.

After a quick phone call, he said, "Make two lefts and you'll be at the entrance of the holding cells. Lieutenant Keeler will meet you there."

I thanked him and proceeded through the white metal door once he buzzed it open.

As I walked, I thought about how I was going to handle this. I was mad, not so much at Josie but at myself for failing to do the obvious. Why was I so quick to believe everything she told me? Everybody lies, especially people who come to private investigators for help.

There was no one at the cell entrance, just me and the locked door that led to the area of miscreants. I'd been here a few times when I'd worked at the paper, but it had been a couple of years. I peered through the small reinforced window on the door, but all I could see was the empty hallway beyond.

Keeler, who was two years shy of thirty years on the force, hurried in. He looked like he wanted to be retired yesterday. His white shirt had gotten untucked and his meticulous combover had gone askew to one side, making him look more unbalanced than usual.

"And I thought I look like shit," I said.

"Your friend ain't making it any easier. Her arresting officer was *this close* to upping her charge."

"What's going on? I've never seen you so stressed."

"Some right-wing gasbag is giving a speech at Lenrock, a guy I never even heard of, but apparently he's famous on YouTube. Demonstrators on both sides are keeping us occupied." Keeler scanned his ID badge to open the secured door. "Cell C. Call me and I'll let you back out. I got another ten fires to put out."

The police station had four cells. Cell A had a homeless-looking guy who was snoring away on his bunk. Cell B's occupant, a young black man with ropey dreadlocks that cascaded over his broad shoulders, grinned at me with vacant eyes.

Cell C.

Josie was sitting in her bunk in her business garb, black blouse and gray slacks, though like Keeler, she was quite disheveled, even her makeup. Her red lipstick on her right side was smeared over on her right cheek, making her look a bit like a lopsided Joker, while on her left cheek, there was an angry red welt the size of a quarter.

"Hey," I said.

She bolted upright.

"What's happening with Penny? Did you make any progress?"

"We probably should talk about you first. Since, you know, you're in jail."

After she stared me down for a good few seconds, she sat against the wall on her bunk with her eyes closed.

"I bet you're happy now," Josie said.

I leaned against the bars and faced the end of the hallway, so I could speak to her without making eye contact. The iron bars, thick and painted in bright white, were cold against my arm.

"Because you haven't changed?" I asked.

"I know you've never liked me, Siobhan. You only put up with me because of Marlene. And as soon as my sister was in the ground, you couldn't wait to get the hell away from me."

I stared at the bar closest to me, the glossy white enamel that looked almost liquid under the clinical fluorescent lights above. "I had every right to leave that house."

"What you're really saying is that you had every right to leave me."

"Yes," I said. "That too."

"You didn't even say goodbye. Did you know that?"

The longer I gazed at the cylindrical surface of the metal bar, the more I noticed the imperfections—nicks, chips, dings. Look long enough, and nothing remains unflawed.

"You're not working for Lenrock," I said.

"No shit. Fancy colleges like Lenrock don't hire people like me."

"What happened this time? What did you do?"

"Saved lives is what I did. This asshole in his fucking truck in front of me, drift, drift, jerk, onto oncoming traffic not once but twice. After the second time, I sped in front of him and forced him to stop."

"Forced him?"

"Put the brakes on and blocked his way."

The way she said it, it sounded like she'd made this move before. Was she aware of the textbook nature of her impulsive action here, that it was an obvious callback to her big sister's death? Probably, because Josie was not stupid, but then again, Josie was just being Josie.

"And then you get out of your car, the guy gets out of his truck…"

"Fucker was texting on his phone, big surprise, I could see it because when he jumped out, he was holding onto his phone, the screen on the texting app. It's as bad, if not worse, than driving drunk. Told him I was placing him under citizen's arrest and he laughed at me and walked away. So I grabbed him and then things got a little out of hand."

"Like the bruise on your face."

Josie tentatively traced her wound with her finger, then smiled. "You should see the other guy."

I don't know if it was because what she'd said was such a well-worn cliché, or because that crooked smile of hers made her eighteen again, but we laughed and the tension between us broke.

I told her I didn't know where Penny was yet but that I was gathering some decent intel. When I got to the part about meeting Faith, I figured it was as good time as any to ask her about the menstrual journal.

Josie shook her head. "So now you think I'm some kind of a basket case who tracked my daughter's bowel movements, too."

"Green Hair, as you called her, had her own version of truth, as you have yours. We all do."

Josie lay down on her bunk so now I was seeing the top of her head, offering me the old school shrink's view.

"Here's the thing, Siobhan, something you don't know because you don't have kids. You end up doing all sorts of crazy shit for them, like keeping tabs of their periods. Because of my daughter's particular kind of hyperthyroidism, she has to adjust her dose when she's on her cycle. And because she's a teenager, she's not very good at keeping track of things, so I do it. That way, she takes her pills at the right time and doesn't get deathly ill. Is that an acceptable answer?"

"How do you know I don't have kids?" I asked.

"Sorry, I assumed. Am I wrong?"

"No."

She laughed.

"You were tight with Marlene, but she used to tell me things, too. Like how she and you saw eye to eye about children."

What a strange thing it was to have someone tell you something about yourself that you didn't remember. It was almost as if she was talking about a different person.

"I can't say I recall telling her that, but I'm amazed you do."

"I was envious of you, Siobhan. I wanted to be close to Marlene like you were to her. My therapist, when I had money to see one, said that's why I ended up adopting Penny."

So much for my powers of psychological deduction. Penny wasn't a stand-in for Marlene, but rather me. How sad was that?

My cell rang: Keeler.

"Knocking off in half an hour. Post your friend's bail, she goes home. Otherwise she spends a few quiet nights here."

Five hundred bucks, that was the bail. So the check that Josie gave me, the one that I couldn't even deposit yet, was going right back. Even though I was a newbie at this running my own business thing, I had a pretty good idea that this was not the way to make money.

"Who was that?" Josie asked.

"The cop that's gonna set you free."

Josie stood up from her bunk and walked over to where I was.

"You're paying the bail," she said.

"Pay me back later."

She put her hands through the bars. A big boned girl, almost six foot tall, but Josie always felt small to me. I took her hands into mine.

"Thank you," she said.

"I'll be back."

As I turned, she said, "Andrew, my husband…"

"…ex-husband…"

"I needed you to take this case, Siobhan. I'm sorry I lied, but I needed you to find my daughter."

"I understand," I said. And I did.

31

After dropping off Josie at the impound lot so she could drive herself home, I thought back to the no kids thing she mentioned. Honestly, I could not remember such a conversation taking place with Marlene, so obviously it hadn't meant much to me at the time. But as I kept mining my own past, something I hadn't thought of in years came back to me. Once I fully realized I was a transracial adoptee, I'm not sure what I thought about more, the mystery of my birth parents or the mystery of my birth life. What I mean is this: every adoptee leads two lives, the one that is and the one that could have been. If my mother hadn't given me up, more likely than not, I would've grown up speaking Korean, eating Korean food, having Korean friends in a land on the other side of the globe. The gulf between those two lives is so wide that it remains beyond the reach of my imagination. That rift is what both intrigued and distressed me during those formative years, right about Penny's age. It was worth noting that Penny might be living in a similar quandary, which may have attributed to her disappearance.

Back in my office building, with my mind marinating in the sauce of my own complicated existence, I walked down the hallway to Craig's office. There was a Post-It on the door saying he wouldn't be back until Friday. His penmanship was font-worthy, the tops and bottoms of his cursive aligned as if with a ruler. I hadn't realized how much I was looking forward to seeing him.

Before I had a chance to truly wallow in pity, the phone rang. I ran back and picked it up just before it transferred over to voicemail.

"This is so boss!" Faith said. Before leaving Llewellyn, I'd left the fake eyelashes I'd found in Travers Hall with either Katie or Carson, and emailed the photos of the mannequins and the wigs to Faith. "Molly scanned the QR codes on the eyelashes and they point to a Park Industries-owned laboratory known for nanotechnology and polymer research. Maybe that's why they have the place under lock and key."

"I'm glad one of us is getting something out of this," I said. "We square now, you and me?"

"Yes, but I don't want us to be. I just held an emergency meeting with the Womyn and we decided that we want to hire you."

I was sympathetic to these girls and their beliefs, but did I really want to get involved any more than I already was?

"Find someone else to break into the next building."

"That's not it. What we need is legitimacy. I want Wheeler to know we are serious about this, and that we are onto her."

"But what are we exactly onto?" I said. "She has every right to steer Llewellyn in a direction that she and the board believe to be beneficial to the well-being of the college."

"But I can't imagine the board would be in support of what she's doing. They're a bunch of fossils on the brink of senility, anyway. What we need is for you to confront her and find out exactly what her plans are."

"What happened to your contact in the media? We're not going to see the team from *60 Minutes* on campus for a riveting exposé?"

"I've already talk to my contact and she isn't totally sold on the idea yet. Which is why we need you to record your conversation with Wheeler."

"A wire."

"An antiquated term. Your phone will be more than capable of recording your conversation—you just need the right app. We'll pay you $500 for your services. That's how much we have in the budget, so I hope it's enough."

Why did everything cost $500? Whatever—that would pay for

Josie's bail, so I agreed. Besides, I was planning to talk to Wheeler anyway about Penny's whereabouts, and actually maybe these girls did me a favor. I could use what I learned in Travers as leverage, possibly.

We said our goodbyes. I turned on the office computer, a hulking black tower underneath my desk that wheezed and groaned like an old man. I read an email from Sven, my brother, writing to let me know that he was going to make it to Thanksgiving next month. He lives in Washington state, in the northwest part near the San Juan Islands, working as a mechanical engineer for a trucking company. We lived on opposite coasts and our parents were in the middle. When I visited Korea those many years ago, I never forgot that the two largest cities, Seoul and Busan, were barely two and a half hours via train. As much as I love the United States, sometimes I resent its geographical girth.

After wading through my inbox, I checked through my notebook and saw "Grace's bodyguard's inside wrist." I hadn't gotten a chance to count the number of stars, but it looked like a bunch. A few tries later, I had it via Google Image search: *Chil Sung Pa*, which translated to Seven Star Mob. According to Wikipedia, it was the most powerful gang in South Korea, their criminal activities so secretive that the Korean Police had trouble containing them. A member of the Korean mafia was protecting the daughter of one of the most powerful companies in the world.

Which reminded me to look up Park Industries. Mainly I was interested in Won Ho Park, the chairman and CEO, the man who'd built the gigantic multinational conglomerate from the ground up. According to the history page on the company's website, his dad was a fisherman and his mom a schoolteacher. There weren't many photos of Park, but because his current wife—he was on his third—was the opposite when it came to public exposure, I found a few photos of him standing next to Cleopatra Park at various ritzy events, benefit galas and such. He was about my height, possibly shorter, but in all the snapshots, he had such a sense of himself. It wasn't exactly confidence, nor was it arrogance, but just a clarity of who he was. He looked like a man who always knew exactly what he wanted.

There were so many photos of Cleopatra that she had her own image timeline on Google, which I thought only celebrities had. But I supposed she *was* a celebrity, because she certainly knew how to pose like one. Her cheekbones were cut like the face of Kilimanjaro and her waist was as tiny as Audrey Hepburn's in *Roman Holiday*. Whether in the glow of natural sunlight or bleached by the harshness of a flash bulb, she was the most alluring person. And, shockingly, she was pushing fifty. Women in general were looking better nowadays, what with plastic surgery and Botox and better diets and Pilates, but this encroached Dorian Gray territory. I couldn't have dreamed of looking that good when I was eighteen. Cleopatra deserved her name.

I blinked my eyes because they were dry. And they were dry because I'd been on the computer for…two hours? As wonderful as the internet was, here was its dark side.

My inbox dinged.

Hey. Now that we've shared cronuts, how about we take it up a notch and go for dinner when I return on Friday?

Craig was asking me out. Via email, which wasn't as personal as over the phone, but I think it rated higher than a text? Or something like that. I placed the computer on standby and headed out for a walk. I felt like whistling, but I was a terrible whistler. I whistled anyway, and it was bad, so I stopped.

32

This day was beginning to feel like it was never going to end, but of course, it was ending because it was already dark outside. While I'd gotten lost in the internet, the sun had set and the Commons, the beating heart of my town, was readying itself for dinner and drinks. The blackboard at O'Reilly's announced a dozen beer-battered chicken wings and a pitcher of Killian's for ten bucks. Next door, Chayo Phaya served flattened and rolled ice cream in addition to their crack-level-delicious pad thai.

I couldn't decide what to eat, which mean I wasn't hungry yet, but the stroll around the Commons felt refreshing, the evening air clean and crisp. On my walk back to the office, my phone rang. There was a bench in front of Buffalo Books, so I sat and took the call.

"The masses have spoken, Siobhan O'Brien," said the voice on the phone. Professor Marks.

"Lawrence."

"You are hereby granted access to our next session of Creative Writing 201. Shall you join us tomorrow at half past eleven?"

"I shall," I said.

"Then it shall be!" Marks declared. "We have declared it so. Grover 107. The class runs for one hour and fifteen minutes. We hold a ten-minute intermission at the midpoint, where we delight in cookies and tea and each other's company."

"Okay," I said.

"And even though you are not an official member of our literary enclave, if you wish to bring something short to read – a few choice verses of a poem, a sliver of a short story—you are more than welcome to do so."

"You mean like something I wrote?"

"But of course."

"I don't think I'll be doing that."

A tiny wren flew down from the maple tree above and pecked at the ground, finding food invisible to my eyes.

"The choice is yours, Siobhan O'Brien. The choice is always yours. Till we meet tomorrow, sweet gumshoe."

I hung up my phone and sat there for a moment. If nothing else, Marks's class was setting itself up to be a solid source of entertainment.

Instead of taking the elevator, I climbed the stairs to my office, my steps echoing up and down the emptiness. Sometimes I do this because I like to feel the effort of my legs and my lungs. Sometimes I do it to clear my head. And sometimes it's because there's something I don't want to do, an avoidance tactic.

Back in front of my computer, I re-read Craig's email.

Hey. Now that we've shared cronuts, how about we take it up a notch and go for dinner when I come back Friday?

I clicked on the reply button. My fingers hovered over the keys. Frozen in place.

Hey right back at you. Dinner sounds great. Let's do it! That's is what I wanted to write. I did want to have dinner with Craig. It did sound great.

My cursor kept blinking. I opened up another tab on my browser and looked up Vera Wheeler's number on Llewellyn's administrative directory.

It picked up on the first ring, and as the administrative assistant spoke, I heard the fake smile she was wearing as she spoke to me.

"Oh, I'm afraid that's just not even remotely possible. President Wheeler is booked solid for the next three weeks."

"Is she there?"

"Excuse me?"

"Is she there now, so if I ask you to go and tell her something, you can do so?"

An edge crept in her voice, the smile losing its shine. "Ms. O'Brien, President Wheeler's schedule simply will not allow…"

So she *was* there. "The mannequins in Travers Hall."

"Mannequins…?"

"That's what I said."

"And why should I…"

"How about this. You tell her what I said, and if she doesn't understand what you're talking about, then you can just hang up. But my guess is that she'll want to open up her very busy calendar for half an hour to chew the fat. Any time after 2 p.m. is good with me tomorrow."

The phone went from annoyed silence to soft piano Muzak. While I waited, I went back to Craig's words for the third time, and my conscious mind finally let in on what my unconscious had been hiding. There I was, sitting opposite Craig at some dark and woody table for two, a votive candle flickering between us. He had a nice, guileless face, almost childlike in its innocence. And then after dinner, a kiss. And then another dinner after that, then going to some *thing*, like picking apples or a jazz concert…and then sitting on the couch at his place, fumbling in the dark for each other, love and hope and fear and disappointment. It was *so much work* to be with someone else—no wonder I was having trouble writing him back. I was already exhausted.

The phone clicked. Did she just hang up on me? Well, I did tell her that was a viable option. But no, it was her coming back online.

"4 p.m. tomorrow."

Click. Well, there's another person who'll never be my BFF.

So tomorrow would be another day spent at Llewellyn. I hadn't signed up for any classes, but I was beginning to feel like a real student.

Back to the email. I took a deep breath, then exhaled a little too aggressively, as I wiped the few dots of spittle from my screen.

Sometimes the best way to get something done is to just do it as fast as possible. I typed:

Okay!

And before I had a chance to change my mind, I hit send.

33

Grover 107 looked more like an old dining room than a classroom, a weathered oval-shaped wooden desk with twelve chairs surrounding it. There was even a sideboard in the back, which I assumed was where cookies and tea would be served. Two large windows offered the view of the quad, which was kind of stunning.

Having arrived fifteen minutes earlier than the scheduled start time, I watched little cyclones of yellow and red leaves form and disappear on these green lawns of academia. There was almost a meditative quality to being here with students and professors and books, like the tranquility found in a church or a monastery. I've always felt safe at colleges, like nothing bad could ever happen. But bad things happened all the time, everywhere. All you had to do was look.

"Well hey there, stranger," a voice behind me said.

It was the black girl with ear piercings that ran all the way from the top of her ear to the very bottom of her earlobe, a Womyn of Llewellyn. Today she had thin gold chains woven through her myriad of holes, ending with loopy, hoopy rings the size of a fist.

"How did your chemistry exam go, Raven?"

"I did all right, I think. I hope. I guess you've forgiven us for pulling a fast one on you the other night, because Sister Faith said you're helping us out."

"Happy to serve, Sister Raven," I said. "Now maybe you can do an honorary sister a solid?"

"I can try, Sister Siobhan."

"There was a fight between Penny Sykes and a girl named Henrietta a week or so ago in this class. Your professor broke them up, but he told me he didn't know what it was about."

Raven nodded. "I heard about it later. It was the story Penny submitted that freaked Henrietta out."

"Submitted it? To whom?"

Raven filled me in on the logistics of their creative writing workshop. The class met twice a week. A week before, two students send out copies of stories they wrote, which then allowed the class to comment on the works to be discussed the following week. Rinse and repeat with the next pair of writers.

"Penny emailed it to everyone the night before, which sucked because that hardly gives us enough time to comment on it, but then like an hour after she sent it, she took it back."

"Took it back?"

"She recalled her email, which deletes it off the server. She said she'd submit something else, but she never did."

"So what was the story about?"

"I never got a chance to read it."

"Did anyone other than Henrietta read it?"

"Doubtful. We're so busy that if something like that happens, it's like a get-out-of-jail card."

"There must be someone else who's as devoted to this class as Henrietta was."

"It's a huge relief when somebody doesn't want you to read their story. We got enough work as it is around here with our seminars and lab sections and whatnot."

"Did Henrietta have any friends?"

The class was almost full now, all but two chairs empty. Raven clapped her hands and everyone looked up at her.

"Did Henrietta have any friends?"

"Whatshername," a short brunette girl said.

"That's real helpful, Brooke," Raven said.

"You know, the one from Israel. Or is it Palestine."

"Better not mix that up," somebody else said, and everyone

laughed.

"Hajira," someone said.

"Last name?" I asked.

"I can pretty much guarantee there's only one Hajira in Lewie," Raven said.

"Thanks, guys," I said. I didn't see any reason to stick around here, so I grabbed my purse and was about to leave when Marks walked in. He was wearing a black broad-brimmed hat that made him look sort of Amish.

"Ms. O'Brien! Don't tell me you're leaving?"

"I'm sorry, but duty calls. Gotta follow leads, magnifying glass in hand, that sort of thing."

I was a lousy student back in the day, and I guess I was a lousy student now.

34

Raven had assumed correctly there was only one Hajira in Llewellyn, and according to the campus directory, she lived on the second floor of Eldred Hall. I was cutting through the quad when something caught the corner of my eye. A little ways up the hill, there was Brent Kim, Mister Special Campus Security, conversing with a really tall young man, like basketball center tall. He might have been imposing, except the kid had a slacker slouch that made him look like he was apologizing for his extended height.

I was still too far away to hear what they were saying, but from the body language, it looked like the guy was pleading something, and now something more, because Brent put his hand out like the Heisman trophy. The kid stopped slouching and loomed even taller, but this was not going to impress Brent, Mister Seven Star Mob. Brent's open palm turned into a pointing finger, and for a moment neither of them moved, just looking at each other, posturing like the way men do when they get angry.

The tall kid turned and stalked away. There were Greek letters on his sweatshirt: TBA. Tau Beta Alpha. Llewellyn had no Greek system, but Lenrock University had an enormous one. I'd look into this later.

I made my way over to Eldred. I didn't know if Hajira was in class, but I figured it was worth a shot since I was on campus anyway. Her door was halfway open and I could hear Taylor Swift crooning over some guy who wronged her. I knocked.

"Hajira?"

The dorm room was decorated quite tastefully. Gauzy red curtains billowed by the open window, and Hajira was reading on her bed, propped against a pile of pink satin pillows. Wearing a red head-scarf with glittery beads, she looked up at me with wide, uncertain eyes.

I gave her my card and stated the purpose of my investigation.

"May I ask how you arrived upon an Irish name?" she asked. She spoke with a British-Indian accent. The student in the creative writing class thought she was from Palestine, but it was more likely Pakistan.

"I'd like to ask you a bunch of questions, so this is the least I can do. I was adopted by an Irish father and a Norwegian mother. My brother, who's black and also adopted, is Sven."

"That is a very cosmopolitan story," she said. "I like it very much."

Hajira offered me her desk chair, so I turned it toward her and sat and caught her up.

"I spoke to Penny perhaps once," she said. "Two shy people do not have long conversations."

"I'm actually interested in Henrietta. You were friends with her?"

Her big eyes turned softer at her name. Maybe it was more than friendship.

"We were roommates," she said. "We chose to live together last year, when we were freshmen."

By my calculation, Henrietta left a little less than two weeks ago, so the wound of departure was still fresh.

"I'm sorry," I said, and I was. Hajira's intensity was like a physical thing in this room, thick and hot and miserable, and I wish I didn't have to keep asking her questions. "Henrietta left after fighting with Penny—is this true?"

"True, but it was not the only reason. She had already initiated the transfer from Llewellyn. The conflict with Penny only accelerated her plans."

"But the story she read by Penny set her off."

"Oh, yes, and if you had seen it for yourself, you might understand."

"Wait, you read it?"

"The first two pages. That was as far as I could go."

"Because the email was recalled."

Hajira shook her head. "Because it was so disturbing. I shudder to think about it. But I will tell you what I remember because I know it may assist in your investigation. The story's protagonist was Penny Sykes."

"I thought creative writing was about writing fiction."

"Believe me, this was fiction, because the character Penny in the story begins as a baby in her mother's womb, and she is devouring herself. She eats her foot, and then her arm, but the parts keep growing back. Then she is born, and she is about to have sex…"

"As a baby?"

Hajira took one of her cushions and hugged it.

"That's when I stopped reading. It was so disturbing – how anyone could write such things…"

I didn't know what to say. All I could see in my mind was that photograph Josie had brought of her daughter, Penny in a yellow one-piece bathing suit staring at the camera. So much for innocence.

35

Hajira was headed for Petty Hall, which was on the way to Broadhurst, for her psychology class. Yesterday had been the perfect autumn day, high fifties with a bright and shiny sun, but today dark clouds and a cutting draft announced the coming of winter. Hajira tucked her headscarf neatly around her neck.

"This was Henrietta's favorite time of the year," she said.

"What did she like about it?" I asked.

"Everything," Hajira said. "The colors, the leaves, the chill."

Up ahead, four Asian men in white turtlenecks and black slacks approached us. They all looked like Brent Kim, strong and quick and no-nonsense. They'd been walking two by two, but since the path was narrow, the two on the left fell back in synchrony to create a single line. The exactitude of their movements was akin to a military maneuver.

They said nothing as they passed us, and as soon as we were beyond them, they resumed their two-by-two formation.

"Does it bother you that those special campus security people are around all the time?" I asked Hajira.

"They stay out of sight. We usually don't see them out much, but they must be getting ready for tonight."

"What's tonight?"

"It's the odd-even basketball game. Puppet show, sing-a-long, comedy skit, fire engine parade…you have no idea."

"My Llewellyn history is rather lacking."

"Grace Park will be playing."

"Basketball?"

"She's actually quite good—I've seen her practicing her highly accurate jump shot. If you wish to see the game later tonight, you're more than welcome to come with me."

"Thank you," I said. "I might just do that."

She rang my phone so we'd both have each other's numbers.

"Thank you, Siobhan," Hajira said. "I must admit, I didn't think I wanted to talk about Henrietta with anyone, but now that I have, my heart feels lighter. You are a fine listener."

I watched her as she climbed the worn granite steps to Petty. Young love, maybe first love, now lost. Did I even remember what that pain was like? Oh yeah, like it was yesterday. His name was Ruben, and his eyes were huge, dark, and eternally calm. But he was a senior and didn't even know I existed. So maybe this wasn't really first love, but rather first crush. Who was my first love? Was it bad that I didn't know? What did that say about me? Maybe I should be the one going to that psych class. Whatever. I was inside Broadhurst now, the chandelier still painfully bright, on my way to see big bad President Vera Wheeler. I made sure the app on my phone was already recording.

Gloria Reedy was still at the front desk, the same lady I'd talked to a few days ago who was the essence of effervescence. But today, she gave me a shoulder colder than absolute zero.

"Ms. O'Brien," she said. "I've been told you have a meeting with President Wheeler. Please proceed to the fourth floor."

Ah, so that was it. Wheeler's secretary no doubt said some unnice things about me. Gloria was another one I'd have to cross off my ever-shrinking potential BFF list.

Three dings later, the elevator door opened and I stepped into a tony lobby that looked like it, too, had been recently refurbished. The spotless red carpet on the floor was of a deep and rich hue, a color you'd find on a luxury automobile. The walls were outlined into panels with trims and moldings of a flawless redwood and covered with a red satiny fabric.

The same elaborate chandelier as the one in the foyer hung here, except the wattage was mercifully toned down. Affixed on the center of each wall was a golden lamp crafted in the same style as the chandelier, and the combined muted glow created a formal atmosphere.

The silence here felt oppressive, mandated, mausoleum-like. In the middle of the room was a desk and a chair, unoccupied. The upholstered straight-backed chair with a fleur-de-lis pattern and the wooden oval desk with a surface as smooth as glass looked like antique pieces that belonged in a museum. This was probably where the assistant sat.

I approached the pair of closed doors straight ahead, ones I assumed led to Wheeler's office. When I reached out to knock, the doors opened slowly, automatically, inward.

"Come, Ms. O'Brien."

Vera Wheeler faced the window that took up the entire wall, her arms crossed and leaning against her desk. She gazed at the view of the campus below and Lake Selene beyond, where the setting sun cast its warm glow over slate roofs and billowing sycamores and gilded the still waters. On the foreground of this stunning backdrop was Wheeler, tall and thin, her straight blonde hair cascading to the middle of her back, black seams down the center of her sculpted, stockinged legs.

36

Five years ago, I'd interviewed Wheeler for the *Athena Times*, a feature story about her experiences as a first-year president and as an educator with an interesting background, a high-fashion model. For that piece, she'd worn a simple white blouse and a black skirt. But now the outfit that she was in, a black two-piece skirt suit, could best be described as a hybrid of haute couture and businesswear. The curves on the collar were almost Elizabethan, and the above-the-knees pencil skirt ended with tuck pleats grazing the hemline. And she was balanced on some serious stilettos; thin leather straps snaked and crossed around her foot and ankle, sexy and classy and quite likely painful. I'd worn heels like these in my twenties and even then, my youthful feet yowled after a night out.

It was a look only a former model could pull off, and did she ever. She was a beautiful woman, even now at fifty. Earlier this morning while I was prepping for this meeting, I'd come across photos of her birthday party in the Hamptons this past July on a fashion blog. There was a shot of her and Vera Wang and Diane von Furstenberg together, holding up champagne flutes for the camera.

Wheeler never reached supermodel status like Tyra Banks or Cindy Crawford, but in her time, she'd been highly regarded, and even more impressive was her business acumen. One magazine profile mentioned her 140 IQ, and she'd put those brain cells to good use, as she parlayed her knowledge of the fashion industry into a consulting firm for cosmetics and clothing companies. Her mother's dying wish had been for her to complete her college degree, so she went a few steps further to get her Ph.D. in Education, which led up to her current gig as president of an American college.

"I remember you," Wheeler said. She had an enviable voice, deeper than most women but still quite feminine. "As a reporter for a failed newspaper. Were you even a reporter? I vaguely recall you specialized in restaurant and movie reviews."

"Even those who write features and reviews are called reporters," I said.

"If you say so. And now you're a private investigator. Goodness, aren't you rather underqualified for that?"

She'd just said this in such a way that it straddled concern and mockery. Did she practice in front of a mirror? Because she was really good at it.

"I'm a quick learner."

"Like learning to sneak around my school, go into buildings you're not supposed to go into."

"I'm not here to cause trouble."

"Now we both know that's not true, Siobhan."

Wheeler gestured toward the chair in front of her desk. It was a modern-looking chair, all black and leather and possibly of Swedish origin. Wheeler sat behind her all-glass desk. She did the cross-and-lean thing that women with long legs did. Close up, her face was made-up perfection, from her trimmed eyebrows to the dark red lipstick that was drawn with painterly precision. For a woman in her fifth decade, there was not a single wrinkle, not even the beginnings of crow's feet at the corners of her eyes. Plastic surgery? She didn't have the look, so maybe she had an expert dermatologist who knew his Botox and fillers. Wheeler and I were both human females, but sitting across this desk, I almost didn't feel like one. Everything about her made me feel...less.

As if reading my mind, she said, "Does my physical appearance make you uncomfortable?"

"Is that the reaction you wish to elicit?"

Head slightly pitched back, mouth open just enough to showcase two rows of bright white teeth, her polite laughter was a master class in grace.

"Your reaction is of no consequence to me."

"I was hired by the Womyn of Llewellyn to look into Travers Hall."

"Ah yes, the girls who purposefully misspell their own gender. Well, let's not waste any time. Let me tell you what Travers is all about so you can be on your merry way." Wheeler rose and walked over to her filing cabinet. She rifled through the drawer and pulled out a folder, then returned to her seat. She took out a photo and pushed it across the desk.

It took about five seconds for me to figure out I was staring at Faith, the leader of the Womyn.

"What do you see when you look at that girl?" she asked.

The photograph, an 8x10 black and white, was Faith behind a desk. Her hair was tied into a neat ponytail, and she wore round-rimmed glasses. Wearing a dark pantsuit and blazer, she looked like…

"A lawyer," I said.

"Looks smart, wouldn't you say?"

"Yes."

"And pretty."

"Very much so. When was this taken?"

"Three years ago, her freshman year."

"Maybe what I should be asking is, how was this taken. Because the Faith I know now…"

Wheeler tapped the photograph with the tip of a red-polished nail.

"…wouldn't touch lip gloss with a ten-foot pole. She and I were going to usher in a new paradigm for Llewellyn, or so I thought."

"What happened?"

Wheeler smirked. "You don't know, do you?"

123

"Obviously not."

"She's my daughter."

37

Jesus. Looking again at the fashionable lawyerly photo, there was no question. Faith wasn't nearly as gorgeous as her mother, so the other half of her genes...

"Her father and I have been divorced for fifteen years, hence her using his last name. I'm disappointed in you, Siobhan. Shouldn't you have figured this out on your own? Maybe you need to have a little chat with this Womyn with a Y."

Wheeler slid another photograph toward me. Here was Faith as I knew her, her makeup-less face overshadowed by her green hair. It was a snapshot from some rally, because she was holding up a sign that read STOP THE TORTURE. In her sleeveless t-shirt, the dark patches of her underarm hair—well, let's just say it wasn't the most flattering shot.

"Tell me, now what do you see?"

"You want me to compare the two photos?"

"Yes."

"It's not a fair comparison."

"Oh, but it is. It is because how we present ourselves to the world is who we are. These Womyn of Llewellyn, and women like you, Siobhan—you can all be so much more, but you choose wrongly every time you walk outside looking like the way you do."

"So I should be putting on a full layer of foundation, hair extensions, fake eyelashes—because otherwise, I'm not fulfilling my full feminine potential?"

Wheeler sat back in her chair and scanned me up and down. "All of those would be terrible choices. You're short, so extensions would only make you look shorter. You have typical beady Asian eyes, so fake eyelashes would actually draw focus onto them. And foundation? Maybe a light layer, but I'd leave your skin tone natural. You are a private investigator. What would be the point of looking like me? You need to look like you, your real you."

I tried to brush off her words, but lord, did they sting. What was it about remarks that disparaged one's physical appearance that hurt so much? There was something downright elemental about it. Maybe because it goes way back to our childhoods, when that was the way you hurt other people and other people hurt you.

"You deal in superficialities, Wheeler," I said, my best attempt at a rebuttal.

She handed me a printout. *A study of the Canadian federal elections found that attractive candidates received more than two and a half times as many votes as unattractive candidates. Despite such evidence of favoritism toward handsome politicians, follow-up research demonstrated that voters did not realize their bias. In fact, 73 percent of Canadian voters surveyed denied in the strongest possible terms that their votes had been influenced by physical appearance; only 14 percent even allowed for the possibility of such influence. In another study, good grooming of applicants in a simulated employment interview accounted for more favorable hiring decisions than did job qualifications—this, even though the interviewers claimed that appearance played only a small role in their choices.*

"I *do* deal in superficialities," Wheeler continued. "Because the superficial is an integral part of life. There's a reason why we were given eyes and ears and noses, so we could see and hear and smell, to distinguish, to categorize, to determine that one person is more valuable than another. This is my mission as an educator, that our human presentation layer matters, and matters greatly."

"So this is what you're doing in Travers."

"The science of beauty. It is a *science*, and we here at Llewellyn will be at the forefront. Not only developing theories but real-world applications. We'll have aesthetic philosophers redefine the very concept of beauty. Our chemists will partner with major cosmetics corporations to develop better materials, better molecules."

"But beauty doesn't last."

"An athlete will age and lose her coordination and her stamina, will she say, 'Why bother. It's all going to pot anyway.' No. The athlete will train, will develop, will cultivate her body so she'll be the fastest, the strongest, the best she can be, for as long as she can."

I shook my head, but she was kind of getting to me. It was possible she had a point, even if it was one I didn't agree with.

Wheeler was on a roll now. "Youth comprises the greatest proportion of beauty, there is no question about that. But that doesn't mean we shouldn't keep trying. There is beauty at every stage of life. Take Catherine Deneuve or Julie Christie—they've been exquisite their whole lives."

"You're asking everyday women to compare themselves to movie stars."

"Not compare, *strive*. Would it surprise you to hear me declare that I am a bigger feminist than Gloria Steinem and Betty Freidan and, yes, even my beloved Faith? Because that's what I am, Siobhan. Believe it or not, the Womyn of Llewellyn and I are on the same side. I want women to be beautiful because it is a great source of power. Use that power to get what we want, to rule who we want, because that's what it takes to be victorious in this androcentric world. We can bring men to their knees, but only if we use all that was given to us, all that we have in our arsenal."

"You seem to have forgotten you've opened the doors to men in this college of yours. Are you going to disallow them from entering Travers?"

"I may be a feminist, but I'm also an educator. If men want to attend these classes, that is their prerogative. I won't cater to them, though, because they do not require this advantage as much as women do."

My phone buzzed. If not for the quiet of this room, Wheeler wouldn't have heard it.

"Your little app didn't quite succeed in its illicit recording," she said. "You're on our network, Siobhan, using our authentication app. I know what your phone is running. Next time, you might want to go old school and use a real wire."

I'd gotten my butt kicked before, but this was one for the ages. Still, I had a job to do.

"There's a second reason why I'm here," I said.

"By all means, continue in your noble quest."

"Penny Sykes."

"Yes?"

"You met with her before she disappeared."

"I met with her before she left the school on her own accord, yes."

"Where did she go?"

"Even if she told me, why would I tell you?"

"Her mother hired me to find her."

Wheeler rose.

"Maybe she should've hired someone more competent. Brent, would you show Ms. O'Brien the way out?"

Brent Kim, who specialized in appearing out of nowhere, materialized behind me.

"Are you kicking me off campus?" I asked her.

Wheeler laughed again. "No, Siobhan. And I'll give you two reasons because I'm feeling generous. One, there's nothing here for you to see, so please, go right ahead and investigate your little heart out. Two, you're a Llewellyn Women in Lifelong Learning. Why would I want a fellow female scholar to leave campus? No, all I want is for you to leave my office now, because our conversation is over."

I'd been thoroughly out-everythinged here, so I figured the best way to keep any sort of dignity was to leave without another word. Brent, being the gracious mobster strongman that he was, followed me out while keeping a respectable distance.

38

"Look," Faith said. "Maybe I should have told you."

I was in Faith's dorm room, which was such a disheveled mess that I had trouble concentrating. I had to fight the urge to pick up the mounds of clothes on the floor and chuck them into a hamper (if not a garbage bag), because they were literally everywhere—on the floor, on her bed, even on top of her bookshelves, a pair of sweatpants draped over a stack of hardcovers. She asked me to sit, but I couldn't find a chair.

"If by *maybe* you mean *absolutely*, then yes, you're right."

"I just didn't want to bias you, Siobhan." Faith, sitting on her bed, pushed away her dirty clothes against the corner and lay down. "I'm sorry."

"Wheeler—your mom—shut down the recorder app on the phone, so I wasn't able to get her on tape," I said. "Not that it matters anyway. She's got her vision for Llewellyn and she has every right to do what she wants."

"Jesus," Faith said. She sounded not only defeated but young, like a little girl trying to stand up to her mother. "This is awful."

"She showed me a photograph of you, black and white, pantsuit and blazer. And declared herself a feminist."

Faith took her pillow, pressed it against her face, and screamed.

"I've been hearing it my whole life. And you know, I just realized something. It wasn't that I wanted to keep you unbiased. The real reason why I didn't want to tell you was…"

"…because you're ashamed."

"Thank you for understanding."

"Your mother is a piece of work. She's sharp, she's ambitious, and I think she's well on her way to turn Llewellyn into her well-Photoshopped image."

"I know."

There was a knock on the door: Molly.

"Sister Siobhan! So nice to see you."

"Sister Molly," I said, and didn't quite know what else to say because there was a lot of purple on this girl. In fact, there was not a single place where there was no purple: purple hair, purple face and neck and hands, and in what could best be described as a purple onesie for adults.

"Why aren't you in your greens, Sister Faith?" Molly asked. "I was under the impression that we would dress in our class colors."

Faith hashed through her pile of tops on her bed and found a forest-green hoodie and held it up.

The purple makeup was thick, but not thick enough to mask Molly's mortification. "But…in our meeting, we talked about how we were going to support our college's tradition in the boldest possible manner…"

"…which is why I'm so thankful we have sisters like you, Molly," Faith said. "Ones who will bravely continue the tradition of Llewellyn."

Molly scampered over to Faith and gave her a great big purple hug.

"I'll carry your words with me for the rest of my life, Sister Faith."

And with that, she was gone. I shot Faith a look.

"A little hazing develops character," Faith said.

39

There were so many students out and about on campus that it felt like another bomb threat. Except this time, people were way more color-coordinated. As promised, Hajira met me to take in the festivities.

"Purple and yellow for the Oddline, those are the graduating classes that end in an odd year, and blue and green for the Evenline," Hajira said. "It's our biggest tradition. A way for the freshmen and juniors to bond against the sophomores and seniors." She had changed her headscarf to a bright blue to signify her sophomore allegiance.

Four big white tents were set up in the middle of the quad, the kind you might see at an outdoor wedding, string lights outlining the roofs and beams to add to the party atmosphere. I caught an intoxicating whiff of fried dough, and sure enough, that's what was being churned out in one of the tents. There was also cotton candy, ice cream, popcorn—it was a regular carnival.

A siren wailed in the distance, and that got the crowd clapping and whooping. The ringing grew louder as flashing red and blue lights cut through the darkness. Two fire trucks followed one another through the entrance of the college, slowly made their way up the hill and parked in front of the crowd. The first truck had long purple eyelashes attached to its headlights, and the second had a blue ribbon running the length of its body, ending with a giant bow on the rear fender.

"The players have returned from their parade," Hajira said. "The fire truck drives them through Selene, where the townsfolk clap and cheer them on the route."

"This is a big deal around here."

"There's always been a close relationship between the town and the school."

"Like the town cops providing security."

"That actually started after President Wheeler's car was defaced last year during graduation."

"What happened to it?"

Hajira smiled. "Someone affixed a giant papier-mâché shell of male genitalia over her entire car."

"A super-sized penis."

"And testicles. Which were quite hairy."

The players were getting out of the trucks now, and there was only one Asian in a purple uniform. The elusive Grace Park, finally in the flesh. She was taller than I'd thought, and watching her make her way down, she was not quite earning her name. There was an awkwardness to the way she stepped onto the pavement, as if where she believed the ground to be and where the ground actually was were at odds. Hajira said she had a good jump shot, which seemed believable. I'd played JV basketball in my high school days, and there was always a girl or two on teams who were not athletic but had a set shot they could count on. Get them moving and they were toast, but they could still make a decent living throwing down one bomb after another from the perimeter. Those girls were the most determined of all the players, the ones who earned every shot. As I watched Grace follow her teammates into the gymnasium, I felt her gravity, her resolve.

Hajira led me to the bleachers of the gymnasium. My high school gym had been twice as big as this one, but then again, we'd had four times the number of students as Llewellyn. Most of the spectators looked like they were from the town, older folks, men in plaid shirts and jeans and the women—also in plaid shirts—and jeans. Selene being still quite rural, it was the default uniform of the town. The place was hopping, loud and obnoxious techno music that was full of beeps and drums blaring out of the speakers.

I had to scream into Hajira's ear to ask if we could sit on the opposite side of the purple team. I wanted to observe Grace before the game started, and I figured it would be easier to see her face than to stare at the back of her head. We found seats in the third row, squeezing ourselves between two men in overalls. They literally looked like they came from working the field—and smelled like that, too, a mixture of hay and dirt and sweat that was surprisingly not unpleasant.

After practicing for five minutes, the team coaches rounded up the players for a chat. Mercifully, the dance music fell silent. The purple team's leader was a whistle-around-the-neck, pencil-behind-the-ear woman with a shock of short red hair.

I watched Grace as she stood in the huddle, and there was something else I felt: loneliness. She stood slightly outside the circle, more so than the other girls. Big surprise. Special security people were always hovering around her, so how could she *not* feel like she didn't belong? And then, it hit me. This whole time, I was thinking it was Grace who dumped Penny, but what if it was the other way around? It was a possibility I would be wise to consider.

Before I knew what was happening, the bottom of a sneaker landed between me and Hajira. Which was impressive, because Hajira and I were basically stuck shoulder to shoulder. The foot cleaved us and pushed us into the bodies of the farmers, who were then pushed into their neighbors—a domino effect that irritated everyone.

The foot belonged to a very tall guy, the same guy with the Tau Beta Alpha sweatshirt I'd seen earlier arguing with Brent Kim. His long gait turned him into a giant step from bleacher row to bleacher row, making his way down to the court.

"What did you say to him, Grace?" he screamed. His voice was so piercing that I half thought he was miked up; maybe his larynx was extra long, like his body. It was kind of amazing that just seconds before, this gym was so loud that I couldn't hear my own voice, and now that this commotion was happening, the entire place fell to eerie silence.

The tall guy was now down to the first bleacher. All eyes were on him.

"What the fuck did you do?"

Now all eyes went to Grace. With everyone staring at her, she did something that only made sense after I thought about it: she folded her arms and turned her back on the guy.

This, of course, infuriated him, but the moment he stepped onto the floor, Brent Kim grabbed the guy, spun him around, then placed him in some sort of a painful arm lock that made him very cooperative. Another one of Brent's flunkies was right behind, I guess for moral support, because Brent sure as hell didn't need any help in subduing the tall guy. The two members of the special security coolly marched down the sideline and headed for the north exit of the gym.

"That's my cue," I told Hajira. "Thank you for showing me around."

"You'll follow that tall man?"

"That's my job, following people who get thrown out of basketball games."

"Well," she said, "okay."

"I'll be fine," I said. "This is what I do."

"I don't doubt it," she said. "Regardless, please be careful."

135

40

Heeding Hajira's advice, instead of trailing Brent straight on, I took the east exit and walked around the gym. I peeked around the corner and watched Brent and his cohort drag the tall guy to the parking lot. They stopped in front of a red hatchback. *Chirp!* The car door opened, and now Brent was saying something to the guy. The guy wouldn't look at him, so Brent grabbed one of his ears and made sure there was eye contact. Then he pushed him into the car, and Brent stepped away, with his arms crossed, waiting for the tall guy to leave the premises.

My car was still parked in the visitor's lot, so I ran to it as fast as I could. The red hatchback was already turning onto Route 9, headed south towards Lenrock. This was not a well-traveled road, so I didn't want to be right behind him. As luck would have it, a pickup truck was also about to leave Llewellyn, so I allowed it to get in front of me and used it as a buffer.

With the moon and stars obscured by clouds, Route 9 was darkness itself. I thought of Grace and her rude little pirouette on the court. It was a move befitting a girl of privilege and power. She knew someone —in this case, Brent Kim—would take care of this little problem, because someone had always taken care of problems for her.

At the junction of Route 43, the truck took a left towards the town of Auburn and the hatchback took a right towards Athena. The tall guy was returning home, as I'd suspected. Two cars got between him and me heading southbound, which was my preference for tailing.

We got on Route 31, the heart of our hometown's commerce.

The hatchback turned left on Brown Street and climbed the hill. It was Thursday night, which meant Lenrock was quiet and subdued; as a top twenty school in the country, it was known for its academic rigor during the week and big-time partying Friday night through the weekend.

I followed the hatchback as it crossed University Avenue, passing by the beautiful old gothic arts and sciences buildings on the left and the ugly blocky engineering buildings on the right. A few more turns later, I saw the sign for the fraternity, Tau Beta Alpha. Tau Butt Alpha, technically, as the middle letter of the wooden sign was replaced with a photo of a man's hairy, naked butt placed sideways. I guess the Womyn of Llewellyn weren't the only ones pulling pranks. As we made our way up the driveway, I was basically tailgating him.

For a fraternity, TBA was surprisingly not a train wreck. Just a few crushed beer cans in the parking lot, and the house actually looked fairly intact. In my day, I'd been to a fair share of frat parties to know what kind of hellholes they could be.

The tall guy and I got out of our cars at the same time. He rubbed his arm, the one Brent had commandeered. He trudged toward the front door.

"Excuse me?" I said.

He turned. "Yeah?"

There was a time when you could tell people you were lost, but in the days of GPS and Google Maps, that lie didn't fly. Besides, I could see this kid was in no mood.

"I saw what happened at Llewellyn. At the gym."

It took him a few seconds to put things together.

"You followed me? All the way from Selene?"

"It's not that long of a drive, but yes."

"What are you, like stalking me or something?"

"No, nothing like that. I just have some questions."

With his wide shoulders sagging, he looked like he was about to tell me to fuck off, but then he stopped. And thought.

"You know what? You're better than nothing."

"Okay…" I said. "I've been called worse. You'll answer a few questions?"

He looked at his phone. "Yeah, whatever. I'm already so late. Jesus, they're all gonna hate me. Just play along."

41

If there was one word to describe Tau Beta Alpha, I'd choose "crest-fallen." Maybe because that was the first thing I saw when I walked through the foyer, the red and gold crest of the fraternity, the wooden engraving nailed on a ceiling beam that ran from one end of the wall to another. And fallen because of the faces of the boys I saw, faces that had momentarily contained hope but which instantly turned to disappointment upon my entrance.

There were five guys standing around an antique octagonal table. They were dressed up, a sweater or sweater-vest over a starched shirt and a nicely ironed pair of slacks. The guy in the middle was wearing a blazer which gave him an air of authority.

"God damn it, Beaker, not only are you an hour late, but what the hell is…this?"

I was glad to be able to attach a name to the tall guy, even if it was a nickname.

"You said to bring girls from Llewellyn," Beaker said. "I brought one."

Blazer guy looked at Beaker, then looked at me, then looked at Beaker again.

"This is not…" he said. Then he turned to me. "No offense or anything, but…"

"Siobhan O'Brien," I said, extending my hand. "No apology necessary, I know I'm past the expiration date. Am I correct in assuming you are the president of this fraternity?"

"Drew Callahan," he said as he shook my hand. "How did you figure that?"

"You just look like someone in charge, Drew."

A little compliment goes a long way, and he beamed like the little big boy that he was. Now that Drew was off his guard, I felt the best way to get him to trust me was to tell him the truth, that I followed Beaker here. When I got to the altercation on the basketball court, he got angry all over again.

"Why the hell did you do that, Beaks?" he said.

"Because he's our brother, Drew," Beaker said. "Or have you already written him off?"

Before they could continue to argue, someone knocked on the door.

"Shut up," one of the other well-dressed guys said. "We got one. Finally."

"We'll pick this up later," Drew said to Beaker, and then the five brothers were all hellos and smiles as they greeted the kid at the door. Beaker gestured for me to follow, so I did, past the large dining room with cafeteria-style tables and through the swinging door that led to the kitchen, which had a line of gigantic pots and pans hanging off a 2x4 suspended on chains from the ceiling. Whoever did the cooking around here probably needed to bench 300. Next to a gas range with eight burners was a griddle that would make any cook proud.

Beaker dipped his entire body into one of three industrial refrigerators and came out with a plastic-wrapped dish. He popped it into the microwave and grabbed two empty glasses from the shelf. He drew water from the faucet and offered me one.

"This is our fall rush," he said. "I think that might be the first guy to walk through the door tonight."

"Don't Lenrock fraternities and sororities hold rushes in the spring?"

The microwave dinged and he took out his rapidly vacuum-sealing meal.

"If you are in a fraternity that isn't teetering on its last legs and has to beg people to join, then yeah, you don't have to do what we're doing now. Unfortunately, that isn't us."

Beaker took his fork and poked a hole in the plastic wrap in the middle of what looked like mashed potatoes, and the steam escaped through the opening. It smelled yummy, the plate heaped with slices of turkey and gravy.

"When I first walked in, Drew seemed angry that I was the only female you'd brought from Llewellyn."

"Drew gets angry about a lot of things."

Beaker led us back to the dining room, where he pulled up a chair for me and actually waited until I sat down before he took a seat himself. And people say chivalry is dead.

He might have been well-mannered in gender etiquette, but apparently he'd missed the lessons in table manners, as he ate like a woodchuck ripping through wood. Bits of food flew within a one-foot radius of his dish as he ate and talked. I slid my chair back a bit, in case he got a little carried away.

"I was supposed to return with a carload of girls." *Spit, spit, spit.* "Usually, they take the van that runs between Lewie and Lenrock." *Spew, spew, spew.* "But because of the Odd-Even basketball game, it wasn't running tonight."

Beaker shoved his empty dish away and sat back and quietly belched. Maybe it was the low lighting in the dining room, but the bags under his eyes made him look older than me.

"So instead of chauffeuring a few girls back here to brighten up your event, you got thrown out by Grace Park's bodyguards."

Beaker closed his eyes and sank into his chair. "She owes me an explanation. I don't care who you are or how much money you have. Christopher ran away because of her, and the least she can do is tell me why."

"Who's Christopher?"

"He and I were going to room together this year. We rushed Tau Beta Alpha together as freshmen last year. He's my best friend, and now he won't talk to me. He won't talk to anyone. We're supposed to be a fucking brotherhood, and nobody else gives a shit that he's gone."

"And Christopher is gone because of something Grace did or said?"

"Christopher is a super sensitive guy, and that bitch did something to him, or to Penny, or…"

"Penny? Penny Sykes?"

"You know her?"

"I've been hired by her mother to find her. That's what I've been doing for the last week."

Beaker looked at me like I was the dunce of the class.

"I thought you said you were a detective."

"That I am, though I bet from what you're about to tell me, maybe not a very good one."

"Penny's at Krishna, same as Christopher."

He saw the blank look on my face.

"You have no idea what Krishna is either, do you."

Beaker took out his cell and thumbed his way to whatever he wanted to show me.

"Here you go," he said, and handed me his phone.

42

The smallness of the screen did not diminish the natural beauty of the place. Serving as the background of the website was a dramatic photograph of a lake surrounded by green mountains. The panorama scrolled ever so slowly, like a camera panning, and then the season slowly dissolved from summer to fall, which is probably what it must look like now, red and orange and mustard yellow dominating the landscape. In a quiet sans serif font in the center of the page, the word "Namaste" faded in and out like a heartbeat.

"I could look at this all day," I said.

"It *is* kind of addicting. There's sound, too—you can choose a chant, rainstorm, a babbling brook, they add new ones all the time."

The Krishna Center for Yoga and Wellness was in Hawthorne, in the heart of the Adirondacks, overlooking Saranac Lake. Tapping the "About Us" link showed me a gray-bricked building that was embedded on the face of a mountain. It wasn't a tall structure, perhaps three stories high, but it ran wide and flat, rather like my old elementary school. Splotches of ivy beautified the exterior, but its plainness stood in juxtaposition to the imposing terrain that surrounded it.

"So is this like a retreat where people go to get away from their busy lives?" I asked.

"That's what it looks like. I've never been there."

I clicked on the "Your Stay" link, then scrolled down to the daily rates.

"Place ain't cheap."

"There's some volunteer program, or something like that. That's how Christopher usually goes there. I don't know about Penny."

"I don't get why you're worried when it looks like he's gone to heaven on earth."

"He didn't just go there—he basically ran away in the middle of the night."

"When?"

"Like a week ago."

A little after Penny disappeared, so the timing made sense.

"You said you and Christopher were going to room together. Is his stuff still in your room?"

"Well, yeah, he just up and left."

"You mind letting me see it?"

After a slight pause of deliberation—I guess he was wondering if it was worth his time to continue to deal with my perceived (and possibly correct) ineptitude—he shrugged. Ah, the shrug, the ever-dependable go-to gesture for the young. I was grateful for its indifferent existence.

After Beaker bussed his dishes, he led me back to the foyer and the base of the impressive red-carpeted staircase. The kid who'd entered after me, who I figured was like a prospect, was being told about the history of the crest. Drew, in full tour guide mode, stole me away from Beaker.

"And here's one of our sisters from Llewellyn I was telling you about. Siobhan? Meet Samir."

"Hi there," I said.

"Umm…hi. Are you…like what grade are you in?"

To Samir, who looked scrawny enough to still be in junior high, I probably looked like a teacher.

"I'm a grad student," I said. "Getting my doctorate in linguistics."

"Oh, okay," he said, visibly relieved.

"It's very nice of the guys here to let me still party hearty with them. We go back. Way, way back."

Drew cleared his throat and turned his attention back to Samir.

"Thanks, Siobhan. Be sure to come by Saturday night for our little thing."

"Wouldn't miss it for the world," I said.

Samir and Drew moved onto what looked to be a meeting room, with built-in bookcases and leather chairs. Beaker led me up the main stairs, which were wide enough for a double-dating couple to walk up side by side. The house was actually quite beautiful, probably dating back to the early century, with an understated black chandelier above the foyer, decorative wooden panels along the walls, a little built-in bench on the middle landing that overlooked the first floor. A few of the oak banisters were missing, but by and large, the house was in livable shape.

"Very smooth there with Drew," Beaker said.

"If this detective thing doesn't work out, maybe I can try improv."

"I'm sorry if I was being harsh. I just thought you'd know about Penny and Krishna, because, you know..."

"I'm the detective."

"Yeah."

"I might have gotten a little sidetracked with all that's going on with Llewellyn."

"Understandable. It's the main reason why we haven't had as many girls come this semester, because they're all legit mad about the integration."

"You can understand why, though, right?"

At the top of the landing, we cut a left and then a right. Along the way, I saw two guys playing video games, another two playing chess, and one in bed, napping. *College, I miss you.*

"I guess. I don't want to sound like some chauvinist or anything, but a women-only college is not an accurate representative of the world out there. I never quite understood why it was seen as something that would prepare a woman for her future if they excluded the other half of the human race."

"It's why I never wanted to attend one, but you can see that some women have difficulty finding themselves when there are men around. You guys are just louder—more aggressive—by nature."

"I guess. I don't know. It depends. The guys in our house aren't like that."

"Which is probably why you've had a sustained relationship with Lewie girls."

Beaker stopped.

"This yours?"

"Yeah," he said. "I never realized just why we meshed so well with Llewellyn until you just explained it."

"So maybe I should be a shrink when I grow up," I said.

Beaker laughed. "Maybe. So here it is, our little man-cave."

Behind the door, a member of the Swedish bikini team greeted me.

43

A life-sized cardboard cutout of a beach-ready buxom blonde woman, that is. A flashing Rolling Rock sign, a Salvador Dali print, a young Arnold Schwarzenegger tight-lipped in his *Terminator* shades—half of this room was filled with such typical male collegiate decorations that I wondered if Beaker was being ironic. There was even a lava lamp on a desk, white goo sticking and unsticking inside neon-yellow liquid.

The other half of the room—which must be Christopher's as it looked neat and undisturbed—was like something out of a New Age bookstore. A trio of framed pictures hung on the walls: a triptych of three blades of grass. In the corner was a literal shrine, a bronze sitting Siddhartha on a pedestal and cones of unburned incense in a white dish. A gold plate with a scoop of white sand and a tiny rake was the prominent decoration on his desk.

"You guys got along?" I asked, disbelieving.

"You'd think we were from different planets, but we're total buds. If not for Christopher, I would've transferred out of here my freshman year to Syracuse. Lenrock's a great school and we'll all be doctors or lawyers or engineers when we leave, but I'm from California and all this rain really brings me down."

"I'd like to search Christopher's side of the room."

"For clues?"

I smiled. "Yes, for clues. It'd be good if you were to stick around, so you can make sure I'm on the up and up."

"Sure."

Nothing out of the ordinary in his drawers: underwear and socks at the top, t-shirts and sweatpants in the middle, and nicer t-shirts on the bottom. There was some room in each drawer since he must've packed them up, but not a whole lot. So either he wasn't expecting to stay that long at Krishna or he left in an emotional frenzy that he didn't think that far ahead. While I moved onto Christopher's desk, Beaker filled me in about the summer session, which was when Christopher and Penny got together.

"I was back home during break to work with my dad—he runs a landscaping business—but Christopher stayed at Lenrock to take a couple of philosophy courses. I came up on the July Fourth weekend, and that's when I saw Christopher and Penny together. In this very room, actually, because this is where Christopher stayed for the summer."

The desk was like a twin of the one in my office, a gray metallic behemoth. There were three drawers on the left side, all impeccably organized, the top one for supplies like staples and Scotch tape, the middle for medium-sized notebooks, and the bottom for larger note-books. Christopher was one neat guy.

"That's the first time you met Penny, I presume."

"First and only. They spent most of their time at her dorm in Llewellyn, but because I was gonna be around for the weekend, they came here. She was really into him, I remember. When he spoke, she'd stare at him like every word was gospel."

"Was Christopher as into her and she was into him?"

Beaker sat on his bed and ruminated over the question. His little twin bed made him look even taller, like a giant visiting regular folks. "I'd say so. They made out a lot, I remember that. Kind of made me feel bad, because I was home for the summer and my girlfriend was back in Long Island and hadn't seen her for a couple of months."

I was rooting through the middle drawer when I came upon something you don't usually find in a college dorm room: a sealed test tube, the kind you see at a diagnostic lab for blood tests. A yellow plastic screw-on cap was on the head, and the label was blank except for the logo, a lowercase "i" inside the empty wedge of an uppercase "P." Park Industries. I showed it to Beaker.

"That is kind of odd," he said. "He's taking organic chemistry right now, but that doesn't look like the test tubes they use."

"Is Christopher sick? Does he get his blood drawn every so often?"

Beaker shook his head. "Never eats red meat, only snacks on organic trail mix, drinks unsweetened soy milk, he'll probably live to a hundred."

"I'll take this, if you don't mind. I promise to bring it back."

Beaker shrugged, which was assent enough for me.

While I searched through Christopher's closet, Beaker told me he didn't think Christopher and Penny were a great match.

"I saw them together for just a couple of days. They were so alike, too much. Like I said, Christopher is super sensitive. Like we have to be careful what we say to him because he can take it the wrong way and then he might not talk for a week. It's just the way he is. I understand him and accept him, but he can be a pain in the ass. And with Penny, it was like this sensitivity thing was doubled because she's the same way. Worse, actually. It was like they were constantly offending each other, but then they'd have this super philosophical discussion and, I guess, make up? It was all beyond me, what they were talking about, something to do with the self. The outer self, the inner self, whatever. I've never had a problem that a six-pack can't solve."

The closet was like everything else under Christopher's domain: stacked, filed, aligned with a ruler. Every clothes hanger faced the same direction, and each shirt was ironed and buttoned at the top. It was like a department store rack in here. I felt bad about moving his stuff around because I knew I was messing it up.

"So what happened? It sounds like they were really together."

"I haven't a fucking clue. That's why I confronted Grace, because after Christopher came back from visiting her and Penny like

149

two weeks ago—this was the end of September—he was a wreck. That's when Christopher found out Penny disappeared to Krishna, and he rushed after her. And here we are, you going through his stuff with mad abandon."

"Sorry."

Beaker waved me off. "It's okay. If it helps you find out what happened to my roommate and brother, then a little mess is more than worth it."

The only thing I saw in his closet that perhaps wasn't for anyone else's eyes was a dog-eared copy of the *Kama Sutra* underneath a sheaf of manila envelopes. I might have had the same edition at some point in my life. Nothing wrong with a little sexual experimentation in college.

"Penny suffers from hyperthyroidism, and she has to take a pill on a regular basis or she gets pretty sick…" I said.

"Heart palpitations, or fast heartbeat, that's it. I remember she had a freak out one time, but then again, she freaked out about a lot of stuff. Christopher had to run back to Grace's to get Penny's pills, and after she took one, she was fine."

"Thank you, Beaker, for everything. Is that okay that I call you that?"

"Sure. That was my pledge name and it kind of stuck."

"Why Beaker?"

"I don't know. I'm not a chem major. I don't have a beak for a nose. Do I?"

I took a step back, then another because of his height.

"No, you have a fine, distinguished nose."

This seemed to make his night. "Yeah? Cool."

As he led me back to the entrance, he mentioned how this was the third night of the fall rush and they had gotten just two prospective pledges altogether. "The other night, I saw like six guys walk by, then for some reason, turn around. I think they were laughing."

"Maybe it's the butt on your sign," I said. "In place of the Beta character."

"*What?*" Beaker asked.

We walked out into the night and I pointed.

"Jesus," he said. "We must've walked by it like a hundred times and didn't see it. Oh man, it's Krazy Glue or something because this isn't coming off."

I wished Beaker luck and walked back to my car. As I drove past him, I waved but he was too busy scraping away the butt picture with what might have been a rock.

Ah, college. Whenever I think I miss you, I actually don't.

44

I hadn't heard back from Craig since I sent him that one-word email (*Okay!*) about dinner. Today was Friday, and he'd said he'd be back from wherever he was, but when I walked by his office on the way to mine, his door was locked. I was relieved. And then disappointed.

What was the next step, me drawing little red hearts on the margins of my notebook? Asking Suzy in math class if he *liked* me or *like me* liked me? This was pathetic. I was pathetic. I closed the door to my office and got to work. I fired up the old beast of a computer, which made an even worse noise than before, like metal grinding against metal, but then it warmed up and the noise disappeared.

I opened up the browser and went to Llewellyn's website, then clicked around until I found the "Partnerships" link. On the first page were two cosmetics companies and one perfume manufacturer, so Wheeler was already on her way to remake Llewellyn in her model image. After a list of scholarships (one sponsored by Jimmy Dean, the sausage people, given to a student who excels in "meat and meat-related studies"—no, it wasn't a joke), I found what I was looking for. Krishna Center for Yoga and Wellness, featured for its summer programs for students and retreats for faculty and employees. Clicking deeper into the website, there were forms for students to apply to the "Krishna Experience" and earn credits toward their degree. I saw no information about anything during the fall or spring semesters. Beaker had mentioned a volunteer program, so I opened up another tab and punched in Krishna's URL when my phone rang. I looked at the clock on my computer and saw it was 10:30 in the morning.

"I knew you'd find her," Josie said.

I'd left her a voicemail last night.

"How about we wait to celebrate until I've actually seen Penny with my own eyes?"

"It's just nice to get some good news for a change. I'm at work, by the way, on one of my two allotted cigarette breaks."

"You're smoking again?"

"No, that's just what we call it, us mindless drones at this lovely office. I'm just glad to get away from the desk and the headset for fifteen minutes. What's up? You said you had a question or two."

"Did Penny have any boyfriends in high school?" I asked.

"Not really. She went to her senior prom with friends, a group thing."

"So Christopher was her first boyfriend."

"I don't...who's Christopher?"

I told her all I knew about Christopher Vachess, mostly what Beaker had told me, plus a little background I'd done on my own. He was from New York City, an English major, and his parents ran a hedge fund. He'd never been fingerprinted and he'd never even gotten a traffic ticket, so at least according to his lack of a record, he was a good kid. When I mentioned Tau Beta Alpha, I heard the change in Josie's voice.

"The guys I met, they're nice kids," I said.

"I guess all the nasty stories I told her about frats didn't scare her one bit."

"It's not like we were angels when we were in school, Josie."

"She never once told me about this Christopher in all our phone calls," she said.

No doubt there was a lot more that Penny had not told her, but that was something Josie would have to realize on her own.

"She's just trying to find herself. Figuring out who she is," I said. Platitudes and empty words, but Josie seemed to appreciate them nonetheless.

"I understand, but more than that, I hope she's taking care of herself. She can lose weight pretty fast with Graves if she doesn't maintain her medicine. She's just a little girl…"

I promised her I'd call again as soon as I found Penny at Krishna.

45

Back in front of my computer, I moved the mouse to wake up the screen, but nothing happened. I clicked on the mouse. Nothing. I banged on the keyboard. Still black. The little orange LED glowed on the monitor's status light, so there was power going in. But when I dipped down below the desk, the computer was silent. I pushed the power button and the hideous grinding noise started again, but instead of plateauing to an acceptable hum, the racket abruptly halted. Pressing the power button again did nothing.

"Shit," I said.

"Knock, knock," Craig's voice said behind my half-closed door.

I walked up to the door and flung it open, and there he was, my guy.

"Craig!" I said.

"Yes!" he said.

Here we were, the two of us, at the threshold of my office door.

"I think we should hug," Craig said.

"I think we should, too."

We hugged, and it was glorious.

"I believe my computer just died," I said.

Craig walked around to my desk and crouched down to take a closer look, which gave me a chance to notice his very nicely shaped head. I hope that doesn't make me sound like a weirdo, but really, it was so very pleasantly round.

"Do you smell that?" he asked.

Now that he did mention it, I did. "Like burnt rubber."

Craig kneeled and leaned further under the desk so he could turn the big black tower around. Now the smell was even stronger, and

I could see the problem. Underneath the power switch was a vent, except this vent was so filled with dust that it wasn't a vent anymore. In fact, it looked like a disgusting hairy stuffed animal, stringy, gray tufts jutting out of the metal grille.

"It must've overheated," Craig said. "It's probably been overheating for a while. Were you trying to look at something on the computer?"

"This Krishna place up in Hawthorne. According to my latest intel, that's where my missing girl is."

"Grace Park is missing?"

"No, a friend's daughter, who seems to have gotten mixed up with Grace in some way."

"I have a working computer and I'm doing paperwork for pretty much the whole day, so you could come to my office and use it."

I offered him my hand. He took it, and I leaned back and pulled him up. Not that he needed my help to rise, but I liked our symbolic teamwork. It was effortless being with him. *Too* effortless.

"What's wrong?" he asked. So not only was he thoughtful, he was perceptive, too.

"Not a thing," I said, "which is what's wrong."

He stared at me, and I stared back. Why wasn't this strange or awkward? It should be. Grown people don't stare at one another like this.

He squeezed my hand. I'd forgotten that we were still holding hands.

"Follow me," he said.

Craig's office was half the size of mine, but it felt bigger because there was virtually nothing in it. The desk was long and oval and white, like a surfboard. There were no drawers, just four spindly metallic legs. No filing cabinet, an ergonomic chair for himself and two black leather armchairs for his clients. It felt more like an office model than a real one.

"Do you have all your client files in the cloud?" I asked.

He pulled out his chair for me to sit in front of his aluminum sliver of a laptop. He dragged over one of his client armchairs and placed himself at the end of his plank-desk.

"I used to have a normal office," he said, opening up his briefcase.

"When you used to be…larger," I said.

He tilted his head, then smiled. "You really are a private eye, aren't you?"

"I try." There were ties from Llewellyn to Krishna, so I wondered if there were any that traveled in the other direction. I brought up Krishna's website on Craig's laptop and typed in "Llewellyn" into the search engine.

"I topped out at 280. Lost more than a hundred pounds since. What else have you figured out about me?"

There were three hits, but not what I'd expected. All links pointed to the profiles of the staff. The Director of Programming, the Director of Development, and the CFO were all from Llewellyn.

"You were married," I said. "But you aren't anymore."

"Wow."

"Please call Beaker for me." I said. "Inform him I do have some detecting skills."

"Who?"

I recounted my visit to Tau Beta Alpha, which Craig found amusing. He found a lot of things amusing. He laughed a lot. He had a nice laugh, not loud but deep, taking time to come up from his belly.

For the next hour, we worked together, and it felt like we'd been doing it for years. I clicked and read while Craig jotted on little yellow stickies and peeled them and stuck them on the pages of his documents. He'd look up from his work every so often to look over at me, and I did the same. Sometimes this occurred simultaneously; other times, not. Either way, I was happy, and I think he was, too.

Krishna, for all of its talk of spirituality and oneness, looked like a serious business, with a corporate org chart, an investors page, and even a mission statement: "To empower people and communities to realize their full potential through the transformative wisdom and practice of yoga." Scouring through their photo stream, I saw one where Vera Wheeler and Cleo Park were standing by an impressively tiered cake, some sort of a fancy anniversary party.

There were several choices for the types of rooms, ranging from a bare-bones barracks-style twin bed to a fancy 100% renewable-energy-run suite with its own bathroom. If I had a client who paid me, I would've gone for the private bath, but since I was on my own dime, I opted for a single with a shared bath. From the description I read, it almost felt like a college dorm, except for the ten o'clock curfew, no alcohol, and silent breakfasts. So actually, it was almost the exact opposite of a college dorm.

I was punching in my credit card number to finish up my reservation when my stomach growled like a tiger.

"Is your tummy trying to tell us something?" Craig said.

"Me want food."

"That means we'll be having lunch *and* dinner. Is that too much Craig for one day?"

"Or is it too much Siobhan?"

We stared at one another. Our smiles could light up a city.

"This is turning out to be a very fine day," Craig said.

46

We decided on Panera Bread, because it was near the downtown Best Buy. Craig, being a techie, offered his help in finding me a replacement computer that wasn't going to bankrupt me. But before going on our technological shopping spree, we treated ourselves to a pair of non-GMO, grass-fed, cruelty-free chicken sandwiches. Craig steered me towards the pesto one because even though it had slightly higher calories than some of the others, it was lower in sodium.

"I gain like two pounds from the water retention," he said.

"So what prompted you to lose all that weight?" I asked.

It was noon on a Friday, the rush hour of rush hours at restaurants everywhere, screaming babies, boisterous teenagers, businessmen barking into their phones between hurried bites of bread and meat. Craig was trying to say something important and I was having trouble hearing him. I leaned forward and pointed to my ear.

"After my wife died," he said.

"Oh," I said. "Jeez, I'm sorry."

We finished the rest of our meal in silence, maybe because he was sad and that made me sad. Or perhaps it was a way to pay respect to her. Whatever the reason, it felt good to get back outside, feel the crisp autumn wind wake me up and make me pay attention to the present.

We walked from Panera over to Best Buy.

"What happened to her?" I asked.

"Multiple myeloma."

"I've heard of it, but I don't know what it is."

"Cancer. Attacks the blood, then the bones. Usually starts out as back pain, then your bones start to crumble, disintegrate. She went fast, not even six months. I'll always be grateful for the existence of morphine.

"You take stock of a lot of things. Martina was always harping on me to lose weight because she didn't want to be a widow. Never said that to me, of course, but I knew that's what she was thinking. So after she died, I went on a diet, and I'm still on it. It really isn't a diet anymore, I guess, once it becomes the norm."

Considering the tenor of our conversation, it felt ridiculous to now be standing inside Best Buy, where everything was bright and shiny and beeping and dinging.

"Maybe we do this another time," I said.

"It's okay. It was eleven years ago. Mostly it feels like eleven years, though sometimes it feels like yesterday."

It took about three seconds before we were accosted by a soldier of the cobalt-blue-shirted sales army. Brandon was his name, and he looked way too muscular to be a hawker of computers. Did everybody pump iron nowadays? His biceps were like boulders bolted onto to his arms.

"Need any help?" he asked.

"I'm good," I said, then pointed to Craig. "I'm with smart."

"Got it, got it," Brandon said. He slapped his shovel-sized hands together and made a minor thunderclap. "If you need anything at all, just holler."

As Brandon lumbered away, Craig said, "Now he'll run into a telephone booth and fly off to save the planet."

There were a lot of choices for laptops, too many. One laptop allowed me to choose from six different shells. Really?

"Last time I shopped for a computer, I was still dialing up America Online," I said.

"I miss those times," Craig said. "Not the slow internet, but there was such hope everywhere, misguided as it might have been."

Craig narrowed it down to two candidates. None of them had

designer covers, which was good.

"They're really all the same, CPU, memory, and storage-wise. You're not doing any heavy graphics work, so the onboard GPU should suffice."

"As a professional private investigator, I'm not allowed to utter the phrase eeeny-meeny-miny-moe under any circumstance. Why don't you do the honors."

Craig flipped a coin, and I headed over to the register with the winner, an HP something or another that was surprisingly affordable, a shade over four hundred bucks. Lots of Xes in the name, so I'm sure it was a good one.

Back in the car with the brand-new computer in tow, I thanked Craig for his help.

"My pleasure," he said.

I kissed him then. I'm not really sure why, but it felt right to cross the gear shift and lean in to meet his mouth with mine. It wasn't a big kiss. But not a small one, either.

"Hmm," he said. Or maybe it was *mmm*. Either way, I liked it.

I drove us back to the entrance of our office building.

"I'll see you at seven?" he asked.

"You'll see me at seven."

I watched him walk away from me. His pants were a little too loose around his waist, and it made him look young, vulnerable. The more I got to know him, the more I liked him, but really, this was too simple, him and me. A shoe somewhere, sometime, was gonna drop. Or was I just a jaded forty-year-old killjoy?

47

After shopping with Craig, I got back on the road and headed to Llewellyn to deal with a few dangling threads. First on my list was Officer David Girard. It was a little past four by the time I arrived on campus, so I hurried over to Broadhurst to catch him before he cut out early. End of the week, nice and sunny for once, small town cop...I just had a feeling.

"Hey there!" Russ said. The young cop who helped me get my ID was in the same seat, in the same uniform, in front of the same computer. It was like I'd never left. "How's that ID holding up?"

"Haven't lost it yet. Is your boss still in the office?"

"I think so. He came back from lunch a little while ago and I don't remember him saying goodbye. Not that he always does."

I nodded and made my way to Girard's office. I knocked and heard a gruff voice, "Yeah?"

I opened the door. He looked up from his iPad, scowled, then looked back down.

"Just have a question or two, if that's all right," I said.

He tossed his iPad aside and rose from his desk.

"Make an appointment with Russ."

He lifted his round brown hat from the hook and put it on.

He pushed past me to the door. If that was all that he had to get rid of me, he'd have to try harder. I followed him to the elevator and got in his face—as much as I could, considering he almost had a foot on me.

He mashed the call button again. I stood right next to him and didn't move. "You think my boss didn't chew me out for the stunt you pulled at Travers? It all comes back to me, all the dumb shit that goes on around here. I got enough problems with green-haired, lip-pierced dykes. The last thing I need is a busybody like you breaking and entering."

The elevator finally came down, and we both got in.

"I'm sorry you got in trouble for what I did."

"Thanks to that fake bomb threat, we got approval from the board for a campus-wide camera system. Install starts on Monday, so it won't be long until this little revolution is shut down for good."

The elevator dinged and we got out. Officer Girard had the most enviable parking space, right behind Broadhurst.

"It's all bullshit, what you're doing," I said.

Girard opened the door of his cruiser. "Is that so?"

"Shared services my ass. The town police lending its security to a college? Please."

"I'm just doing my job, and you're getting in the way of that. I promise you, if I catch you or anybody else opening doors that are supposed to remain locked, I'll personally make sure you see the inside of a jail cell."

He got in his car, slammed the door, and peeled out.

That went even worse than I'd thought.

48

Next on my must-annoy list was Dr. Christine Collins, Assistant Professor of Chemistry. With my luck, she'd probably chuck a rack of test tubes at me. But my luck was so poor that she wasn't even around. She was supposed to be teaching the final class of the day, but the instructor standing in front of the dry-erase board was a substitute, who was super pissed that I interrupted his lecture on oxidation reduction.

"Do you have any idea where she went?"

He made a face. Maybe everyone I see today was going to make a face.

"The sooner you tell me, the sooner I get out of your hair," I said.

"Just email her!"

"Okay!" I said.

The guy might have been a grouch, but he was right. I guess it was some sort of faculty-wide policy, but one quick email was all it took for the autoresponder to reply.

I'm currently away at the Krishna Center in Hawthorne for the Anti-Aging Consortium until Monday, so I will get back to you when I return. If you require an immediate response, please email the administrative assistant Karen Knight at kknight@llewellyncollege.edu.

Was it fate? It sure smelled like it. Not only was Penny over there at Krishna, but now Collins would be there. From what I'd overheard in Travers Hall, that meant Wheeler would be there, too. Anti-Aging Consortium—this must've been what those two professors had argued about, Val and Roberto, complaining about how Collins was go-

ing to present something that was perhaps scientifically unsound. I'd
looked them up in the directory: Drs. Valaria and Roberto D'Onofrio,
also professors of chemistry. According to their faculty profiles, Roberto was the head of the department while Valaria was an associate
professor. That meant Collins was the lowest on the tenure-track to-
tem pole, since she was an assistant, yet she was the one who was
going to Krishna with the president.

The D'Onofrios shared an office in Parker Hall that looked well
lived-in. You could just feel it: the coffee pot with its permanent
brown ring, the fern whose branches were twined into an opening
in the bookshelf, the bag of Pepperidge Farm Milano cookies that
probably got replaced weekly. The one who won the sweepstakes to
talk to me was Valaria.

"My husband and I share this office, yes," she said, "but never at
the same time. It was one of the rules we had, so we don't spend every waking moment together. Have a seat, Ms. O'Brien. So, you're a
private detective? That sounds like an exciting profession. Way more
exciting than teaching kids about organic molecules."

As I recalled from my eavesdropping session at Travers, Valaria
was the level-headed one, and that assessment was further promoted
as we discussed the changing landscape of the Llewellyn campus. I
told her about my current case; she couldn't remember Penny being
in any of her classes. I wanted to know more about what was going
on in Travers and what Collins was doing over there at Krishna, and
since Valaria seemed a reasonable person, I thought I'd approach this
from that point of view.

"I had a couple of questions about you and your husband's work
in Travers," I asked.

"Travers, yes, so what do you know about Travers?"

She was trying to play it cool, a little too cool.

"I spoke to Professor Christine Collins before she left," I lied.
Then I lied more, because Valaria wasn't buying what I was selling.

"She told me about the boxes there, the false eyelashes, the wigs."

Valaria nodded to herself as a slash of a bitter smile lined her lips.

"We all signed nondisclosure agreements, but I guess since Christine is the chosen one, she can do whatever the hell she wants."

"She told me your talents were being wasted," I said. Too much? Possibly. But it felt like the right thing to say.

"Oh really? How magnanimous of her. You know, if not for her glomming onto this entire ridiculous shtick of Wheeler's, she would've been fired. That's how inept she is. She's a terrible teacher, you should see her students' evaluations for the last four semesters. Her research, astonishingly, is even worse than her ability to instruct."

"But she's got Wheeler's ear," I said.

"The joke will be on her, in the end. That paper she's presenting is a fraud. The peer review was done by some pretend-doctors in the Ukraine, and her data analysis is too uniform to be real. It's the very definition of academic corruption. But you know what all this is for, don't you?"

I shook my head dumbly, riding the wave.

"It's for that vacuous Barbie doll Cleopatra Park."

"I don't understand."

Valaria picked up her bottle of Evian and took a nice, long drink.

"I thought you came to talk to me about Penny Sykes."

Oh well. It was good while it lasted.

"My job as a PI is to gather information. Information doesn't come with a label. I have no idea what will or will not be useful, so I try to accrue as much as I can."

Valaria took another sip of her water, then cleared her throat. "What color is Christine's hair?"

On the faculty page, all the photos were in black and white. I said nothing.

"You never talked to Christine."

"No."

"Don't I feel stupid."

"Smart enough to stop."

"But now you know things you aren't supposed to know."

"What is going on in Travers, Valaria? I give you my word that whatever you tell me will not go beyond my case. I have a strong hunch that what's happening here in Llewellyn is tied together with Penny's disappearance. Will you help me?"

Valaria pressed the speaker button on her phone and tapped four tones on the keypad.

"Public Safety." It was a familiar voice, Russ.

"This is Dr. Valaria D'Onofrio. Can you please send someone to escort Ms. Siobhan O'Brien off our campus?"

"That won't be necessary," I said to the air between us. "I'll leave now, Russ."

"Is that acceptable, Dr. D'Onofrio?" Russ asked.

"Yes," Valaria said. "That will do."

I walked back to my car. I drove away. I guess you could say my academic career at Llewellyn had come to an end.

49

On the drive back from Llewellyn to Athena, I got two calls. The first one was from the Athena Police Station.

"That test tube you dropped off?" Keeler said.

That was the test tube I'd found in Christopher's room.

"Yes, anything?" I asked.

"There wasn't much left in there because whoever used it rinsed it out good, but not quite good enough. Male ejaculate."

"Excuse me?"

"Spunk. Jizz. Cum."

"I know what semen is, Keeler."

He chortled. "Just wanted to say some of that urban lingo you street-savvy private eyes are used to."

"Is it worth running through the database?"

"Already did. No matches."

Then it was Craig's turn to ring me on my cell. He asked if I liked linguine in clam sauce for dinner.

"I do," I said.

"Would you still like it if I were to make it for you at my place?"

Hold your horses, I almost said, but then I thought there was no faster way to get to know a person than to see his home.

"Sounds lovely," I said.

He told me his address.

"I know exactly where that is. On the corner of Geneva and Stewart, two blocks from the county library."

"Then you've known where I've lived for the last twenty years," he said.

I pulled up to a beige house with green shutters, a duplex with a slate gray roof. It was a well-maintained home, the lawn clear of fallen leaves, the water hose neatly looped by the bushes. I stepped out of my car and saw the front door open.

Craig was wearing an apron in the shape of Bugs Bunny's head, with the slogan, "What's Cookin', Doc?" He waved, and I waved back. He watched me walk up the stone path, and my stomach tightened. Was it just nerves or something else?

"Welcome," he said. He opened his arms and I embraced him as unreservedly as possible.

"You smell like home," I said. He did: pasta, tomato sauce, garlic. Even though my dad was Irish and my mom Norwegian, Italian cuisine was what I grew up with.

Something beeped between us, the black timer that hung from his neck like a charm.

"That's the garlic bread. Come with me," he said, and took my hand and led me to the kitchen.

It was a kind of a mess. There was no can or jar of tomato sauce, Craig making his own from scratch. Ditto with the noodles, as attested by the straggler squiggles from the mouth of the pasta machine mounted on the counter. The center island was where everything was happening, and the butcher block looked like a Jackson Pollock painting, streaked with the red tomato juice, smudged with fingerprints of white flour, black dribbles of balsamic vinaigrette around the edges.

"Holy shit," I said, overwhelmed. No man—no woman, not even my own mother—had ever gone to this kind of trouble to make dinner. "What I meant to say is: wow."

A second buzzer, magnetically attached to the fridge, buzzed a similar tune. Craig brought out a large white bowl and picked up a handheld blender.

"I hope you like gazpacho," he said. He plunged the silver spinners into the mash and proceeded to create a liquid tornado. "My little immersion blender. You can just stick it anywhere, and it blends."

"Okay," I said.

He switched it off, and the kitchen was plunged into silence. Without meeting my eyes, he said, "This is all too much, isn't it? Way overboard."

"No, no, it's fine," I said. "Maybe we're just both a little nervous, because even though…"

"I ate an entire box of cupcakes an hour ago," Craig said. "I haven't done that in…oh jeez, excuse me." He clutched at his stomach and ran, I presume, for the bathroom, except his foot caught the blender cord. Not tragic for a small appliance to go flying, except the blender was still in the bowl and the bowl got caught up with the blender and I wasn't fast enough to move out of the way of the cold soup as the reddish slop went airborne and splattered against my blouse and pants, as completely as if someone took a bucket and had aimed its contents right at me.

Craig, in his haste to reach the porcelain goddess, didn't see any of this, so there I was, all alone and dripping with gazpacho. I licked some off my sleeve and tasted tomato, cucumber, lime, and garlic. It was good.

I heard the toilet flush and watched Craig leave the bathroom. He was about to say something but stopped when he saw what had happened.

He grabbed a stack of dish towels from a drawer and held them out for me like an offering.

"It never amazes me how something I'd imagined in my mind can be so far away from reality," he said.

"Like you thought we'd be sitting at the table, enjoying your soup instead of me wearing it."

"Something like that."

While I was doing my best to soak up as much of the soup as possible, Craig just stood there, wallowing in self-disappointment.

"I've gotten to all my girl parts, but my pantlegs can use some dabbing?" I said.

It brightened him to help, and I felt good about that. He went through three towels before he was done.

"You might want to get out of your clothes," he said.

"How convenient."

"Oh yes, now you realize my grand plan, to humiliate myself and get you naked."

"The garlic *is* particularly strong," I said.

"I put a whole clove in there."

"I'll need a change of clothes."

"I can get you something," he said.

There were two full baths in the house, but only one of the showers was working, by the master bedroom. As soon as I entered it, I knew what was wrong with Craig, and from the look of mortification etched on his face, he knew it, too.

The bathroom that he had once shared with his wife, more than a decade ago, was painted in a warm peach outlined with powder blue molding. It had two sinks, and the one on the left was his, the bowl surrounded by aftershave, cologne, deodorant, and razor. That was fine. The issue was the one the right, which was littered with feminine accoutrements: a cluster of nail polish, a bottle of Midol, hair curler with its power cord dangling off the counter, a pair of teardrop-shaped silver earrings crisscrossed in a pile.

"Why don't you get undressed? I'll be right outside, and you can just toss your clothes to me and I'll throw them in the washer."

I did just that. But before I stepped into the shower, I took a finger and ran it underneath the hair curler. As suspected, there wasn't much dust at all, which meant that either Craig or his hired housekeeper still cleaned here but continued to leave this item, all of Martina's items, frozen in their final repose.

I didn't have to wash my hair as the soup had gotten me only from the neck down. There were two choices for liquid soap, a manly blue and a dainty pink; I went with the blue because the pink one looked also to be preserved. I lathered and washed and re-lathered and re-washed to get all the gazpacho smell off me.

I've often found the shower to be an excellent place of rumination, enabling thoughts to run freely like flowing water. Eleven years was a long time to be carrying a torch, even for a dead wife, but who was I to judge? People moved on at their own personal velocity. Maybe things had gone south tonight because Craig pushed himself to go too fast. I envisioned him stuffing himself with a box of cupcakes, his stomach turning sour from the onslaught of processed sugar, and it bummed me out in a major way.

There was a loud knock on the door.

"Just me," Craig said. "Is it okay if I crack this door and slip a bathrobe to you?"

"Sure," I said.

After I dried myself off, I picked up a white bathrobe still in its brand new package. A large black "M" was embroidered on the chest, so obviously a gift intended for Martina. Whatever weirdness I'd initially felt went away when I put it on, the sheer comfort of the material trumping my reservations. The terrycloth robe was substantial and soft, like a wearable blanket. It had a lovely thick collar that caressed my neck like a stole. A matching pair of slippers lay by the door, equally luxurious.

When I exited the bathroom, I found Craig in the kitchen, which was now looking a whole lot neater. Also, he was wearing the same bathrobe over his t-shirt and pants, except his had a "C" on the chest.

"I didn't want you to feel odd, wearing just a bathrobe while I'm in my regular clothes."

"Except now *you* feel odd."

"A little. Your clothes are drying now, so our collective oddness will end soon. These are both new, by the way, gifts from years ago.

It was meant for me and Martina, but she never got a chance to wear it."

I nodded.

He nodded.

Silence.

"Well," we both said at the same time, giving us a welcome entry into laughter.

"You first," I said.

Craig let out a sigh. "I don't even know why all of her stuff is still here. I used to know, but I don't anymore."

"Just easier to let things be."

"Maybe. Inertia is a powerful force."

"You must have loved her a great deal," I said.

"I did, sure. But she's now been gone for longer than we were married. Well, I don't think I'm going to solve all of my problems tonight, so how about we finally have our dinner?"

I asked if I could help, so Craig put me on table-setting duty while he got the food going again. What was to be a four-course meal became a three-course meal, a bowl for the salad, a plate for the linguine, and a small plate for a chocolate cheesecake, the only thing that was store-bought. The freshly-made pasta was fantastic, so different than the boxed kind, and the sauce, topped with finely-chopped bits of parsley and cilantro, enlivened the dish. It felt good to return to normality, do what was expected tonight. With each course, I could see Craig relaxing a bit more. He told me about his work in Syracuse, a labor contract dispute between the haves and the have-nots. By the time we'd arrived at the dessert portion, I'd caught him up with my own case.

"Scope creep," Craig said.

"How the scope of any work tends to slowly but surely get larger as time goes on."

Craig nodded.

"More creep, the better," I said. "Even in my rather brief experience at this profession, I've never seen it work any other way. It's like you start off at a clearing, and ahead is this forest you have to hack your way through. And as you hack, stuff piles up. The key is to keep moving forward."

"Fast enough that the piles don't come down on you."

Craig topped off my decaf coffee, then his. He made it stronger than Starbucks, my kind of joe.

"So, you're now off to Krishna for...?"

"The weekend for sure," I said. "Could be longer. All depends on how quickly I can find Penny."

"Why wouldn't she be there like this Beaker said?"

"It never hurts to have low expectations."

Craig raised one eyebrow, Mr. Spock-style.

"You don't subscribe to that idea?" I asked.

"I believe in positive thinking—imagine it just the way you want it, and it'll happen."

"Does it work?"

"Not always, tonight being an excellent case in the point, but, regardless, I've always been attracted to the brighter side."

As we did the dishes together; him doing the washing, me doing the drying, I thought about Craig during his wife's sickness, how he must've tried to imagine her getting stronger, recovering—and seeing the opposite. If he had opted for my low-expectation theory of living, would he have been better off?

After handing me the cutting board, the last item to dry, Craig turned to me. "I'd like to ask you something. Totally up to you. Please feel free to say no."

"All right."

"I have a fully furnished guest room. Would you consider spending the night there?"

Baby steps, I thought. But they were steps nonetheless, and the first one was always the hardest. I stared into Craig's blue eyes and saw his struggle, his strength. I wanted to help.

"I have to leave pretty early in the morning," I said. "I probably won't see you."

"That's fine," he said.

I leaned into him and grabbed his hand.

"Okay, then," I said. "It's a deal."

51

I usually sleep in on Saturdays, but not today. My phone's alarm annoyed me to wakefulness at five. I had to go back to my house and pick up my suitcase; I wasn't looking forward to the long drive ahead of me.

Craig's house was as dark as night at this ungodly hour. Outside of the kitchen, I hadn't seen much else, so I took the scenic route on my way out with my phone's flashlight on. Descending the staircase, I examined the photographs on the walls. It became clear to me just why Craig had trouble letting Martina go—he'd known her for just about his entire life. Even when they were toddlers, they looked like tinier versions of themselves, their faces unmistakably theirs. Martina looked quite bookish when she was a kid, with very large glasses that threatened to overtake her small round face, but as she grew into a woman, she definitely exuded that sexy librarian vibe. They went to the prom together, which was when Craig started to get a bit plumper. They both attended Lenrock University, because the second set of graduation photos was of them in cap and gown, in front of the Jebediah Lenrock statue on the main quad. Wedding pictures of the happy couple, honeymoon pictures in front of the Eiffel Tower, and the two final photos were of Martina by herself, one where she's looking radiant with a slightly protruding belly, and the last where she's definitely lost weight and maybe the baby, too. It's the only shot where she's not looking at the camera, half her gaunt face in shadow, her eyes downcast.

Twenty years together is considered to be a lot nowadays. Craig was around my age, which meant Martina died a year or so shy of hitting thirty. That meant they'd known each other for more than a quarter of a century. This woman wasn't just the love of his life; she *was* his life.

On the first floor, in addition to the kitchen, there was a living room, a TV room, and a formal dining room. Above the mantel in the living room fireplace, there were picture frames of what looked to be Craig's parents and also of another family whose young mother could've been Craig with a wig on—probably his sister. A pair of pictures of children, one with Craig's sister, another with Craig's brother-in-law. There was space here at the end of the mantel, and seeing that gap made me sadder than anything else in this house.

In my life, I've been seriously involved with two guys, almost getting married to the second one until we realized, thankfully, that we actually sort of hated each other. That was the extent of my romantic career, which upon reflection would ordinarily get me down for its brief duration and lack of intensity, but here was the flipside, the dark side: having it all and having none.

Standing at the kitchen counter, I hovered over a memo pad, struggling to come up with the appropriate set of words. What were we at this point, exactly? Before last night, it seemed like we could be something, but now I wasn't so sure.

Craig, thank you. I'll see you after I get back from Krishna.

That could've been a note for a UPS driver. I ripped off the sheet and put it in my pocket.

Craig – the road to happiness can be rocky

Who did I think I was, a Hallmark card? Rip, pocket.

After standing there for another ten painful minutes, I figured it out.

I drew a heart on the middle of the page. Signed my name underneath it. And jotted inside: *See you soon.*

When in doubt, be vague.

52

Speaking of hearts, the road that led to Krishna was not for those with a faint one. There were no guardrails as the graveled path spiraled its way up the peak, and things got really hairy when another car came barreling down the mountain, as the road was barely wide enough for two vehicles.

According to Google Maps, the drive from Athena to Hawthorne was three hours. The first two were New York Thruway, but the last leg of the trip was pure uphill, cresting up almost four thousand feet.

What a view. It was past peak foliage, but not by much. When I saw the sign for a scenic overlook, I parked in the little lot and got out. I've always loved the Adirondacks for their gentleness, that even at these soaring heights, its mountains were calm, curvaceous mounds. A river snaked between the base of four mountain ranges, and from up here, the curls of that bright blue water were two perfect continuous S's under a cloudless, endless sky.

Another half hour of gravelly low-gear ascent later, I laid my eyes on Krishna. Half of the gray block of a building, the left side that was embedded in the mountain itself, was in shadow even under the full gaze of the late morning sun because of the overhanging trees above it. Solitude, fortitude, aloofness, majesty: that's what I felt gazing at it, a diametrical combination of severity and grandeur.

The open gate at the bottom of the hill was a giant circle of black wrought-iron steel, and around the campus were emerald green arborvitaes planted in such a way to make a fifteen-foot-high natural fence. At the top of the gate were seven skewered letters, gunmetal gray: NAMASTE. Seeing those giant capitals didn't exactly fill me with peace. It was more like a command.

The driveway up to the main building was well-marked, so I followed the one for guests and parked around the back, which was where registration took place. As soon as I opened my car door, a man and a woman, about college age, greeted me. They put their hands together as if in prayer, in front of their chests, then closed their eyes and lowered their heads.

"Namaste," they said in unison.

When in Rome, so I mimicked their gesture and slogan.

"Welcome to Krishna. May we help you with your bags?"

I showed them the duffel I'd brought.

"Light packer," I said.

"To have nothing is to have everything," the girl said. Yellow flowers were woven through her golden hair. She was in an all-white tunic and so was the guy, both in matching white sandals. The girl was wearing a name tag: Chandini; the guy: Udai. Considering they were both as white as Wonder Bread, neither looked like their names, but then again, maybe I shouldn't be the one to talk.

They pointed me to the entrance, which they didn't have to because of the excellent signage, but I thanked them anyway and let them bestow their low-key charms onto the next visitor.

At the Guest Registration counter, Aadrika signed me in.

"That's a beautiful name," I said.

"Celestial," she said. "That's what it means in Sanskrit."

"Everyone seems to have interesting monikers around here."

"It's because we get to choose our own. We're told who we are from the moment we are born, so why not empower ourselves and choose? If you had a choice, wouldn't you pick something unique and interesting?"

I handed her my driver's license and credit card.

"I see you have a pretty cool one already."

"Especially when I get all fancy and slash that awesome accent over the 'a,'" I said.

"Oh yeah, that's the stuff," Aadrika said, laughing.

She placed me on the third floor of the main building, which was called Meadowlark. "We refer to it as the Meadow," Aadrika said. "The new addition is called Javani, which is 'child' in Sanskrit." She handed me two key cards like the ones at hotels.

"The meadow and her child," I said. "Even the buildings have interesting names around here."

"Interesting is an excellent descriptor for what we do around here."

"Speaking of interesting, a friend of mine is staying here. Penny Sykes?"

I pulled out my phone and showed her the photo. I was hoping my question in the middle of our pleasant conversation would catch her off guard, and it did. Something crossed Aadrika's face, but she reset herself quite nicely.

"I'm afraid it's not ringing a bell. I only man the desk for a few hours a day, so…will there be anything else, Siobhan?"

"Yes, just one more thing, if that's okay with you?" I said. Aadrika wanted nothing more than to be done with me, which was why I was pushing. Sometimes you push, and the other person pushes back, and something valuable might come of it. Or not. All you can ever do is try.

"Yes?"

"Christopher Vachess."

"The bell remains unrung."

I showed her a photo Beaker had texted me, Christopher in a suit and tie.

"That's Prasad? Wow," Aadrika said.

"Prasad?"

"That's how I know him."

"His Sanskrit name," I said.

"Helps out in the kitchen. I'll let him know you want to speak to him."

"Sure, that'll be fine," I said. Actually, it wasn't fine—I wanted the element of surprise on my side. But I didn't want to tell that to Aadrika, which meant I'd have to find my way into the kitchen sooner than later. Like right after I was done here. I thanked Aadrika, raced up two staircases, found my room near the end of one of the many branching, identical beige-bricked hallways, dumped my duffel onto the bed, and got out my map of Krishna to see where the kitchen was. It wasn't marked, but I figured going to the dining hall on the second floor and seeing the food traffic would reveal its location pretty quickly. No rest for the weary—I ran right back out.

53

Lunch was being served, and damn, did it ever smell good. I watched a man in a brown apron and a hairnet replace two large trays of yellow noodles in the buffet line. When the empties were on his cart, he rolled it to the far end of the hall and turned a right then disappeared through a set of swinging double doors that read: STAFF ONLY. Two round windows on the door revealed him waiting for the service elevator. The arrow pointed down.

I watched him and once he disappeared, I pushed through the double doors and watched the floor number indicator blink from 2 to 1 to LL. Next to the elevator was the entrance to the staircase, so I descended two flights and prepared to act like a lost tourist in case anyone questioned me.

LL, which stood for Lower Level according to the very large sign on the wall next to the door, was teeming with activity. I was greeted with more signage: laundry to the left, kitchen to the right. I could've just followed my nose, as the spicy aroma of turmeric led me to the hustle and bustle of the brightly-lit industrial kitchen. There were perhaps twenty people in here, all of them similarly dressed in white hairnets and brown aprons. With the equipment running, I couldn't make out anything that anyone was saying. I did my best to stay as inconspicuous as possible, but it wasn't long until a tall woman spotted me. She flipped off her oversized Cuisinart and approached me.

"Can I help you?"

"I'm looking for Prasad," I said.

"You know you're not supposed to be here, right?" She pointed to her kitchen ID bearing her name, DEVAPRABHA.

"I wouldn't be here unless it was important. All I need is five minutes of his time, possibly not even that."

"You're not going to upset him, are you?"

Strange question, but then again, strange place. "Don't intend to."

"Because Prasad is having a hard time right now."

"Just one question, that's it."

She walked over to a half-open door that was labeled PANTRY, entered it, and closed it behind her. I watched the continuing procession of these dining workers. It was almost like a dance, a few twirling around each other to rush from one task to another. A girl sat on a stool next to a white plastic container as tall as a garbage can, chopping up broccoli with speed and dexterity that comes with practice. Two well-muscled guys were making pizza crusts, one kneading the dough, the other tossing and spinning it like a professional.

The pantry door opened, and there he was, Christopher, walking over with Devaprabha. He looked thinner than the photo I had on my phone and older, too, probably due to the goatee. When he saw me, concern crossed his face.

"Five minutes," Devaprabha said. "We're about to run out of sage, so you need to re-stock those first."

"All right," Christopher/Prasad said.

"Can we step out into the hallway? It's tough to talk here with all the noise," I said.

"I have no idea who you are," he said.

"Beaker told me where you were," I said, and Christopher relaxed at the mention of his friend's name. "Siobhan O'Brien, private detective." And just like that, he froze up pretty hard.

"What do you want?"

"I was hired by Josie Sykes, Penny's mother."

I hoped Christopher never played poker, because he didn't have the face for it.

"Penny's not here," he said.

"Beaker said you followed her here."

"That's not true."

Except he couldn't look at me.

"Then why would Beaker tell me that?"

"I don't know!" he said, on the verge of tears. And then he was crying, like really hard, like *baby* hard. Was I supposed to go to him, placate him somehow? It wasn't fake, that much I knew. The poor kid was shuddering now, and wailing loud enough for Devaprabha to hear, because here she was, pushing me out of the way and taking Christopher into a hug.

"You told me you wouldn't upset him," she said.

I actually hadn't said that, but arguing wasn't going to get me any gold stars, so I kept quiet and let them pass. I was going to need a higher level of access to this place, and the best way to accomplish that was by way of media credentials. I took the elevator back up to the third floor and my room. On the morning of the day the *Athena Times* had laid everyone off to be subsumed into the *Binghamton Bulletin*, all the reporters received brand-new press passes; if there was a more perfect display of corporate stupidity, I couldn't think of one. We were supposed to have turned in the badges as we vacated the building, but I never did. It had already come in handy a few times for me. I hoped this would be another.

I brought up the Krishna website on my phone and found the number for Media Relations. I was about to dial it, but stopped myself when I saw the inscription above my door:

take a breath. take another. there you are.

I did take a breath, and then another. I'd been in such a hurry to find Christopher that I hadn't even seen my room. Not that there was that much to see, because it was almost as bare bones as Josie's jail cell. A stripped twin mattress on a well-worn metal frame sat in the corner, taking up half of the room's space. A small wooden desk and a chair were on the other side. On the desk were my linens, so I made my bed. The room was free of décor, but that was fine because I had a window that displayed the full natural splendor of the environs, from the green of the forest to the silver of the lake. I sat on the bed and stared out for a good five minutes.

Now that I was spiritually rejuvenated, I rang up Media Relations. After three rings, voicemail kicked in; a very cheery Cynthia's recorded voice answered. A normal non-Sanskrit name. Strange—I'd think if anybody had a unique name, it would be the spokesperson. I left Cynthia a message that I was the culture reporter for the *Bulletin* and asked her if she might meet me after I grabbed some lunch.

53

With the afternoon sun shining through oblong windows that ran along the entire wall, the high ceiling of the dining hall seemed even higher. Still, there was nothing ostentatious here. Like the rest of the building, this, too, was spartan, with just two paintings adorning its beige walls, a side profile of a Buddha in meditation and a large lithograph of Meadowlark, which was the main building on Krishna's sprawling campus below the Adirondack Mountains.

There were two buffet lines, one for regular and one for vegetarian. I went to both, picking up the real turkey sausage *and* its ersatz soy counterpart, a wedge of tofu quiche, plus a mango scone made from chickpea flour. I drew a hot cup of water and lingered in front of the wooden chest of teas featuring seven by six drawers, a total of forty-two to choose from. I didn't know there were that many teas in existence. Himalayan Hibiscus sounded daring and sophisticated, so I dunked a packet into my steaming water and let it steep.

Holding my lunch and beverage on a tin tray, I surveyed the dining hall. Just a few days ago, I was sitting with those kooky old ladies in Llewellyn's cafeteria, and now here I was, déjà vu-ing all over again. I flashed back to high school, where I sat with the basketball team, one of the many cliques that divided us and gave us an identity, which we held onto for dear life. Confusing times, high school. Christopher was only a few years removed from those days.

And speak of the devil, there he was, sitting at a corner table for two with a girl with blue hair. Which begged the question: Did anybody have normal-colored hair anymore?

I didn't want Christopher to see me, since he might suffer another terrifying crying jag, so I sat two tables to his backside. Christopher was leaning into her, and the girl was feeding him soup with a spoon while cradling his head—the result of my polite barrage of a single question. Christopher was so addled that he needed to be held and hand-fed. I guess this was what Beaker must've meant when he called Christopher 'super sensitive.' I might have chosen less flattering words to describe this particular facet of his personality, but whatever. I didn't want to approach him again right now, so what could I do to find out Penny's whereabouts?

Not knowing what else to do, I took a bite of both sausages. Surprisingly, I liked the soy one better than the turkey. I ate the quiche in three enormous, delicious bites. Christopher sat up. Was he feeling better? No, because now Blue Hair handed him a handkerchief, and after he blew his nose, he put his face into his hands and Blue Hair rubbed his back like she was polishing a window.

I felt a tap on my shoulder.

A short blonde woman didn't say hello but waved furiously, enthusiastically. When she saw my confusion, she pointed to the nametag on her lapel.

CYNTHIA BARD
Media Relations

I was just about to say something, but Cynthia crossed a finger over her lips. Then she pointed to a sign: SILENT DINING SECTION. Good thing I hadn't been talking to myself. I wiped my mouth with my napkin, but she held up both hands and waved them once again, this time adding a shake of the head. She mimed an eating motion. I shook my head, then added a tap to my tummy, to show her I'd eaten enough. Cynthia tipped her head then made a gesture with her hands, some sort of air drumming that I couldn't decipher. This was turning out to be a frustrating game of charades.

"I've had my fill," I whispered.

Cynthia made an "okay" gesture with her fingers then motioned for me to follow. I didn't want to lose sight of Christopher and Blue Hair, but I didn't know what my next move should be, either.

Times like this, it helped to conjure up some wise words from Ed.

An investigation is a living, breathing thing. Go with what happens, because what happens then is what was always supposed to happen.

I'm fairly certain Ed was drunk when he gave me that little tidbit of advice, because he wasn't that much of a talker. Except when he was drunk. Then I couldn't get him to shut up.

I rose and followed Cynthia, missing Ed.

54

Cynthia was in love, of that there was no doubt. At one point in our walk on the fourth floor of the Meadowlark building, she placed her hands on the wall.

"You can feel the soul of this place," she said. I managed not to lose my tofu sausage.

We were in the Meditation Room, which overlooked the rounded peaks of the distant Catskills. The day was mostly overcast, but a few shards of sunlight poked through the clouds and beamed temperamental spotlights onto the forest below. This wasn't a huge room, enough for perhaps twenty people to meditate. A built-in wooden bench wrapped around the back, and there were round red cushions for people to sit on.

"I imagine the very molecules of these cinderblocks are in a higher state of serenity," I said.

"My goodness!" she said. "You should put that into the article you're writing."

"I really appreciate you taking time from your day to introduce me to Krishna. My managing editor at the *Bulletin* thanks you, too."

"I spoke to Margaret right before I came to get you," Cynthia said. "She asked me to be your guide, which I'm more than happy to do."

Margaret was actually Stacy, my part-time bookkeeper, who'd sounded more than thrilled to play the part of my boss when I'd asked her to do so.

"The angle I'd like to approach with this story is the volunteer program," I said. "The backbone of Krishna, could you say?"

Cynthia looked like she was about to cry, and I felt a tiny bead of guilt for lying to her.

"The unsung heroes. That's so wonderful that you want to highlight these giving, selfless people."

"Can you tell me a bit more about the program?"

"Volunteers make a minimum six-month commitment to live and work here. We always need help in the kitchen, washing dishes, prepping veggies, that type of thing," Cynthia said. "But there are many other areas, too, like taking care of the lawn and housekeeping, and those who can't perform the more physical duties due to age or disability can work in the administrative offices."

And while they performed these physical tasks, the volunteers lived together in a large dormitory with bunk beds. The women lived in the east wing while the men lived in the west.

"I'd like to interview a couple of the volunteers, too, if that's okay."

"Of course."

"So…through labor and dedication to self-awareness, people find their true selves here at Krishna."

"Karma. Work goes in, enlightenment comes out. A virtuous circle. I'm so glad you'll get the word out."

A bald man with a white beard that flowed down to his belly walked into the room. He put his palms together and bid us a "Namaste," so we did the same and exited so he could meditate.

We took the stairs down. Inspirational quotes greeted us at each turn. Above the second floor landing, Plato told us, "Be kind, for everyone you meet is fighting a hard battle." Cynthia was telling me this was her ninth year at Krishna, that she, too, was once a volunteer who'd found such solace that she never wanted to leave, when we heard what sounded like an argument coming from one of the offices we were passing. Finally, something real going on around here. The office door was open enough that I could see a silver-haired man in a white jumpsuit pacing in front of a desk.

"It can't be done. I just spent the last two hours in the Orchard Room to reconfigure the space. Not only does it feel wrong, it *is* wrong, Michelle. You know this as well as I do."

"You can come here a thousand more times, but it's not going to make a difference."

The woman's voice was as firm and final as a schoolteacher's. To the left of the door was a nameplate:

MICHELLE WEST
Programming Director

"Let's keep moving," Cynthia said, and ushered me down the hall.

"Can't keep everybody happy all the time," I said.

"Michelle's job is perhaps the most difficult one we have here, but if anybody's up to the challenge, it's her."

Cynthia, as expected, was toeing the company line. The most I got out of her about Michelle was that this was her second year with Krishna and that she was also a computer whiz. "She's so good with all the cool stuff like Instagram and Snapchat. Revamped iPhone and Android apps are coming out later this year!"

Coming towards us was a group of twenty or so people, all looking straight ahead and saying nothing. Clipped on each of their lapels was an oval sign:

in loving silence

Folks like these didn't exactly seem like the kind who'd tweet or take selfies, but technology was infiltrating every bit of our lives, so if anything, Michelle was probably ahead of the curve.

We walked past the dining hall, now in cleanup mode. The tea station was still open, but the pans of food and the lines of people were long gone.

On the wall past the dining hall was a matrix of posters that displayed the various programs going on this week, and I now saw another familiar face.

THE BREATH OF MINDFULNESS
All That Matters Is Now
Dharma Benjamin Roth

The photograph smack in the middle of the poster was the same man I'd just seen in Michelle's office, except here, he was the epitome of calm. Standing waist-deep in a forever field of sunflowers, Dharma, again clad in his white jumpsuit, held his arms straight above his head, like a football ref signaling a successful field goal. His smiling face was slightly upturned to the blue sky above. It was quite a picture. I wondered how many takes it took to get it right.

"Dharma looks like he's been coming here for a while," I said.

"He was here when the building was inaugurated," she said. "One of the Seven Roots, as the old guard refer to themselves."

We arrived at the end of the hall, a set of closed double doors in front of us. STAFF, it said in stark black letters, carved into the wood.

"There are about a hundred volunteers here at any given moment at Krishna. More women than men...about seventy-five, twenty-five, which is also the split for our visitors."

She held the door open for me, and I almost ran into Blue Hair, the girl who had been accompanying Christopher in the dining hall.

"Dido!" Cynthia said. "Just the gal I was hoping to see. Are you busy right now?"

"I got half an hour before I need to get back to the bakery," Dido said. She looked like she recognized me, which seemed odd because she never saw me in the dining hall, unless she had eyes on the back of her head. Which, around here, was perhaps more of a possibility than any other place.

"Ms. O'Brien is a newspaper reporter writing a story about the volunteer program," Cynthia said. "Can you show her around and talk to her for a bit? About the program, what you've done, what we do, etc. I have a meeting in five."

"Of course."

Cynthia gave me her cell number and was off.

I extended my hand. "I'm Siobhan." Flecks of flour floated around her hair like fairy dust as we shook.

"I see pink," Dido said.

"Pink?"

"Around you. Your aura."

"And pink signifies…?" I asked.

"Deception."

Dido, a bandana wrapped around her spiky blue hair, stared at me evenly. She'd made up her mind, so I didn't want to waste her time or mine.

"Penny Sykes," I said.

"Good," she said. "Kick off your shoes and follow me."

I kicked off my shoes and followed her.

55

The women's dorm was about the size of a small gymnasium. There were ten columns of bunk beds five rows deep. At first glance, it felt almost military, the stark white sheets against the black metal railings, but upon closer inspection, every occupied bed was sneakily personalized. One woman had bright red and blue beads wrapped around her headboard. A lower bunk had origami mobiles hanging off the bottom of the top bunk, yellow and pink cranes spinning lazily as we made our way over to Dido's, who had a corner bed. She had affixed a procession of tiny wooden elephants on the bottom railing, trunks raised triumphantly to the sky.

"Minimal decorations allowed?" I said.

"You could say. We're encouraged to cleanse ourselves of unnecessary material."

"I like your elephants."

"Thank you. My quiet space is on the second floor," she said. "There's nobody above me right now, so that's where I go for my morning meditation."

She scampered up the ladder. I thought of my time at the Korean camp back in Minnesota, the creak of the metal as it gave and took our daily abuse. I'd always preferred being on top because where I slept, there were skylights that showcased the moon and the stars on clear nights. This high ceiling had no such openings, but it was painted in a soothing sky blue and cloudy white that made it feel even higher.

Dido took the head of the bed so I took the foot. From this height, the top of the lake was visible from the window, the late morning sun bedazzling an oval sheen of water. She straightened her legs, drew her right foot into her left thigh, then grasped her right knee with her left hand and turned the top of her body completely away from me. Downstairs on one of the posters, I'd seen this yoga pose. I'd throw out my back if I'd tried it.

"So you knew Penny," I said.

"I have no idea who that is," Dido said.

I know this place was supposed to instill patience and virtue and acceptance and love, but what I really wanted to do right now was to shove Dido off the top bunk.

"Then why did you bring me up here?"

When she smiled, her whole face softened, almost became someone else's. I saw how pretty she was, despite the blue hair and the lip ring and the tattoo of a spiderweb on the side of her neck.

Dido reversed the pose, left foot to her right thigh.

"Because you needed to be here."

"Said my pink aura."

"Exactly."

"I thought the pink aura meant I was a liar."

"Should an aura's hue be limited to a single meaning?"

"I hope that's a rhetorical question."

Dido returned to sitting position and put her hands together, her fingers splayed. She placed her thumbs over her heart, breathed in, then exhaled with a quiet *om.*

"Complication is the blood of life," she said. "It lets us know we're alive."

I slid over to the edge of the bed to climb back down before I hurt this silly girl, but then I had a thought. Dido was most likely not her name. Maybe Penny wouldn't be using hers, either. I took out my phone.

"That unnatural device is not allowed in this sacred space," Dido said.

"Both the unnatural device and my unnatural self will be leaving this sacred space soon enough. Just look, okay?"

After giving me a lingering look of disapproval, she looked. "Hae Jun."

"That's her Korean name. You *do* know Penny."

"By way of Prasad."

Prasad was Christopher. Hae Jun was Penny. Whoever thought up this thing here where people chose their own names never took into consideration that this would make a detective's work rather trying.

"And where may I find Hae Jun?"

"She tried to kill herself," Dido said. "Last week."

Shit.

"How?"

"I don't know the details, and I don't care to know."

"Is she still here?" I asked.

"The next day, she was gone."

"And…has anyone been informed? Or does nobody care?"

"People who come here to be volunteers…they come for many reasons, but one of the more common ones is that they're running away from something."

Dido told me she had been at veggie prep and was transitioning to the bakery, so she was tasked to train Penny to work in the basement kitchen, chopping, coring, and dicing enough vegetables to feed six hundred people three meals a day. It was not an easy job, but not a difficult one, either. There is a meditative quality to doing the same thing over and over again, a rhythm you find as you dump one container after another of potatoes into the industrial combo food processor to make a hundred gallons of sweet potato fries.

"We play music real loud, we dance, we sing. It's like a working party, and there's also a great sense of accomplishment because things come in and go out and disappear. Bins of prepared vegetables are filled with our work and our love, and off they go upstairs to the hot kitchen, for all to feast on. When the day ends, we power wash and squeegee our floors, literally wipe the slate clean."

"Penny danced and *sang*?"

"Just because she tried to kill herself doesn't mean she's moping around all day. Depressed people probably laugh more than regular people."

"Why was she depressed?"

"None of my business. Everyone has a right to suffer in their own way, and I respect that. I did notice, though, that the day Prasad arrived was the day she disappeared."

Dido scrunched her shoulders tight, then scrunched them even tighter. With an explosive exhalation that sounded like "*Huh*" she slacked her body to a slouch, her head lolling like a doll's. And then slowly, inch by inch, she woke herself back to an alert, straight-backed sitting position.

"I'm due for my shift, and I can see the red rising off of you like steam. This is as good a time as any for us to retreat inside ourselves and do our own work. Let's talk again when our spirits are better aligned."

She hung her legs over the side of the bed and jumped, landing on the hardwood floor without a sound. A few other volunteers were now milling about the room, making a cup of tea by the kitchenette, one older lady doing tai chi.

"You can stay for as long as you like."

"No, thanks," I said, and took the longer but safer route down the ladder.

56

Dido made her way towards the doors and I followed.

"Do you know the concept of mindfulness?" she asked.

"No, but I saw a poster with that word on the way over here."

"See," Dido said, and slipped her shoes back on. I did the same. "This is karma. This is the magic of Krishna. It's no coincidence that of all the posters on the board, you saw and remembered Dharma's. Go and talk to him. He might even let you sit in his program, because he's one of the old-school guys."

"I'll see. I'm here until tomorrow and I still need to talk to Prasad and…"

Dido smiled. "Karma once again, Siobhan. Prasad's gone."

"I just saw him in the dining hall. With you."

"Yes. And right after his meal, he left."

I was beginning to get the feeling that Penny and Christopher were not just difficult to find but actively trying to avoid me.

"Can you tell me where he went?"

"You want to follow him?"

"At most he's got an hour's head start."

"Even if I knew where he was headed, I'm not sure I would tell you."

I'm no fan of violence, but Dido was getting me very close to that edge.

"Is it still because of my pink aura? Or fuchsia? Or whatever the fuck it is?"

She laughed. "No. It's because you're fighting it."

"Fighting what?"

"The flow."

I sighed, for what felt like the hundredth time since I started talking to this girl.

"Go with the flow. Uh-huh," I said.

I considered my options. If I could get the license plate number of Christopher's car (which Krishna must have somewhere in their system), then I could contact Keeler, who then could look up the toll tag in the car. Most had these nowadays, and they doubled as a homing beacon, because there were a couple of tolls along I-81 north-south, a bunch of them on I-90 running east-west…

Dido cupped my face in her hands, breaking me out of my thoughts.

"What is happening now is what should be happening, because it is exactly what *is* happening."

"Dido," I said, "please get your hands off me."

"There are no accidents. Prasad leaving was what was meant to happen. Do you know why? *Because that's what happened.* Siobhan, let it go. Let it happen. Because that's how things work around here. It's actually how they work everywhere, but here especially, it becomes self-evident."

An investigation is a living, breathing thing. Go with what happens, because what happens then is what was always supposed to happen.

Ed, if you're speaking to me beyond the grave through this girl, please stop.

"I'll consider it."

Dido held open the door back to the main building for me.

"Namaste."

I put my hands together and wished her the same. She took the stairs up while I took them down.

Was it time for a little breaking and entering? That would probably be the fastest way to get what I needed, though there were no guarantees. Dido's words kept repeating in my ear. *There are no ac-*

cidents. Prasad leaving was what was meant to happen. The problem with this fatalistic line of thinking was that you could end up doing nothing of consequence, ever. If everything happened for a reason, then there was never any reason to do anything, since whether you did something or not, it was all meant to be.

I had to try, didn't I? If I didn't try, how would this case move forward?

But what if not trying was trying in itself? Let the universe do the heavy lifting?

Jesus Christ, my brain was tying itself into a pretzel. Christopher was just here, and if I'd kept a closer eye on him, if I hadn't let that woman in the kitchen dissuade me...

Reality: The likelihood of me catching up to Christopher within a reasonable timeframe was basically zero.

Where would a kid like him go? Probably back home, which, as I recalled from my background check, was Ronkonkoma, New York. Or back to Lenrock. I could find him if I tried a little harder. But if I did find him, what good would it do if he screamed and yelled and went boo-hoo nutzos on me again?

Maybe the best thing would be to give him some distance, a little time.

Or was pressure what he needed to fess up to whatever it was that he needed fessing up?

I didn't know what to do. I had to do something, or else I was gonna drive myself insane.

57

I didn't start running until I was thirty. It wasn't a milestone-birthday thing. It was a fat thing, or perhaps more accurately, a fear of fat thing. Right around this time was when my pants and skirts started to groan under the pressure of having to contain my burgeoning waistline.

As luck would have it, that autumn, a group of co-workers at the *Athena Times* decided to form a running group. We even had a name: The Paper Route. Leave it to a bunch of writers to come up with something like that. It was three women and four guys, none of us remotely athletic, and it took us twelve huffing minutes to run one mile. A week later we were down to six runners, but we managed to shave off a full minute. This attrition of people and time occurred steadily until two months later, when tiny snowflakes caught in my eyelashes, I was a group of one who ran an eight-minute mile.

For the last twelve years, I've run the same loop twice a week: Wednesday evenings and Saturday mornings, along the red-bricked church and past the dog park and through the apartment parking lot, the path so ingrained that I imagine the calluses on my feet have molded to the medley of cracks and potholes on the asphalt. No matter how hot or cold or rainy or snowy, I'm out there, my body cutting through the wind, a smile plastered to my face.

Running helps me think, and right now, I had some thinking to do. The pocket map in my Krishna welcome packet laid out a route that took me to the center of Hawthorne, along the shoulder of East Street, a three-mile round trip. In my running uniform of a black pullover and black tights, I jogged lightly down the long driveway and headed for the town.

The temperature couldn't have been more perfect, in the mid-fifties, where my run starts off chilly but never gets hot. It was Saturday afternoon and the cars were few and far in between. On both sides of the road, tall, thick evergreens held me in their natural grace. For a while, all I knew was now, my feet stomping on the pavement, the scent of pine needles, the breeze running through my hair. I was hitting that magical equilibrium where it felt like every step on the ground generated the same amount of energy on the rise.

At the one mile mark, my GPS watch beeped, and I ran by the sign:

HAWTHORNE
Settled 1750
Incorporated 1767

In the center of the white metallic sign with black letters was the image of a red square building with a steeple, which was exactly what I was running towards. It was the town hall, fancy and impressive, fitting for the well-to-do Hawthorne. I ran past an antique store located in a classic Victorian, its beige clapboard shingles painted so exactly that they looked like vinyl siding. A hair salon aptly named "The Cutting Edge" was also located in a historic-looking building, but seen through the windows, the inside was almost futuristic, all chrome and white ceramic—yet not in a clashing or displeasing way. There was an inn/spa for pets, a musical instruments store, a yoga studio—every restaurant was a non-chain, not a single Starbucks or McDonald's to be seen.

Three athletic men wearing white turtlenecks and black slacks, all with crewcuts, exited a café; one of them held the door open. Sashaying through was none other than Cleo Park, just a flash of her as she made a beeline for another open door, a black Cadillac Escalade. Wearing enormous sunglasses and a skin-tight slate-gray yoga outfit, she looked like a Hollywood actress escaping the paparazzi. So, in addition to Professor Collins and President Wheeler of Llewellyn being here, Cleo Park herself was in attendance. And there was one more. I'd only seen her once, at the basketball game, but that was most definitely Grace. I might have lost Christopher, but this was an excellent development.

At the intersection of three roads was a traffic circle, and in its center was a bronze statue of a guy on a marble pedestal, the namesake of this tony town, Henry Hawthorne, according to the plaque. REVOLUTIONARY, SCHOLAR, FATHER, it read. The circle was a natural place to turn around, so I started on my return to Krishna, with my mind in a relaxed state, ready to process the bits of information I've gathered so far.

Mid-July, Josie drops Penny off at Llewellyn for their six-week incoming freshman program. Penny is painfully shy, but she meets Christopher and they begin a relationship. By the beginning of the semester, late August, she's fully adjusted.

Penny is assigned a roommate, but she doesn't live with her. Instead, she lives with Grace Park, the daughter of a Korean billionaire, who also has a connection to Christopher, according to Beaker.

Penny writes a controversial horror story in a fiction writing workshop and has a physical altercation with another student over what she wrote. After this incident, Penny moves out of Grace Park's dorm and enters Tender Llewellyn Care, a safe house for students run by Faith, who is the daughter of the president of Llewellyn, Vera Wheeler.

By the end of September, Penny asks Josie, her mother, not to call anymore. Josie goes to see her and is turned away by Faith.

Two weeks ago, Josie receives a call from the dean, who informs her that Penny took a leave of absence. Christopher's roommate Beaker says she's at Krishna, but she isn't anymore after she tried to commit suicide. And Christopher was here because he wanted…what?

That was the million dollar question, wasn't it? And I'd let him get away.

Was what was happening in Llewellyn, especially at Travers Hall with the wigs and the fake eyelashes, related to any of this? Or was it just a distraction? Wheeler was definitely turning the college into something it was not, and even though the fight between her and Faith was perhaps a mother-daughter fight as much as an ideological one, there was definitely a rottenness there. Town cops acting as security, special personal security for Grace Park….

Christopher, Penny, and Grace. A triangle. Thinking over my bullet points, that was the glaring hole, between two and three. Finding out what happened between these three kids had to lead to Penny's whereabouts. Grace would no doubt be surrounded by her guards, but I had to find a way to talk to her.

I was so deep in thought that I hadn't noticed.

Someone had joined me on my run.

58

"I hear you're writing a story about our beloved Krishna."

The man who jogged next to me was none other than Dharma Benjamin Roth. Clad in a white bandanna, a white training suit, and white sneakers, his craggy face led me to think he was probably in his sixties, possibly even his seventies, but the way he moved suggested someone far younger. His stride was light and relaxed, the mark of a veteran runner.

"You heard correctly," I said.

"And I believe you are a seeker of truth and justice," he said.

I guess I should've expected it. This was just the way people talked around here, and the more I accepted it instead of resisting it, the easier it would go down.

"If you say so."

"Do you not believe in the freedom of the press?"

"Of course I do."

"You can call me Dharma," he said.

"I know your name. I've seen your poster."

"It's a nice poster, isn't it? One of my better ones."

Now that we ran up the final hill on this path, the peak of Krishna's Meadowlark building rose beyond us.

"Do you desire to hear the real story of Krishna, about what truly matters?" Dharma asked.

"Absolutely. I'm getting a bit out of breath here, so how about if we meet up at the downstairs café at, say, 4 p.m.?"

"That café," Dharma said, "is an utter abomination."

"Well, okay, we certainly don't have to meet there."

"I know you are fatigued, but if you will allow me, I'll lead you on a different path, a road not as often taken. Which is always the road more fulfilling. It'll bring us to the western side of Lake Ondaga, a quarter of a mile from the Meadowlark."

"I didn't know there was another lake besides Lake Hawthorne here."

"It's the same lake, just the original name. The name of the American Indian tribe massacred to make room for a yoga retreat that now features wifi and women wearing $300 Lululemon outfits."

"Lead the way, Dharma," I said. For about five seconds, he accelerated like a V8, flashing his true foot speed, then he shifted down to my level again.

"To the path of enlightenment," he said.

What started off as a normal trail soon became an unruly route with grass as high as the knees in spots, and after another minute of delving deeper into the woods, I wondered if following a stranger to the middle of the forest was a smart move. I did have my phone with me, so I couldn't get that lost with a GPS in hand, but still, it was a bit unsettling. Dharma seemed like a decent human being, but all I knew of him was that poster on the wall.

My fears were somewhat allayed when a trail re-emerged, a faint one. There were even markers every so often, roughly whittled wooden arrows on posts pointing the way, but we also had to jump over a fallen tree and run around another one. It was a path that was no longer maintained, which was a shame because it was gorgeous. Mostly the forest over here consisted of sugar maples, so the leaves were either a mustard yellow or a pale green. Peeking through the more sparse section of the forest was the lake, its still surface mirroring the sky and the clouds.

"We're almost there," Dharma said. I looked toward his voice and saw a blur of white, then nothing. Up ahead was a massive thicket of hollies, and he'd disappeared behind them. I stopped. Birds chirped around me, and to the right, some animal darted away, its feet rustling through the thicket.

"There's nothing to be afraid of," came Dharma's disembodied voice.

"Said the guy before he murders and buries his victim."

Beyond the natural wall, Dharma's arm poked through like that of a ghost.

"That's not helping," I said.

He opened his hand and wriggled his fingers. "Please, Siobhan, just hold my hand and I'll pull you through. Close your eyes so the branches don't poke you."

There had to be an easier way to make a buck, but too late now. I grabbed his hand, closed my eyes, and felt my body being yanked through some serious brush.

"Wow," I said.

"Yes," Dharma said. "That's what everybody says when they lay eyes on Ondaga Plain."

Standing at the outer edge of Ondaga Plain, the vast field that expanded in front of me was a potent combination of overwhelming and calming. Ensconced within the boundary of wild hollies with their glossy green leaves and bright red berries, these flat grounds stretched about as long as a football field.

"I don't remember seeing this on the map in my welcome packet," I said.

"I can't even tell you how much it took to keep it that way. They wanted to turn this sacred space into a concert venue."

"Who is *they*?"

Dharma sat down and unlaced his sneakers.

"Krishna, LLC, a limited liability corporation."

I sat down, too. There was some grass, but not much of it. Instead, a groundcover plant had proliferated, short and curly dark-green leaves that were surprisingly soft.

"I like what's growing here," I said.

"Periwinkle. Hardy as hell, totally naturalized now. In May, the entire field flowers, lavender petals everywhere. No need for gas-guzzling mowers to choke our air or chemical weed killers to poison our earth. The hollies make a natural permanent barrier. I helped with all these plantings a long, long time ago. We also spread clover seeds, too, so nothing grows above four inches here."

"I hear you're a Krishna Root."

"One of the seven."

"So you've seen a lot of changes."

Dharma put his hands together flat then placed his thumbs against his heart and tilted his head just so, like I've seen in some Buddha statues. I had to admit, this guy really rocked this pose. I could see the years he spent meditating in this position, ingrained in him like the lines on his face.

59

As the sun slowly set over the row of tall evergreens to the west, Dharma recounted the Krishna story from the beginning. The year was 1960. Guru Dev Krishvananda, who'd come from India to study philosophy at Princeton, quit before completing his degree because by the time he was a sophomore, he already had over two hundred people attend his weekly yoga class. Five years later in Morristown, New Jersey, four men and three women, in their twenties and full of energy and hope, set up an ashram, a spiritual monastery for full immersion into the yogic experience. They formed the Yoga Center of New Jersey, which was set up as a nonprofit and sounded official but hardly was. Krishvananda had rented a large three-floor house and ran his yoga classes in the basement.

It took just two years for them to outgrow their house. It was an enormous jump to go from what they had to the Meadowlark building, but in addition to being a master of yoga, Krishvananda was also a master of business. The Meadowlark used to be a Roman Catholic seminary, and it was in financial trouble. Krishvananda formally established Krishna as a nonprofit religious order and was able to convince the banks to give him a very friendly loan. By calling on the small army of devotees he'd already amassed, he used volunteering to bring the building to a state where it could house one hundred visitors.

"The volunteer program is just about the only thing that reminds me of how things used to be. That's what's real. Everything else is… shameful."

"If I have the timeline right, this is right around when America was in its hippie period. Open your mind, tune out, etc.?" I asked.

"Our guru was never afraid of going against the grain. He held his beliefs rock steady. Falsity surrounded us, supposed enlightenment by way of chemicals, but Krishvananda knew the true path to a higher level of consciousness was best achieved by the body and mind in clarity and concert."

A full day began at 4:30 in the morning, when Krishvananda led the congregation with Krishna Flow yoga, the kind that did not rely on a caravan of set poses like most classes.

"The closest analog would be jazz—spontaneity within a structure," Dharma said. "Everyone sitting in that room was connected to one another. It was like we flowed in and out of each other, our individual movements forming a greater whole. Once you experience something like that, your world changes."

Meditation was taken seriously, a minimum of two hours each day. The diet was strictly vegetarian, no coffee, no caffeinated tea, not even any processed sugars, so no desserts. The highlight of the day was the time Krishvananda sat with his disciples and guests in the Great Room and answered personal questions and problems.

"What kind of questions?" I asked.

"Anything."

"So he just sat there like Oprah?"

"If our guru had wanted to have a TV show, he could've had one."

"Can you recall what some of these questions were?"

"When I say anything, I wasn't exaggerating. *I'm having trouble sleeping. I wish I ate less chocolate. I've been passed over for a promotion at work. I feel like my life is not my own.* Some of the questions were more general, philosophical in nature. Others were extremely subjective and limited in scope. Our guru welcomed them all and responded with humor, insight, and praise."

The day ended at nine sharp, lights out and everyone going to bed.

"Except Guru Dev Krishvananda's night wasn't over," I said. "Even though he was preaching celibacy to his unmarried disciples, I read that he was having sex with a coterie of women."

Dharma set his hands on his knees and set his angry eyes upon mine.

"You think you know all there is to know about that part of the story."

"I'm not saying anything that can't be found through Google."

"When the disciples are ready, the guru vanishes."

"I remember that phrase in one of the articles.. They said the ashram residents were already on their way of breaking away from your guru."

Dharma raised his arms and spread them out. The sun was directly behind his head, outlining his hair in a yellow blaze. "There's nothing quite as malleable as history."

"So it's not true?"

"It certainly wasn't the truth for me, and not for any of the other Roots. At that point in our history, we had over fifty yoga instructors and ten bodywork professionals. To think that all those people found instant gratification with the guru's resignation is firmly in the realm of fiction. At that point in our history, there was a faction who wanted to push Krishna into the mass-market, solipsistic entity that it has become. It was a power grab. They frightened the board of trustees into dismissing our guru, and ever since, it's been a gradual erosion of the Krishna mission. Once upon a time, we were an organization that asked people to look inward. Now we hold spiritual retreats for corporations, Siobhan. Oil companies that bleed our planet, soft drink purveyors that poison our young, pharmaceutical outfits who provide pills to numb our minds and bodies.

"And if those atrocities weren't enough, we are now ushering in technology into our sacred space. Yoga apps that will capture a selfie video and assign a grade to your postures, then showcase on the

Krishna website for people to click on the 'like' button as if it were a contest. Maybe that sounds innovative, but it is ultimately destructive. It completely ignores the mind aspect of our practice, which is a thousand times more important than whether you can swing your leg over your head. The Krishna Futurists, as that silly department is now calling themselves, have already begun to work with Silicon Valley on augmented and virtual reality equipment, figuring out more ways to dump our souls into the electronic trash. They'll tell you it's progress, but it is exactly the opposite. Every step they have taken forward is ten steps backward."

I didn't know if I agreed with Dharma, but one thing for sure, this guy's faith was unshakable. Every word was delivered with belief so strong that it sort of made me sad. Because, let's face it, he might have wasted his entire life on believing in a guy who liked being in the center of attention and enjoyed bedding young women. An old newspaper story I'd dug up in preparation for this trip mentioned that Krishvananda earned a quarter of a million per year for the eleven years he was guru, so obviously he liked money, too. In short, he was like most dynamic, successful people, courting the popular triumvirate of power, sex, and cash.

"So why are you still sticking around, Dharma?" I asked. "From what I've read, a number of Krishna-certified instructors did strike out and set up their own shop."

He rose slowly, and I followed. He raised his arms and breathed in a breath so big that I thought his chest would explode. His arms were like a valve, lowering ever so slowly as he exhaled with measure and control.

"Because this is home, Siobhan. I will not abandon my home. Not without a fight. And that time is coming."

"What do you mean?"

"After twenty years of self-exile on an island off India's coast, Krishvananda has returned."

"To where?"

Dharma smiled. "Where else?"

"Here? Now?"

"Yes and yes. When the time is right, I'd like you to meet him. Would you be amenable to that?"

"Of course," I said, remembering who I was supposed to be. "That's why I'm here, to capture and relate the complete story."

"Very good," Dharma said. "The sun has almost set, so let us return."

On the way back, he told me a bit more about the sex scandal, information that had been purposefully kept away from the public, that Krishvananda had been stuck in a loveless arranged marriage and ended up marrying one of the women with whom he'd cavorted. And regardless of his extracurricular activities, in ten years, Krishna went from a $1.5 million-a-year business to $25 million, almost entirely because of the work Krishvananda had done. He'd worked tirelessly to promote himself and Krishna, and in the end, it was all taken away from him, and for what? Because he fell in love? At least that was Dharma's point of view.

"And what's happening this weekend...we may have reached Krishna's nadir."

"What's going on?"

"Have you heard of Cleopatra Park?"

"I just saw her leaving one of the cafés."

"For twenty years I've done my mindfulness workshop in the Sunrise Room, but because of her, they've relegated me to the Orchard Room, which is not even half its size. And for what? Take a look at the schedule for that room for tomorrow morning and you'll see the embarrassment."

By the time we'd climbed up the hill and reached the entrance of the Meadowlark, it was five o'clock, the sun almost done for the day. I was soaked with sweat. Dharma looked like he could sprint another fifty miles.

"I'll be in touch," he said.

"You don't have my number."

"I'll reach you."

He headed down the hall and I headed for the staircase, then thought better of it and stopped at the elevator to the left.

"Siobhan?"

I knew that voice. I turned around, and there he was, Craig, suitcase in one hand and a bouquet of flowers in the other.

Roses, red ones. I tried to remember when I last received flowers from a man. Since that was taking me way longer than it should, I decided to enjoy the present instead of bemoaning the past. I placed my nose fully into the velvety redness and breathed in.

"Thank you," I said.

"I finished checking in like thirty seconds ago. Your timing couldn't have been better."

"Perhaps good timing, but terrible presentation. I went for a run, so I'm a sweaty mess."

It was actually good to have this excuse, because I didn't know whether to shake his hand or hug him or what. Still, it was an awkward moment, but I was further saved by the procession behind him.

Two of Park's guards were at the head, and following them were Cleo Park, Vera Wheeler, Grace Park, and a tiny mouse of a woman with a tight perm—Christine Collins, Assistant Professor of Chemistry at Llewellyn. Her hair was as red as Little Orphan Annie's. Bringing up the rear were two more guards, the last one being none other than Brent Kim.

"People of interest?" Craig asked.

"Or interesting people."

They cut across the lobby and headed up the stairs, on their way to the dining hall.

"I'll have you know, I did a little detecting of my own to get here," Craig said.

"Oh yeah?"

"I'd forgotten the name of the place you'd gone to, but since you used my laptop, I searched my browser history and found it. Used the same links to make my reservation."

"This might be a second career for you if that lawyer thing doesn't work out. Let's get you settled in and then grab some dinner."

Like myself, Craig had gotten a room on the third floor, except he was in the eastern wing while I was in the western.

He laid his suitcase on the desk. "I feel like I'm back in my college dorm."

"Is that good or bad?"

"I'm not sure. I took up more room. I was almost three hundred pounds."

Together, it took no time at all to make his bed. With the sheet tucked in neatly, we sat on it together.

"How did you get so big?"

"Just ate all the time. It was even easier in college since the dining halls were all-you-can-eat buffets. It's not hard, at least not for me, to gain weight. Both of my parents are overweight, so I'm genetically predisposed. I bet you've never been fat."

"I was a fairly chunky baby."

"Sorry, but that doesn't count."

"I've never been skinny. I'm certainly not skinny now."

"But you're not fat and it's highly unlikely you ever will be. It's protection, you know? That girth around you. People literally cannot get close."

"And why did you want that distance?"

Craig opened up his suitcase and hung his shirts and pants in the nook besides the mirror.

"I think I was afraid. Of being away from home for the first time, failing out, the usual nightmares colleges are made of."

"The only thing we have to fear...*is feeeaaaarrr itself*!" I said.

"I think what we need to fear," Craig said, "is your FDR impression."

Skin Deep

61

Back at the dining hall, I scanned the communal tables for Park and Wheeler. There they were, at the tables by the back wall, four women flanked by six bodyguards. The place was bustling, the line for the buffet snaking halfway down the length of the room. Within a minute of Craig and I joining the line, a dozen people followed us up. As before, everything smelled divine. There was something fried tonight, the scent of grease made my belly growl. I picked up two trays from the stack and handed him one.

Like lunch, there were two lines, one for vegetarian, one for meat. And like lunch again, I got both the real honey-fried chicken and the fake tempeh-fried chicken.

"My eyes are bigger than my stomach," I said.

"I'll happily help you with any leftovers."

"Mind if we go sit over there?" I asked, gesturing to Park and Wheeler.

"Is it going to cause a scene?"

"Quite possibly."

"Then, absolutely."

Each cafeteria-style table sat a dozen, so there were two empty seats at the end. We were still at least ten paces away when two of the guards stood up and blocked our way.

"There are many other available seats," one of them said to me.

"Are these reserved?"

The guards looked at each other, like maybe they should lie. Underneath their neat white turtleneck and black slacks, they had bodies of professional wrestlers, and they also had similar levels of brainpower.

"The more the merrier," Wheeler said. "How so very nice to see you here, Siobhan. And I see you've brought a friend."

"Craig Barnett, attorney at law," he said.

"A private eye and a lawyer. Sounds like a team ready to do some investigating and suing."

She was trying a little too hard to be cool, which was good. Because it meant she was actually nervous, if not about me, then about something else.

"It's nice to meet you, too, Ms. Park," I said.

Cleo Park paused in her dainty mastication of a baby carrot and slowly turned to me. In person, her beauty made me suck in my breath a tiny bit. She'd be stunning without any help, but with the flawless makeup and jet-black straight hair that shone and swayed like a shampoo commercial, she was jacked up to eleven. It was like looking at a very bright light: I could only stare for so long. How the hell was she almost fifty?

"Uh-huh," she said. *That voice.* I'd seen countless photos on the internet but hardly any videos, and in them she'd been silent, and now I knew why. Her Minnie-Mouse-on-helium squeal made Kim Kardashian sound like Lauren Bacall. Cleopatra wasn't so perfect after all.

"And you must be Dr. Christine Collins," I said. She looked just like the photo on the Llewellyn faculty page.

"Somebody's been doing her homework," Wheeler said to me.

Collins was about to say something but stopped and glanced at her boss, Wheeler. At which point she must've seen something I didn't see, because she averted my eyes and stared down at her food instead. Nicely trained.

"Just doing my job," I said. "And you must be Grace. I saw you at the Odd-Even basketball game. I hear you have an impressive outside jumper."

Now it was Grace's turn to play the part of Collins, and her mother to play Wheeler. Except it wasn't exactly the same. Grace wasn't asking for permission here but rather seeking its sadder counterpart, approval. It was a glance that might have lasted not even a second, but I'd gone through it myself as a teenager enough times to recognize it. Did Cleo not think much of her daughter's on-court skills? No surprise there.

Wheeler took her knife and sliced off a chunk of chicken breast. She shook out a few grains of salt from the shaker into the palm of her hand and turned it over, sprinkling it on the glistening white meat. It looked quite good, so I had myself some chicken, too.

"Will you be tailing us 24/7 while we're here? That's the proper term, right, tail?"

"Or you can save me some time and energy by telling me all the interesting things you'll be doing," I said.

"I don't feel so good," Grace said to her mother.

"In your mind or in your body?" Cleo asked. An odd question, but then again, she was an odd woman.

"Body," Grace said. "My stomach."

Cleo rose, and everyone else followed. They were all just going to leave their trays on the table.

"Don't be rude. You bus your own trays here," I said.

Cleo leveled a look at me, her pissed-off model pose, I guess.

"I don't *have* to do anything," she squeaked.

She turned and left. Wheeler instructed the guards to clear the table, which made them my very best friends. They clinked the dishes and cups so hard that I thought they'd crack them, but the Krishna dishware was tougher than they looked. After much clatter, they were gone, too, and it was just me and Craig at the table with lots of people looking at us.

"That was a very noir moment," Craig said.

"I try my best to please the public."

"Ugggggggggh!" came a sound from behind me.

I turned around and saw an older man grab his belly. Someone asked him if he was okay as he slumped on the table in agony.

"What the hell is going on?" Craig asked, but I couldn't quite tell him, either, because the searing pain from my own stomach brought tears to my eyes. "Siobhan? Are you okay?"

I was not.

62

Having never delivered a child, I couldn't say with certainty that what I was now feeling was akin to giving birth, but lord, it had to be pretty close. At first it was like my intestines were tying themselves into a knot, but now it was like there was a knife deep in my gut, stabbing me from the inside out. The cramps came in waves and were so intense that I feared I'd black out.

"I think I just peed a little," I said, writhing in Craig's car.

I vaguely recalled Craig almost carrying me, but just when that happened was a mystery. Time had lost meaning. Craig was driving as fast as he could to the hospital, darting in and out of this two-lane road.

"We're almost there," he said, and we were. There were ten cars ahead of us and probably a hundred behind us.

"Hold on," Craig said, and his SUV bucked like a horse as we crested a curb, climbed on the grass, and bumped over the flower bed to become the fourth car in line, right behind two ambulances that were unloading a pair of grunting, flailing Krishna diners.

A nurse with a wheelchair rolled up right by my window. She opened the door and loaded me in.

"Please park your car in the lot, sir," the nurse told Craig. "I've got her."

Craig said something to me before he left, but I hardly heard it through my own anguish.

"My name is Dolores. You're cramping?"

I nodded. I concentrated on breathing, in and out, in and out. Small, shallow breaths because stretching my stomach in any way brought sharp jabs to my sides. Dolores rolled me through the automatic glass doors of the ER entrance and into a nightmare. The lobby of the hospital had turned into a torture chamber, dozens of people moaning in distress.

"You're doing great. A few have lost consciousness from the pain, so things could be worse, believe it or not."

"I'm back," Craig said, out of breath. He crouched down and held my hand. With his other hand, he gave Dolores my driver's license and insurance card, and she took it over to the desk.

Everybody was wearing the same lanyard Craig and I were, the Krishna barcode that let us into the dining hall.

"It has to be the food," I said. "But you're not affected."

"I didn't get the chicken, just the fake stuff," Craig said.

Behind us, we heard a piercing shriek. It came from Cleo Park, whose entourage looked like they had also gotten whatever this was, all but one of the guards, who had his hands full trying to shepherd everyone through.

"Nice to see the rich and famous didn't get a pass," I said.

"Rotten meat? Salmonella?"

"Can't imagine either of those would work as quickly as this."

Dolores returned with a clipboard and my IDs, which she handed back to Craig. "Okay, Siobhan O'Brien. Let me just say I never would've guessed your name if I had a million tries."

"I get that a lot," I said.

"You can come, too," she told Craig as she took a hold of my wheelchair. "I can use the help."

Dolores wheeled me through a set of automatic doors and hurried down the corridor that was full of belly-aching patients.

"How many so far?" I asked.

"You're number seventeen, but it looks like there's another dozen behind you. And who knows how many more after that."

Dolores brought me to a bright, ballroom-sized space, each bed sectioned off by circular green curtains. It looked like a makeshift job, which it probably was since they usually didn't have to treat so many people at once. There were steady groans coming from someone to my right, though not as bad as some I'd heard on the way in.

"We're trying to keep the affected in groups of similar distress," she said. "This is the five group, on a pain scale from one to ten."

"Thank you," I said. When I tried to get up from the wheelchair, I felt a stitch in my lower stomach that made me immediately fall back into my seat.

"Let me," Craig said.

"Let *us*," Dolores said. "The last thing we need is for you to throw your back out."

Together, they lifted me off and placed me in bed, which was cold and hard. Or maybe I was the one who was cold and hard.

She took my temperature. "You're one degree lower than when you first came in, but still at 101."

A doctor with a stethoscope around his neck rushed in. She looked young enough to be a kid playing doctor, but there was nothing kidlike about her demeanor.

"I'm Dr. Novakovic. Please open your eyes real wide so I can shine this light into it?" I did as I was told. "Resistance to dilation, that's good. Nausea and cramps, but I bet no diarrhea?"

"At least not yet."

"Consider yourself lucky—you might be with the half that won't have it."

"Food poisoning?" I asked.

"Too early to tell."

"When do you think you'll know?"

"What are you, the food police?"

"Actually," Craig said, "she's a private investigator."

Novakovic took a look at my chart. "Siobhan O'Brien?"

"You should see me Riverdance."

"While drinking a pint of Guinness, no doubt. For now, Dolores will IV less exciting fluids into you to dilute the toxicity in your system. You won't be doing any gumshoeing if you don't get better." She turned away and was on her way out.

"I'll call you later and you'll let me know what you find out?"

Novakovic didn't reply, but at least she knew she'd be hearing from me.

Just watching Dolores's expertise and efficiency at doing her job—the effortless insertion of the needle into my arm, the practiced pitch of the solution onto the metal hook above the bed, turning on the flow of the liquid with a quick flick of her thumb, all these actions happening in an uninterrupted flow that was downright orchestral—made me feel better, and I told her so.

"Aww, that's sweet," she said. "Though you're probably improving because your body is working through whatever it was that got to you. Now I gotta make my other rounds, but I'll be back in half an hour to check on you."

Craig, meanwhile, had found a folding chair. He slid the curtain closed and took a seat by my side. There were still groans and complaints aplenty around us, but their collective volume was softening.

"Is this the sort of thing that I should expect," he asked, "hanging out with you?"

"At least you won't get bored."

"What do your spidey senses tell you about what happened?"

"You know, it was real easy for me to get to the Krishna kitchen earlier today. Took a while before anybody even noticed me. Wouldn't be hard for someone to come down and do something to the food."

"Maybe someone that everyone knew already."

"An inside job is always more likely than not. And even though Krishna is all about peace and tranquility, there's cracks and bumps underneath those cushy yoga mats." I told Craig about meeting Dharma on my run and the soapbox speech he'd delivered.

"But poisoning people…I mean that's a pretty serious crime. Like somebody's going to jail."

"You've certainly seen your share of people doing terrible things in your line of work."

Craig shook his head. "Not personally. I don't take on criminal cases. That's for…wait, what are you doing?"

Getting up still smarted, but not like before. I unplugged the IV drip from my arm.

"Grace Park," I said. "She just passed by."

Craig turned around and peeked through the small opening in the curtains. "You saw her through *that*?"

"It's one of my super powers. Come on, help me to my feet." Grace was heading to the back of the room, beelining for the restroom sign.

He wanted me to stay put, but I had to do what I had to do. This was my best chance to finally talk to that girl, and I wasn't going to let a sore tummy get in my way.

"Let me come," Craig said.

"I'd rather not attract any more attention."

I navigated past the nurses and orderlies who rushed past me. Through the thicket of human traffic, I saw Grace as she indeed slipped into the women's bathroom. No bodyguards followed her in. I went in after her, and my luck was riding high because I only saw one set of feet in the stall. In the corner of the bathroom was a yellow plastic sign that read "IN MAINTENANCE – PLEASE WAIT." I took it out and propped it up outside the door. Then I kicked in the little rubber door stop from the inside to keep the door from opening.

You proud of me, Ed? I learned from watching you.

63

Silence, then a flush. I might have avoided the diarrhea part of the bug, but Grace wasn't as lucky. The metal door opened and there she was, her face drained of color and her eyes sunken in. The harsh fluorescent lights above made her look a bit like Gollum from the *Lord of the Rings* movies. Grace probably had half a foot and twenty pounds on me, but in her present condition, she wasn't getting past me by force.

"Excuse me," she whispered. She had an IV bag that she rolled next to her. She shuffled to the sink and washed her hands, then leaned against it for support. I pulled down three sheets of paper towels and held them out to her.

"You obviously ate a lot more chicken than I did," I said.

"That's all…wait, you're that detective woman who was sitting at the end of our table."

"You're going to answer a few questions. Then you can go back to your bed."

I watched for her reaction. Using my authoritative voice, I was playing the role of a no-nonsense hardass. I wasn't entirely sure this was going to work, since Grace was a girl who'd been brought up in a life of privilege and protection. I couldn't imagine many people talked to her like this. Except, my gut told me, her parents—that moment at the dinner table, that forlorn look she bestowed on her mother when I'd brought up basketball.

"All right," she said. "Can I sit on the toilet? Because I don't think I can stand for much longer."

I nodded. Grace held onto her IV post and gently lowered herself onto the toilet. She might have stood six feet, but right now, she looked like an overgrown child. I felt terrible for doing this to her, but there was another girl who was missing, who could be in an even worse situation.

"Where's Penny Sykes?"

I didn't think it was possible for Grace to slump any further, but somehow she managed it. In a voice so small that I asked her to repeat it, she said, "Mama said she was here. But she's not."

"Your mother? Why would your mother know?"

Grace laughed emptily. "There's nothing Mama doesn't know."

"Did your mother take Penny somewhere?"

She leaned her head against the stall and closed her eyes. Her words fell quickly, rushed, as if they were falling out of her.

"Me and Christopher, we tried to help her. We did help her, I know we did. God, she was so mad, so angry, but it wasn't our fault, none of it. Everybody wants what they want, right? She wanted Christopher so she got what she wanted there, too. Oh, if only I could go back to that first week. I would go back to the three of us, sitting in my dorm room, playing cards and sipping peach schnapps—it was terrible, but it was all we could get our hands on. Everything was so simple."

There was a very loud bang on the bathroom door.

"Open up!"

Grace's eyelids fluttered open.

"You better get that," she said.

"No worries," I said. "Somebody else will get it."

"Oh good," Grace said.

Another bang, even louder, most likely a very large boot against the door. The rubber door stopper held, for now.

"I just want to sleep," Grace said.

"You can, if you just answer one more question. What were you and Christopher and Penny doing together?"

"I told you already, we were helping! Helping Penny get rid of her problem. Getting Mama the new blood so she can be beautiful and young and love me. Helping Christopher's parents so they could stay. Saving, saving them all."

The next bang was so loud that I instinctively put my hands around my ears. The entire doorframe, which was made of metal, shook; dust and debris fell around the seams.

"Are Christopher's parents going somewhere?" I asked, but she must've not even heard the question because she started to break down.

"I told him what to do with the condom…okay? Jesus. That was *me*, that was my idea, maybe it wasn't…"

The door swung open. The guard wasn't so dumb after all, I thought, as I saw him put away his credit card which he used to push out the rubber stopper under the door. He came right for me, shoved me hard enough that I banged my shoulder against the paper towel holder and fell to the floor. He was rearing back to kick me but I pointed at the stall. Lucky for me, Grace was stumbling out and he had to hurry to catch her.

"You're gonna answer for this," he barked at me.

"That's enough," Craig, who had snuck in behind the guard, said. "You better not lay a hand on her, *hombre*."

The guard glared at us then hurried out of the bathroom with Grace and her IV pole in his arms.

Craig helped me up.

"Jesus, are you okay? Did he hurt you?"

"It's fine, I'm fine," I said. "He was just doing his job, and I was doing mine."

"You didn't tell me you were going to take her prisoner in the bathroom."

"Sort of happened on the spot, *hombre*."

"I don't know what I was thinking. Just blurted it out."

"It's kind of adorable."

We made our way back to my bed. It was good to lie down again, though I was feeling a lot better than even just half an hour ago. Except now my shoulder hurt a bit.

"So did she spill any beans?" Craig asked.

"You could say. She was borderline delirious, I don't know how much of it made sense."

But some of it did. Christopher had sex with Penny, and something was done with the condoms he used. The reason behind... whatever she'd done...was because Grace wanted to help her mother (though new blood – what the hell did that mean?), and also to save Christopher's parents from...leaving? But then her mother found out and had Penny moved yet again? That wasn't clear. What was clear was that I'd need to delve deeper into Cleo Park's business, which wouldn't be easy since she lived in her own sequestered bubble. But there were ways into everyone's lives, even that of the rich and the powerful, because no one lived in a vacuum.

Dolores stopped in. "How're you feeling?"

"Good," I said. "Ready to be discharged."

She cocked her head and walked over to me. "Really?" She took my temperature and shined a bright light into my eyes. "Yeah, you've recovered nicely, despite getting off the IV early. We can use your bed, so you can go ahead and check out."

I thanked her. It was almost ten o'clock.

"She takes a licking and keeps on ticking," I said.

"Back to work?" Craig asked.

"Back to work."

"Glad I'm a lawyer. Better hours."

Back at Krishna, things were returning to normal. Some disgruntled guests were packing up their cars and leaving, but the main lobby was cleaned up and looking like its usual soothing white and beige self and the people returning from the hospital were like me, tired but feeling a whole lot better.

As soon as Craig and I got in the elevator, Cynthia Bard, the PR lady, jumped in.

"Third floor, right?" she asked, bubbly as always.

I nodded.

"On behalf of Krishna, I'd like to personally apologize for this evening's extra-curricular activities," she said. "We've already con-ducted an internal investigation into the matter and I'll have you know that we're now working closely with Hawthorne police."

"Really?" Craig said.

"In all the years I've been here, we've never had something like this happen. Our bodies are our temples—no one believes this more strongly than our Dining and Nutrition Department. You can imagine how utterly destroyed they are. They're just sick about it."

The elevator dinged and the door opened.

"But not really *sick*, like the people who actually got sick, like myself," I said.

"Sorry," Cynthia said. "Poor choice of words. From what we can gather, it was just one batch of the chicken that was affected, so a minor portion of the guests. But still, even one sick guest is one too many."

We all got out onto the third floor lobby.

"Thank you for being here," I said to Craig. "You saved the day."

"It was the least I could do."

I kissed him, and he kissed me back. Nothing too grand, just really nice. It gave me hope, and I think it gave him hope, too.

"I'll call you in the morning, like eight?" Craig said.

"Perfect."

As soon as he was out of earshot, Cynthia said, "It's always lovely to come here as a couple. Next time, I suggest you guys stay in Javani, our newest addition. I didn't get a chance to show you those lovely rooms."

"Look," I said. "You don't have to worry about me writing about what happened here tonight."

Cynthia broke open a smile that actually felt genuine. "I can't tell you how relieved I am."

I guess I could've made her feel even more relieved by telling her that I would be writing no story whatsoever, since I was a complete fraud.

Back in my room, I fell face-first onto my bed. I was beat, but I had to return Josie's call. On the ride back from the hospital, my phone had notified me of a missed call from hours ago.

She picked up on the first ring.

"She's run out of methimazole," she said. "Her drug for Graves'."

"How do you know?"

"I have an alert set up with the pharmacy when her refills need to be re-upped. Her final set of pills are still at Llewellyn's health center, waiting to be picked up for a week."

"I'm afraid I still don't have great news," I said, and gave her the rundown including the latest gastronomical incident. I left out most of what Grace told me about Penny and Christopher, since I still needed to investigate what she'd said.

"You had a long day," she said.

"I'm getting close, though. I can feel it."

"Without her methimazole, she can drop ten pounds in a week, and she's already so thin as she is…" There was a long pause. "I've been thinking about how little I actually know her, you know? I just thought…I thought it would be different between me and her. I thought I would be the kind of mother my daughter could confide in."

"Just you and Penny against the world," I said, which I immediately regretted, because now she was crying. But maybe it was good for her to get it out.

"This is all so fucked up," Josie said.

"It's a mess, I agree. But all messes start somewhere. Don't forget that."

"I won't. Please find her, Siobhan. Please."

"I don't have your daughter yet, Josie, but I will. I promise you."

I hung up, but my night wasn't over yet, I had a doctor to track down. I rang the hospital and asked for Dr. Novakovic. By now, I hoped the influx of the Krishna sick would've abated.

"You should be in bed, Ms. O'Brien," Novakovic said.

"That's actually exactly where I am, doctor. In bed, lying down, calling you."

"Jack-o'-lantern mushroom. I'm looking at it right now, it's distinctive because of a tiny flap of orange on the bottom. Omphalotus illudens. Can easily be found near the base of hardwood trees around these parts. We get a few cases a year, mostly from overzealous mushroomers."

"Krishna isn't the kind of place that'd serve wild mushrooms. More likely they'd source them from a local farm," I said.

"Yes, this is definitely not that. These mushrooms were freeze-dried."

"How do you know that?"

"The lab report. Most of the mushrooms were pulverized to a powder, but not all. When you freeze vegetables, you can see a particular type of cellular destruction that's consistent with the damage of freezing. Some vegetables are fine, like broccoli, but spinach becomes mush when it melts. Mushrooms keep their shape, but under 100 times magnification, you can see everything."

"Thank you," I said.

"Sleep," she said. "Doctor's orders."

I turned off the overhead light and stared at the almost full moon through my window. There was a hazy ring around it, fog or a thin layer of clouds. I thought of Penny's pills; I thought of orange mushrooms. I closed my eyes.

Early morning light beamed down on the barefoot people lying on spongy rectangular mats. From where I was standing, just inside the wide double doors of the sanctuary, I could see how this spacious room used to be a chapel. On the opposite wall sat a giant bronze Buddha, his right hand raised as if to swear to tell the truth and nothing but the truth.

"Excuse me," a quiet voice spoke behind me. I was standing in front of the tall wooden cabinet that contained stacks of purple yoga blocks, so I moved out of the way.

Christine Collins, the professor who'd come to Krishna with Cleo Park and Wheeler, picked up a pair of foam bricks. It took her a few seconds to recognize me, as it was six-thirty in the morning. From what I'd read, the morning yoga session was the most popular one at Krishna, but after last night's mass food poisoning, attendance was sparse, the room not even at half capacity.

"How are you feeling this morning?" I asked her.

She avoided my gaze and grabbed a mat and a cushion and made her way to the far left. Of course I followed her.

I'm sure if I were into yoga and detox and all that healthy stuff, I'd possess a more discerning view, but as it stands, yoga people are like country musicians to me: they all look and sound alike. So the instructor who walked up to the stage and started speaking to the people in the room was like everybody else at Krishna: wiry, content, and calm. Dressed in a tight red t-shirt and silky white capri-length pants, he turned down the background music of faint chimes and birds chirping with a remote and spoke into the tiny ear-clipped microphone.

"A glorious morning to you all. My soul is your soul; the sun is the love that binds us together. Welcome to the start of another beautiful day here in Hawthorne, in the heart of our Sanctuary. This is First Light Gentle Yoga. My name is Hiran and I'll be your guide."

He sounded like a golf commentator, quiet and precise. He asked us to put our right hand over our hearts, then feel the beat as we breathed.

"Straighten your legs and feel the floor beneath you. Connect to the earth below and bless its strength, the tendrils of its loving stability."

Tendrils of its loving stability?

The lady next to me touched her nose to her kneecap. If my arms were twice as long, I might have been able to grab my toes, but that was all right. I wasn't here to become Rubber Woman. My shoulder was still achy from last night's run-in with the bodyguard.

"Raise your right hand, lean to your left, breathe in. Now breathe out as you return to center."

Breathing, as it turned out, was a big part of yoga. And so were women in tight little pants that showed off their well-toned booties. When we all assumed the Downward Dog pose, hands and feet on the floor, butt raised high in the air, everywhere I peeked, female buns of steel encased in black and gray tights mooned me with poise and vigor, and I felt guilty for scarfing that Big Mac on the drive down yesterday.

After spending half an hour waking various sleepy muscles, I was surprised at just how alert and energized I felt. Now New Age harp music filled the room, and the instructor employed a metronome: lying down, we were to breathe in through the nose and into the belly for six beats, hold for two, breath out through the mouth for four beats, hold for two. A dozen repetitions later, I was in rhythm, except my synchronicity was being disturbed by what sounded like sobbing. It was Collins. Tears streaked down her cheeks. Crying softly, she looked like a little girl lost.

The harps faded to silence, and the instructor put his hands together and doled out a flurry of namastes. He suggested we do the same to our immediate neighbors, so I blessed and was blessed by a silver-haired gentleman to my left and a pregnant young woman to my right. People rose from their cocoon of meditation, rolling their necks and stretching out their arms. I crawled over to Collins, who had her face covered by her hands.

"I don't know what Wheeler is doing to you, but you know you always have a choice."

Collins, through her reddened eyes, stared at me. "You don't know anything."

"You've gone from lecturer to assistant professor in six months. You've worked on a PowerPoint presentation you'll be giving this morning, *Aging Is a Disease, and There Is a Cure: The Path to Perpetual Youth.* You're also a trained chemist, someone who spent many years honing her academic craft, but now you're about to spout a whole bunch of ridiculous hokum, and your boss Vera Wheeler has you by your short hairs. You're trapped. How am I doing so far?"

Collins' small round face drained of color.

"In case you didn't know, I'm here to find Penny Sykes. Her mother has asked me to find her because she disappeared earlier this month. I don't know how Penny figures into all of this, but I have a feeling you might. Do you?"

"Yes," she said, so quietly that I almost didn't hear it.

"She suffers from hyperthyroidism. Without her medicine, she can get sick quite quickly." I placed a hand on her shoulder. "Can you tell me where she is?"

"No, she can't."

Wheeler said from behind me.

66

She was in an all-white business suit, jacket and blouse and knee-length skirt, white hose and white stilettos. Virginal and sexy, all in one.

"That's very gauche of you, Vera, wearing shoes in here. Didn't you see the sign outside?"

Collins quickly wiped her eyes with the sleeve of her shirt and scrambled up off the floor to stand behind her boss.

Wheeler crouched down and spoke into my ear.

"So," she said, "how's your little brother Sven?"

I wanted to grab her face by her ears and yank her to the floor. Perhaps seeing my flash of menace, Wheeler stood up quickly and backed off.

I shouldn't have been surprised that she knew something about me. Maybe she had hired a detective of her own. I thought of my brother, who was actually not so little—six-foot-two Sven could handle himself, but he also had a wife and a toddler, my beautiful nephew with his sparse brown curls and impossibly tiny fingernails.

Threats, Ed once told me, come from a place of fear.

I rolled up my yoga mat nice and slow to buy myself time.

Spin it to your advantage.

I gathered the foam blocks, stacked them together. The best way to couch this threat was to see it as a desperate personal attack to get me off her back. I felt my wits returning to me.

While I was taking my mental break, Wheeler had done the same. With her arms akimbo, she stood her ground. In fact, she walked right up to me again.

"Cleo doesn't know about the little stunt you pulled on her

daughter last night at the hospital. If she knew? If I told her?"

I smiled.

"What the hell is so funny?" Wheeler asked.

"If you wanted Cleo to know, you would've told her already. Now get the fuck out of my way."

I placed the mat and the blocks back in their cubbyholes and walked out of there, feeling Wheeler's seething eyes behind me.

Waiting for me at the bank of shoes was Craig, holding out my sneakers. I was grateful to see a friendly face.

"You okay?" Craig said.

As we made our way upstairs to the dining hall, I related my encounter with Collins to Craig.

"Shit. That's pretty low, to threaten your family."

"I'll text Sven later, it's like five in the morning there."

"So you think Collins knows where Penny is."

"Even if she doesn't, I think she can lead me there. The problem is, now that I've interrogated her, my chances of doing so again are slimmer."

"Kind of like what happened with Grace."

The dining hall wasn't as busy as it was last night, but there were still a good number of people. The big difference: not a single diner was on the meat aisle. A heaping of fatty, glistening bacon sat on the serving dish, untouched.

"If somebody wanted to make a point about vegetarianism, I suppose the point has been made," Craig said.

Dharma's words came back to me: *Because this is home, Siobhan. I will not abandon my home. Not without a fight. And that time is coming.* Sounded like posturing at the time, but now? I wasn't so sure.

"Feeling brave?" Craig asked, pointing at the bacon.

"Not really," I said, and we did like everybody else, opting for the vegetarian aisle.

Once we got in line, we stopped talking as per the dining hall rules of silent breakfasts. When I sat down with my dish of tofu frittata, cup of fresh fruit, and mug of Himalayan Hibiscus tea in front of Craig, it felt good to say nothing at all. All around me, I heard the clinking of utensils and dishes, an almost musical quality to these ordinary sounds that were magnified due to the complete lack of human conversation. The man sitting cattycorner to me chewed slowly with his eyes closed and his hands clasped together.

There was an innocence here at Krishna, though I'd think the Hawthorne Police might deem it closer to negligence. Cynthia Bard had said last night that they were working with the cops to get to the bottom of the food poisoning, and I'd imagine they took one look at the lax security around food preparation and thought these people were living in a fantasy world.

By the time we made our official exit from the dining hall, it was ten before ten.

"I can stay a few more days, you know," Craig said.

He'd already checked out, his luggage lined up outside the dining hall like all the others, everyone respecting each other's property, no one worried about theft at this Shangri-La.

"Don't you have to be in Albany for the state supreme court in like five hours?"

"Sounds pretty important, doesn't it? It's not, though, just a patent ruling."

I pulled his rolling suitcase off the wall and handed it to him. We made our way to the bank of elevators.

"You have your work," I said, "and I have mine."

We rode the elevator down with four others with suitcases in tow. At the lobby, Craig held my hands in his hands.

"I'm sorry about what happened at my place."

"No worries," I said.

"After work today, I'm seeing a therapist about my…I don't

even know what to call it. A kind of hoarding. Inability to move on."

"You're not doing that for *me*?"

"No. For me."

"Good answer," I said, and hugged him hard.

Craig turned back before he exited through the open doors to shoot me a final glance. Framed in front of the distant Adirondack Mountains, he was commercial-ready. He waved, and I waved back. Now that he was gone, I sort of wished he hadn't left.

I turned and walked towards the Sunrise Room.

67

If I had come a minute later, I would've been shut out—the place was teeming with people, almost entirely women, and mostly women of a certain age and look. It wasn't necessarily that they looked *bad*... but rather eerily similar, in the uniform way women who've had work done look, a rebuilt, reconstituted mask with their sinewy arms and platinum blonde locks. The only available seats were in the very back row, so I took one next to an extremely made-over woman.

"I always say, you can never start too early," she said. There was something about this woman's voice that sounded familiar, but I couldn't place it.

"I'm just an observer," I said.

I took out my pocket notebook and got my pen in hand.

"A reporter, huh?"

And then it suddenly came to me, who this woman was, how she knew so quickly that I was a reporter, or at least faking to be one. Annabelle Wolinsky, a.k.a., A-Wol, one of the vacuous women in one of those *Housewives* shows on reality television. It wasn't Beverly Hills but rather an East Coast city, one of the old moneyed places like New Canaan or Greenwich. Gold Coast, that was it – *The Housewives of the Gold Coast*.

"I've gone A-Wol," I said, and it delighted her to hear her catch phrase.

"Wonderful to make your acquaintance...?"

"Siobhan O'Brien. Reporter for the *Binghamton Bulletin*."

"I see," she said, and I could see her thought processes run across her well-preserved face in about two seconds: surprise at my name, disappointment that I wasn't from *The New York Times*, recalling

Binghamton's location, considering the media reach of the said paper, shrugging and accepting the possible exposure, however slight it was. "I might have something for you, a rumor that might be more."

"Oh yeah?"

"Let's chat after this session. A little girl talk, shall we say?"

"Perfect."

Rising from the front row were two of my favorite people, Vera Wheeler and Christine Collins. Next to their empty seats were four black heads, Cleo and Grace Park flanked by two guards. Wheeler walked up to the podium and leaned over the mike. She was coiffed to the hilt, her short wave of yellow hair channeling Marilyn Monroe. She smiled, then started...singing?

Forever young
I want to be forever young
Do you really want to live forever
Forever, forever young.

Wheeler was no Adele, but she could carry a tune. Alphaville's "Forever Young" was huge in the 80's. Wheeler's singing had the immediate effect of loosening up the audience, light laughter filling up the room. She leaned into the microphone.

"Some people say that song is really about suicide—that the only way to stay forever young is to end it all," she said. "Kind of a downer, wouldn't you agree? And terribly misguided, because, as our seminar states, Aging Is a Disease, and There Is a Cure. Perpetual youth is what we're here to discuss, because it is undoubtedly the future. Here to tell you the scientific nuts and bolts is Dr. Christine Collins, one of the brightest researchers we currently have on faculty at Llewellyn College."

Collins, who was mousy to begin with, did not take to the eager crowd. When she cleared her throat in front of the microphone, the crackle startled her and she actually jumped.

"Hello?" she squeaked. She was amplified by the sound system, but somehow all it did was magnify the smallness of her voice. Once the colorful PowerPoint presentation beamed itself onto the white screen, she found her bearings. She pointed her red laser dot at what looked like a blue worm in the shape of a C with black caps at its ends.

"This is a simple representation of a single DNA strand. Notice what happens when a cell divides."

As it divided from one cell to two to four and so on, the black caps shortened until they disappeared altogether.

"These ends are telomeres, and they are akin to the plastic tips at the end of our shoelaces. Without the protection, our shoelaces would become frayed. Same with our DNA strands. Once the telomeres run out, the cells no longer divide. We call this state *senescence*, the scientific term for *dead*. The enzyme telomerase has been shown to slow, stop, or even reverse the shortening of these telomeres. Hospitals themselves would no longer have the burden of extending the life of the elderly since everyone would remain in the prime of their lives. Now I will elaborate upon the scientific details."

For the next half hour, Collins tossed out more egghead terms— amyloid plaque, apoptosis, protein cross-linking, mitochondrial mutations—which made me feel like I was back in a college lecture. But most everyone else in the room looked riveted, and as far as Wheeler was concerned, there was only one person who mattered anyway. She sat off to the side of the stage, but I noticed her constantly glancing over at Cleo Park.

There could only be one reason why Wheeler was courting the likes of Cleo Park: money. It wasn't difficult to put two and two together. Llewellyn had a paltry endowment. Perhaps the creation of Travers Hall was a way to woo Park. By showing her how seriously Llewellyn was treating the science of youth as well as beauty, by way of Western paradigms like Christine Collins and Eastern paradigms like Krishna, this felt like an all-out assault by Wheeler to get Park to pony up.

As I was jotting down my thoughts, a hand touched my arm.

68

Annabelle pushed a folded sheet of paper to me. I glanced at her, and she mimed opening the paper and reading it. So this was what my fabulous private eyeing life had come to—passing notes in class.

Amrita. Do you know what that is?
I wrote back: *No.*
It is the elixir of life.
My reply: *How many bottles can you spare?*

That got her to smile, or at least slightly crease her surgically modified face. Collins was now taking questions from the audience. A woman asked her about cancer and Collins' response was more scientific jargon, an acronym named WILT, Whole-body Interdiction of Lengthening of Telomeres, whatever that meant. A few people were leaving; Annabelle tipped her head toward the exit to do the same.

I hadn't realized how much hotter it was inside the Sunrise Room until we walked out. Annabelle extended her well-manicured hand and ushered us to the large multi-limbed bronze statue of an Indian goddess that stood at the end of the hallway. To my surprise, on the opposite side, the statue was hollowed out and two red cushions were inside the cavity.

"You must be a regular to know a spot like this," I said.

"Welcome to Durga, the form and formless, the goddess of creation, preservation, and annihilation. Krishna is rife with secrets," Annabelle said. "Like amrita."

"The elixir of life. Very Indiana Jones."

"Amrita is a fluid that flows from the pituitary gland down the throat during deep meditation."

"One of those nice side effects of quieting your mind."

Annabelle frowned beautifully. "No. Amrita only flows for the chosen few."

"Ah. Let me guess, for the master yogis, like Krishvananda."

Annoyance crossed her face, but only for a microscopic moment. "You know of Krishvananda?"

"By way of Dharma."

"Oh yes, Dharma. He's got quite a lot to say, doesn't he. But does he know that Krishvananda…"

"…has returned?"

Now *that* pissed her off and she was past hiding it. "Well, did he also tell you amrita can give you eternal youth?"

"No, he didn't mention that."

"You don't believe."

"I think living forever would probably be less a blessing and more a curse."

"I saw you yesterday at the dining hall, talking to Cleo Park. So I know you've seen her up close. You know she's almost fifty, right? No surgery, and she could easily pass for thirty."

"Amrita?"

"You think her being here at the same time that Krishvananda is coincidence?"

I shrugged.

"Phone, please," Annabelle said.

I handed her my phone. She rang hers so we had each other's numbers.

"You're gonna get a call from me. You won't want to miss it. God knows I want to see it, finally – I've waited long enough."

"It'll be great to have you as an integral part of this feature story I'm writing, Annabelle."

She rose to leave. Our transaction finished, she offered her hand,

I shook it, and she was off.

Annabelle, Cleo, Dharma, amrita. All of this was interesting, but I was beginning to feel like I did at Llewellyn, when getting involved with Faith and Wheeler and Travers Hall didn't get me any closer to finding Penny. It was the chance encounter with Christopher's roommate Beaker that furthered my case more than anything else, though I had to remind myself that I wouldn't have even been at the basketball game to see Beaker if I hadn't been chasing everything else. Glacially slow, achingly slow, frustratingly slow: this was how cases got solved. I had to be patient. Except Penny *couldn't* be patient; wherever she was, she was running out of time.

As I sat alone inside Durga and bemoaned the tangential threads of this case, I recognized a familiar voice nearby: Wheeler. It came from the other side of the statue.

"…establishing new standards at Llewellyn. Michelle and I have already laid out the framework for additional synergies between us and Krishna."

Michelle had to be Michelle West, Krishna's programming director.

"We're standing at the tip of the proverbial iceberg, Cleo." That was West. "There's going to be so much more. Anti-aging is going to be a significant portion of Krishna's programming going forward. The board has already approved it."

"That's great to hear," Cleo said in her Minnie Mouse tone. "I do have one concern, though. How will you integrate Krishvananda into your programs?"

Silence.

Wheeler: "Krishvananda?"

Cleo: "Yes, Krishvananda. The guru who once led this institution."

West: "I don't…this is… Krishvananda is part of Krishna's legacy, but I don't understand…"

Cleo: "I see I've caught you both off guard with my question. My aromatherapy appointment is in a few minutes, so I'll let you figure this out amongst yourselves. Bye now."

A few seconds later, West: "Krishvananda?"

"I thought he was still in Mumbai," Wheeler said.

Their voices faded as they moved away from the statue. I waited a few moments before I walked over to the other side, to make sure they wouldn't see me. I wanted to hear the rest of their conversation, but that would have to wait because a cop almost ran into me.

69

As the officer made his way to the lobby, three more joined him to form a quartet of navy-blue uniforms heading in the opposite direction of the Sunrise Room and toward the other side of the building, the Orchard Room. As the cops approached the entrance, they negotiated through the rush of the crowd that had been just let out. I waited until they were halfway to the front of the room before I entered. By the door was a tall chest like the one in the sanctuary, housing yoga mats, blocks, and blankets, so I leaned against it for cover.

"Benjamin Roth?"

The cops spread out and surrounded Dharma.

"How may I assist you, Officer…Salazar, is it?"

"Sergeant Salazar. We need you to come down to the precinct in relation to the food poisoning that occurred last evening here at Krishna."

Dharma, clad in his usual all-white garb, looked so relaxed that he almost looked sleepy, as if being questioned by a cadre of cops was something that happened on a daily basis. "Is this a formal request or something voluntary?"

"I have a warrant for your arrest," Salazar said, and took out the document and held it out. Dharma took it, read it, and handed it back to him.

"So you're giving me an opportunity to walk out with you quietly and willingly so as not to make a scene or embarrass myself or Krishna."

"Couldn't have said it better myself."

"That's very kind of you, Sergeant, but I don't think so," Dharma said. He walked around to the back of the lectern, as if ready to deliver a lecture. "I think I'll make you folks earn your keep today."

Nobody moved or said anything for a good ten seconds, the air tight with tension. Salazar broke the silence.

"Resisting arrest would be another charge against you. And if you hurt us in any way while trying to escape, that'd be another charge, a very serious one, attacking an officer of the law. I'd ask you to reconsider and come peacefully."

Dharma leaned forward against the lectern to get closer to the microphone. His voice now boomed throughout the room and out the door, drawing the attention of passersby. "I won't lay a pinky on any of you. What I will do is give you a rushed tour of Krishna as you try to arrest me. Consider it a more active version of civil disobedience, if you will."

A cop in the back moved up and stood next to Salazar. He was a smaller guy with biceps that bulged underneath the uniform. "Sarge, let me grab this asshole so he'll stop yapping."

Dharma was behind the lectern, and an eye blink later, he was halfway across the room. He ran so fast that he did that thing that Trinity did in the beginning of *The Matrix*, running sideways on the wall for three impossible loping steps, then did some kind of a somersault in mid-air to a standing dismount that deposited him in front of the door. It was like watching Cirque de Soleil, except cheaper.

"Enjoy the show, Siobhan," Dharma said as he walked out. The cops were frozen as I was, and then they snapped awake and rushed after him.

I ran, too, to follow the unfolding chaos. Like Dharma had said, he was going to make the cops work, because not only was he faster than them, as someone who'd worked and lived here in this building since its very inception, he knew the layout better than anyone. Down the hall, Dharma had enough of a lead that the police had no chance of catching up to him, but now he ducked into one door and then came out in another door. And then he did it again, except this time, he came out through a door across the hall, which meant he had either run upstairs or downstairs through a set of stairs I didn't know existed, or maybe he'd scurried up the ceiling through ducts or dumb waiters or god knows what. As I stood and watched with everybody else as Dharma toyed with the four cops, I couldn't help but laugh. It was a farce on stage, like *Noises Off* or a Roadrunner cartoon.

Dharma dashed back out into the hallway with a very tall stack of papers, and as he ran down the hall, sheets flew off and fluttered all over, like very large pieces of confetti. One caught a cop right on his face, and he ran blindly into an unlucky bystander, tumbling onto the floor and entwining in each other's arms like lovers. Another of the cops had gotten smarter and had run way ahead to wait in ambush, but no chance; even though he'd guessed the right door, Dharma fell into a roll and spun away from his grasp, then pushed off the wall with both feet to come right back up and continue on his entertaining escape.

How long could this go on? Not long, considering these were just small town cops. Salazar, who was doubled over and trying to catch his breath, ripped the walkie-talkie off his belt.

"Jones, radio for backup. Not SWAT—it's not like that. I don't know, we just need more uniforms here because this guy is fast as hell and pulling that *parkour* shit."

"You should've seen him thirty years ago," said a melodious voice.

70

I turned and faced a tall, thin man in a beige tunic, his long white hair tied in a loose ponytail. He was of Indian descent, and here at Krishna, his mode of dress and the way he held himself did not stand out. Except when I stared into his eyes, I felt a little swimmy. They were enormously round, a shade darker than caramel, and slightly wet, as if he'd just heard something that touched his heart.

He wasn't young, but he wasn't old, either. Sixty? Fifty? Maybe even forty, or possibly seventy. Not that it mattered, because what he exuded in every cell of his body was wisdom and intelligence and… danger? No, more like mischief, the fun kind of peril that every girl secretly craves. I'd heard of animal magnetism, but I'd never experienced it to this extent.

"Krishvananda," I said.

"You've been foretold of my arrival, I see."

It was almost too much, talking to him this close, one on one. My mouth had gone dry.

Another Indian, an older woman in a yellow sari, briskly walked past Krishvananda and handed him a gray folder, then disappeared into the crowd that was moving outdoors, because Dharma was now outside the building and running full speed down the grassy hill. When a cop tried to intercept him, Dharma juked and dodged him like an NFL running back.

Krishvananda opened the folder and thumbed through the pages. When another Indian, a bald old man who could've been Gandhi's twin, walked by, Krishvananda reached out to him and said, "This is good. Dharma is done." And then that man disappeared into the crowd, too.

Another police cruiser arrived with its red and blue lights flashing. Dharma, who at this point was all the way down to the visitor parking lot, stopped running and walked right to the car. He raised both arms in a gesture of surrender, and as soon as a cop got out of the car, kneeled on the grass with his hands clasped behind his head, ready to be cuffed.

Krishvananda and I watched all this from the lobby window. I turned to him and saw his smile, which rounded his face into a boyish expression of unadulterated joy. It made me smile, too.

"I have heard that you are a reporter," he said.

"That's right."

"I'd like to share something with you, something that may, how do you say, break open a story?"

He offered me his arm and I took it. I can't say I know what it's like to be a queen, but walking down the Krishna hallway with this man had to be something like it. I don't think many people recognized him, but their heads turned, regardless, at his innate regality, and I stood up straighter and let him lead me to the elevator, where he pushed the button for the 4th floor.

"You said I should've seen Dharma thirty years ago?"

"He could've been an Olympic gymnast. He had muscles in places I didn't think muscles could exist. Like here," he said, and took my hand in his hand and traced a line on the flesh between my thumb and index finger with his fingernail. I felt for the elevator wall with my other hand, trying to find support because his touch was alternately soft and hard, gentle and spiky. I blinked twice and looked up at his face and that's when I found a few tiny drops of resistance to pull my hand back.

"Is something wrong?" Krishvananda said.

"You're enjoying this," I said. "You know the effect you have on people and you take pleasure in the power you have over them."

The elevator dinged and he gestured for me to exit.

"To your left, ever-observant Siobhan," he said. "Follow me."

Was this a good idea? This was not a good idea. I drew in a long breath and exited the elevator. The fourth floor was deserted, like the way it was when I'd come up here with Cynthia Bard. Krishvananda led me past the Meditation Room and then a series of office doors — Chief Financial Officer, Chief Technology Officer, Chief Executive Officer—and towards the end of the hall, where there were two sets of identical vases, each as tall as a person. They were both made of silver, gleaming against the spotlights above and below. The vases were set in front of a rectangular inset of mirrored walls so it looked like there was an infinite number of them reaching far into the horizon.

"Where are we going?" I asked.

"Up."

"But we're on the top floor of Meadowlark."

"One can always aim higher," Krishvananda said.

As he walked behind the vase on the left, I watched him expand into a million identical copies through the reflections of the mirrors... and instead of appearing on the other side of the vase, he vanished.

"Just do what I did, Siobhan," his echoing voice said. "I will not lead you astray, my child."

I walked his way and shielded my eyes against the spotlights and smacked an elbow into a wall.

"That hurt," I said.

"I didn't realize you were going so fast. You're fearless, aren't you?"

"Just following your directions, Krishvananda."

"Now feel the wall in front of you and go as far left as you can, then as far back as you can, then left again, and finally forward."

It was like I was inside a maze, a narrow one that only allowed one person at a time. Though I wasn't claustrophobic, if I stayed here much longer, I probably would be. I was completely enveloped in darkness and there were spaces so constricted that I felt my own breath against my lips. The walls felt weird, soft but almost...skin-like? Like it was alive. Was my breathing becoming labored because I was freaking out or because I was walking uphill?

Thank goodness for sunlight. I saw it and I rushed to it, though when I finally got out, my eyes took a good thirty seconds to adjust. I was in what looked like a small greenhouse, except instead of plants and irrigation apparatuses, it was a living area. A twin bed, a wooden table and two matching chairs, a tub and toilet behind a curtain in one corner, the bare necessities of existence. But I hardly saw any of that because my eyes went wide angle on me. Located at what must be the highest corner of the Meadowlark building, I was surrounded by the ravine and the river below, the smoky Adirondack Mountains beyond, and the crazy beautiful splotches of yellow, green, and red of autumn worn by all the tree leaves in between. Because all the walls were glass and because we were situated right at the edge, it seemed like I could step right into the vertiginous vista below. And if that wasn't impressive enough, on the opposite side was the granite slab that Meadowlark was built into. The afternoon sun transformed that rock face into an ever-changing display of silvery sparkles.

"How is this place not visible from the ground?" I asked.

Krishvananda poured hot tea from the electric pot into two cups that were sitting on the desk. Also on the desk was the same gray folder he'd been handed a few minutes ago. He sat on one chair and I sat in the other. Strong mint tea, hot and cool at the same time on my tongue.

"Ankh—that's what I call this personal sanctuary—sits at the northeast corner on the roof. I know Meadowlark looks like a box, but it actually isn't. On the right side, it's angled out as it rises, enough so that from the ground, you can't see Ankh at all. Also, the outside is coated with the same white paint as the roof, except this is see-through paint so we can look out but one can't look in."

"Openness and privacy at once," I said. "Seems a shame it's only for you."

"It's fun to be the guru," he said. "But you know what else is fun? A private detective pretending to be a reporter."

I took another sip of the tea and said nothing.

"Of course I know your little secret. There is nothing that happens inside this building that escapes me, even when I was in Mumbai. I don't care about your ruse because our motives are aligned."

He pushed the gray folder towards me.

"This was why Dharma put on his show just now," I said. "A distraction."

"Dharma made his willing sacrifice," Krishvananda said. "What you will find in that folder are financial documents that show some rather creative lending between Llewellyn and Krishna in the last twenty years. Highly questionable transactions, quite possibly illegal. Krishna is a non-profit, and Llewellyn is an educational institution, and they have been commingling their assets without the knowledge of either board, to make up for their budget shortfalls. In short, they have been cooking the books. Those documents, Siobhan, will give you leverage over Vera Wheeler and Michelle West, the two who are doing everything they can to ruin what I have built here."

"And you're doing all this just to help me out," I said, doubtfully.

"You still have contacts in the media. Once you verify what I've purported here, I'm certain you'll do the right thing. You were a reporter once. Your moral compass hasn't changed direction."

"And you get to bring down Krishna once more so you can pick it back up."

"It's not that simple, but it can be. As long as we deal in plain facts instead of lies. Do you know what bothers me most about all this anti-aging initiative at Krishna and Llewellyn? It's just another gateway to push drugs and surgery when there is a better path."

"Amrita."

Krishvananda beamed his winning smile once more. "You *have* been paying attention. I want to show you, Siobhan," he said. He reached out with his beautiful hands, palms open. "Will you allow me?"

And now here was that mischief at full power. I knew this was bad news, I knew *he* was bad news, but my body wanted it. My body wanted *him*, I could feel it, the tingling, the itch, the ache. It would be so easy to give in to him, just take two steps forward and let him take me away. My desire for him grew hard in my bones, primal and nasty and dirty and hot.

I took the folder and ran down the stairs as fast as I could. Thrust back into the darkness of the maze, bumping against its supple walls, I heard Krishvananda's laughter fading behind me.

71

No wonder he'd had the whole place following him like a god back in the day. As I rode the elevator down to the third floor, I still felt Krishvananda's pull on me. That guy—that guy was dangerous.

Back in my room, I opened the folder he'd given me and looked through the sheaf of spreadsheets and statements, all of it beyond my level of comprehension, but I knew Stacy could tell me if there was any truth of what Krishvananda had alleged, and Craig would be able to determine the legal implications. Moving large chunks of cash around was never a good sign, so if that indeed turned out to be the case, we were probably talking about jail time for a few unlucky scapegoats.

And one scapegoat in particular caught even my numerically neophyte eye—Vachess Holdings, which came up over and over again throughout the sheaf of documents. I flipped back to my notes and saw that Christopher's parents ran a hedge fund. Universities and colleges often employed hedge funds to enrich their endowments.

Helping Christopher's parents so they could stay.

A quick Google search brought the serious faces of Brandon and Sabine Vachess from their website, standing together with their arms folded in front of what looked like a classic rich-person's office, a huge dark mahogany desk and an Old Master painting on the wall. Their "About" page listed their clients, and both Llewellyn and Krishna were on there.

There was a knock on my door.

"Good evening, Siobhan!" The ever bubbly Cynthia Bard. "I was afraid maybe you'd left already."

I glanced at my watch—five o'clock. I'd asked for a late check-out but I'd blown even the extended deadline.

"I was supposed to be out of this room two hours ago. I'm sorry."

"Oh please, don't be. In fact, I'm so glad you're still here, because I'd like to show you something. May I?"

After fighting off Krishvananda and his sexy Jedi mind tricks, what I wanted more than anything was to take a little solitary breather, like just close my eyes and conk out for half an hour or something, but duty called.

"Of course," I said, and followed her out.

"We're not going far, just back to the Sunrise Room."

Following the Dharma show, there were still a few objects askew in the main hallway, a couple of chairs facing the wrong way, a sheet of paper peeking underneath the curtains. Cynthia saw it and picked it up immediately.

"I know I've already said it, but it really isn't usually like this. Between the food poisoning last night and the police chase this morning, it must seem like Krishna's a center of bedlam."

"I'm fully aware these are extenuating circumstances," I said. "You really don't have to worry about me writing about any of this." Really, she didn't.

"That is so very gracious of you, and we at Krishna thank you from the bottom of our hearts for your understanding. And as a gesture of our gratitude, I'd like to offer you something that shows us in a more positive, forward-thinking light."

She opened the door to the Sunrise Room and the enormous banner on the wall behind the lectern:

THE NEXT ONE HUNDRED YEARS
THE FANTASTIC FUTURE OF KRISHNA

"It's time that we shared our concepts with the rest of the world in the most impactful manner," another voice said behind me. It belonged to Michelle West, who strode forward with an outreached hand. "So nice to finally meet you properly, Siobhan."

I'd seen her when I'd encountered Wheeler, but only briefly. She was about my age, her wavy brunette hair salted with strands of gray. In a tight black pantsuit with sharp creases, she had the air of someone who told people what to do and relished doing so.

"It's very impressive," I said, wondering why West was being so cordial. I'd thought by this time, Wheeler would've told her I wasn't a journalist at all—unless, of course, that she and West weren't close at all, just using one another.

"We'd originally scheduled this presentation for next week for our board members and trustees, but we pushed it up a week to tomorrow morning. I know you were ready to leave today, but would you do us the honor of sticking around one more day? You'd be our guest, of course, and since you're already all packed up, I'd like to offer you a room in Javani, the new, green-certified annex of ours."

As bribery-y and pleasant as that sounded, I felt I'd gotten what I needed and it was time to move on.

"Look," West said. "Can I level with you?"

"Please do," I said.

"I know you met with Krishvananda. I know he's here. I've known it since the day he slithered back into the building."

"I overheard you talking with Cleo Park and Vera Wheeler. By the statue. You feigned ignorance…"

"…for Vera's benefit. The less she knows about Krishvananda, the better."

"So his secret hideout up there isn't much of a secret."

She laughed. "Let's just say we have hospitality go up there once a week to change his sheets and empty the garbage."

"And you accept his presence because he still wields power over a number of Krishna devotees."

"At this point, our relationship is less like a treaty, more like a cease-fire. Kicking him out would cause more problems than it would solve."

Cynthia cleared her throat. "Michelle, I believe two of our board members are waiting in the lobby for us?"

West clapped her hands. "Thank you, Cynthia. Siobhan, the four of us will be dining tonight at Iron, a lovely restaurant in the city center, and we'd be honored if you were to join us."

It was almost six o'clock now and the prospect of driving for the next three hours didn't seem too appealing. But then again, being stuck at a restaurant with these two people plus another two, all of them barraging me with anti-Krishvananda propaganda, didn't feel so hot, either. But maybe I'd learn something that would help me with my case, and I would be able to get a good night's sleep for an early departure tomorrow morning. There was no way in hell I was gonna stick around for another useless presentation, but they didn't have to know that.

72

The board members were a silver-haired couple, Nolan and Cressida Brooks, bluebloods to the core. Three times in our two-hour conversation, they mentioned their son was at Harvard. But in their youth, they'd been wild and crazy kids, some of the earliest disciples of Krishvananda at the Krishna ashram.

What West and Cynthia wanted me to hear was from primary sources on the other side, and as expected, the Brooks' stories were not flattering of the experience. In fact, they sounded borderline criminal. The disciples who broke the rules—which could be as innocuous as kissing another member or drinking a cup of coffee—were "disciplined" by having to keep a yoga pose for hours at a time. It reminded me of stress positions, what is used in modern "enhanced interrogation" techniques. Repeat offenders were kept in pitch-black rooms for days, a way to purify their desires, and of course, while the disciples were struggling to maintain their ascetic lives, Krishvananda had at least six girls he banged regularly.

"Yes, he did marry one of them, that is true," Nolan Brooks said. "But that was because he was painted into a corner. He married her to save face. They divorced not even a year later."

I nodded and jotted down notes into my notepad. I didn't doubt that these things happened, but I couldn't see how any of this was going to get me closer to Penny. Except I *did* know. Time to rattle the cage a bit.

"Krishvananda mentioned something about loans between Krishna and Llewellyn College. Would you guys know anything about that?"

If the Brooks had been involved, they were master actors, because it was news to them. West, on the other hand, wore a fake smile that put the Joker to shame.

"Michelle?" I asked. "Have you heard about this?"

"Just sounds like more deflection," she said, but she sounded neither convinced nor convincing. "I'm sorry, guys, but I need to take care of some stuff back at the office. I need to call it a night."

Sitting in my fancy-schmancy room in the Javani building, I put my feet up on the ottoman and took in the moonlight. It was quite soothing here, the walls painted a pale green, wooden blinds on the window, a flare lamp that washed a soft light over the room. A speaker embedded into the ceiling could be hooked into a phone or play New Age music, so I chose the latter, tranquil electronica flowing forth from the grille.

My only regret of the evening was that I hadn't brought up the loans earlier so I wouldn't have had to slog through their pitch, but no matter. Now that I was alone and had a few hours before turning in for the night, I had the time the space to think this case through. It hadn't been quite two weeks yet since I started a search for Penny, but it felt longer. Ed had told me about a missing persons case that took him three years to solve, having to travel to three countries to finally find the man who had changed his name, his Social Security number, and even his face. I didn't have three years. From what Josie had warned me of Penny's disease, I barely had three weeks.

I sat at the desk and turned on my laptop. I placed my notes around it. My mind was clear and focused. And of course, my phone rang. It was a number I didn't recognize.

"Siobhan?"

"Yes?"

"It's me, Beaker. You remember me, right?"

Dance music with heavy bass drowned out his words. "Of course. I can't quite hear you because of all the noise. Can you either speak louder or…" A few seconds later, Beaker came back on the line, with the music more muted.

"I'm sorry, there's a house party still going here and it's kind of crazy. There was also an ambulance here, and that sort of stuff turns a party even crazier."

"Did somebody get hurt?"

"No, well, yes. I'm calling about Christopher. He's here."

"If you handcuff him to a radiator, I'll pay you a thousand dollars."

"The ambulance was for him. He took a fistful of pills, but luckily it was mostly my allergy meds, which apparently you can't OD on. So he's okay, but they just took him to Athena General. He's staying there for at least a couple of days for observation. It's really fucked up, what he tried to do. He was kinda drunk, but I didn't…nobody expected him to pull something like this."

"Thanks, Beaker. But you know, I did ask you to call me as soon as you saw him."

"I was gonna, I swear," he said. Just like that, he turned from a concerned adult to a pleading teenager, which I suppose he still technically was. "He came in yesterday but I had two prelims plus a twenty-pager for my lit class so I didn't even see him until this afternoon."

I thanked him and hung up.

I was exhausted, and could have used a few hours in a bed, but Christopher was the key to finding Penny. I'd already lost him once, and this time, I wasn't going to fuck it up.

73

I got behind the wheel under the starry night sky, about to crank my engine but stopped when I heard singing. Or, more accurately, chanting.

I ducked down in my seat and rolled down my passenger side window, as the noise had come somewhere behind me, getting closer.

Two figures made their way from the Meadowlark building, dressed in matching all-white robes. The material was something shiny, like silk or nylon. Under the full moon, they glowed like a pair of ghosts.

From their high voices and their lithe body shapes, I was reasonably sure they were women. They walked holding hands. One of them held a phone with its flashlight on, using it to illuminate their path.

They were coming right for my car. I slunk down even farther. They passed me and headed for the trees.

My phone chirped, a text from Annabelle Wolinsky, the Housewife of the Gold Coast that I'd met at the Krishna anti-aging seminar:

you want2c amrita
you want2b at parking lot
follow robes

Visiting hours at the hospital weren't for another ten hours, so I had time. I got out my flashlight from my glove box, zipped up my windbreaker, and quietly exited the car.

Following the two ladies was easy, as they continued to chant and also kept their light on. I gave them a good lead.

"Ooooom-ma, oom-ma," they sang in unison. They did not hesitate at all as they made their way through the path, which meant they'd done this before. After they walked under a fallen tree and around another one, I realized we were on the same trail as the one Dharma had taken me a couple days ago, the one that lead to Ondaga Plain. Sure enough, the ladies, like the way Dharma had disappeared before me, slipped through the thicket of hollies.

Crickets chirped and an owl hooted into the darkness. The yellow moon had risen high in the clear night sky. As I followed the chants of the two women, their singing joined up with others. It was a chorus, and their collective voices rose as the wind picked up, and as the wind died down, so did their pretty, creepy melody.

A fire glowed from afar. Ondaga Plain was about the size of a football field, and whatever was happening was all the way on the other side. I kept along the edge of the surrounding forest to give myself cover, in case there were eyes looking out for curious passersby like myself. No longer under the thickly populated pines, the ladies in front of me didn't need their flashlight anymore, and neither did I. All of us could have just followed the scent of burning wood, which grew stronger as we approached the dancing flames.

This was no mere bonfire—the giant pit that contained the blaze was large enough to sacrifice virgins. I remembered seeing lines of rocks along the periphery of the plain when I was here with Dharma, so somebody, most likely a whole bunch of somebodies, must've moved them with great, sweat-producing effort to create this elaborate circle. Because of the sheer size of the inferno, my eyes took a bit to adjust seeing what lay beyond.

The two figures I'd been following were now almost directly in front of the flames, and they stepped out of their robes and let them fall to the ground. They were indeed women and of a certain age, because their breasts and behinds were a testament to the constant pull of gravity. The two took an exaggerated bow then separated, one going around the flame to the left, the other to the right. I took a few steps back into the forest because at this distance from the fire, I needed more cover. I ducked under a pair of low-hanging branches, scampered around a fallen log, and hid behind a nice big tree trunk.

After the two women I'd followed took their places, nine naked women sat in a semicircle around the fire, their bodies swaying rhythmically to the same chanting I'd heard before, "Ooooom-ma, oom-ma." On a raised stage in front of the flames, Krishvananda sat cross-legged in a comfortable pair of gold-fabric pajamas, mumbling something unintelligible. No surprise that the women took off their clothes while he stayed fully clothed—this kind of power trip was right up his alley.

You never knew when weird shit like this could come in handy. I started recording video on my phone and pointed the lens at the spectacle unfolding in front of me.

I recognized one of the nude women: Annabelle. Like her reconstituted face, the rest of her body featured strategic nips and tucks. If there was one part that was spectacular, it was her ass, as round and firm as a twenty-year-old's. How much was flesh, how much silicone?

Annabelle knelt in front of Krishvananda with a wide white bowl in her hands, placing the dish under his mouth. His chanting rose to a higher pitch. Like a conductor orchestrating his musicians, all the ladies followed his lead, the chorus gaining urgency. Some raised their arms and waved while others flailed their limbs, as if their bodies were out of control. Somewhere in the distance, a wolf let out a primal howl. Krishvananda opened his mouth and a pale golden liquid started to seep out, drip over his chin, and fall into the dish that Annabelle held.

Amrita. Had to be. It wasn't saliva because the liquid ran down with hardly any viscosity. Since he'd been chanting, there's no way he could've held that liquid in his mouth. I wouldn't have believed it if I wasn't seeing it with my own eyes.

Behind Krishvananda, a tenth woman emerged. She must've been lying down behind the raised stage because a moment ago, she hadn't been there. While Krishvananda kept spewing his elixir, she stood upright in all her glorious nakedness. Cleo Park, in the buff, not one extra cell of fat on her body. It was like looking at a Photoshopped photograph, a physically perfect female specimen. Even with the world's best nutritionists and personal trainers and plastic surgeons, it wasn't natural for someone almost fifty to look like this. Older people in the best shape of their lives were still sinewy, the passage of time impossible to mask. She should've looked more like Annabelle, her body an unwilling map to the years of her life. So what did this mean—that the effects of amrita were real?

Krishvananda closed his mouth. Annabelle gave the dish to Cleo, who put it to her lips and drank. I had to suppress an involuntary gag—that was like swallowing someone else's spit, but I guess this was the disgusting price of everlasting youth. "Ooooom-ma, oom-ma," the crowd kept chanting.

It was at this unfortunate moment that my phone rang, my ringtone of New Order's "Blue Monday" blaring out its techno beats. I fumbled for the Do Not Disturb button, but it was too late. Cleo stopped her imbibing and all eyes turned toward the source of the noise. A pair of very bright flashlights, the kind that you see advertised in gun magazines as military-grade, almost blinded me.

"Stop!" somebody yelled. Since Cleo was partaking in the festivities, most likely it was one of her Seven Star Mob guards. I had no desire to confirm that in person, so I sprinted through the woods. With their brilliant illumination behind me, it was easy to retrace my steps, but the forest was full of stuff that could trip you, which almost happened twice. Visions of falling down and cracking my head against a tree invaded my brain, but I shook them off and kept my eyes focused on the ground.

White lights of civilization, the tall lamps in the parking lot, peeked through the pine trees. The beams of the flashlights behind me had receded to some degree, but they were still coming. As my tired legs and spent lungs started their earnest complaint, I considered my options. I could run back into the Meadowlark building to try to lose the guards, but that's also where there were even more guards and they'd probably already radioed ahead. No, the simplest choice was the best choice here. I was already packed, my car ready to go, so I pumped my legs and made my final push, out of the trail and onto the asphalt. I yanked my keys from the pocket of my pants, pushed on the fob, and dashed to my black Accord. I hazarded a glance back, and there they were, two of the Mob, in their usual white turtleneck and black slacks, the scariest looking waiters in the universe. Even though they all looked like clones, the one on the left was as tall as Beaker and galloped toward me like Usain Bolt.

I threw open my car door and jumped in, cranking the engine, whose rise and hum had never sounded sweeter. As I peeled off, I caught the human gazelle in my rearview mirror, close enough to my car to jump on it. He looked like the kind of guy who might do just that, clamp onto my roof with his vice-like grip, but instead, he reached for something in his pocket. A gun? No, a phone. To take a picture of my license plate.

74

I got to my office by 3 a.m. I managed to fall asleep on the couch, but by seven, the room was bathed in full sunlight and I woke up with a crick in my neck and a cramp in my leg.

I made a cup of coffee from the Keurig and felt slightly more alive. I picked up the financial statements Krishvananda had given me and stared at the columns and rows of tiny numbers. They seemed innocuous enough, official-looking digits with accounting labels like *capital depreciation*, *net cash flow*, and *EBITDA*. I emailed Stacy and asked her if she had time today to look it over, telling her to consult with Craig on anything.

I flipped through my snail mail: junk, junk, junk, bills, bills, bills, and then a package from Keeler, the test tube I'd had him put through forensics, the one I'd found in Christopher's desk. Perfect, as it would save me a trip to the police station because I wanted to ask Christopher about it in person.

I fished out my toiletries from my suitcase and walked over to the bathroom in the hallway, where I washed my face and brushed my teeth. Nothing like cold water and mint to start the day off right. My t-shirt and jeans felt a bit lived-in, but they were gonna have to do as everything else in that suitcase was in worse shape. On the way back to my office, I walked beyond mine to Craig's. Looking through the window on his door, I imagined him in his chair, hunched over his desk. He really came through for me while I was sick at Krishna; I owed him one.

The sun lasted just long enough to wake me up, as the skies turned gray by the time I got back out to my car. Another fine Athena overcast day, at your service.

Driving to the hospital to see Christopher, I thought about how I was going to approach him. The first and only time I'd talked to him, he'd run away crying. Hyper-sensitive, that was the word Beaker had used to describe him. Screw it, how about if I just go for broke this time, put the fear of god in him, tell him he's in a world of trouble, that he's an accessory to a kidnapping and could be tried for manslaughter. But then again, Beaker did tell me he tried to kill himself, so that was probably a terrible idea.

It was times like these that I missed Ed the most, having someone with the knowledge and experience to give me guidance, or if not that, just to be able to bounce off some ideas. I imagined his deep voice speaking to me, as he often had across the car seat. A lot of our detective work was spent in cars, though our positions would've been reversed, with me in the passenger seat while Ed was behind the wheel.

It never hurts to triangulate.

Christopher, Penny, and Grace. Three people, three sides, a triangle. Beaker had said Christopher dated Penny during the summer. Grace and Penny then become BFFs, until something happens and Penny disappears. That's what it looks like, after the fact. But what about before the fact? What if…?

After parking my car in the visitors' lot of Athena General, I called Beaker on his cell. He picked up on the fourth ring.

"It's way too early to be calling a college student," he said.

"I need you to check something for me. I assume you are friends with Christopher on Facebook, but what about Grace?"

"You called me to see whether I was Facebook friends with Grace Park?"

"Yes."

"I have no idea. Probably. You want me to check?"

"Might as well make this huge inconvenience worth something, right?"

Beaker did not find this funny, but he did bring up Facebook and confirm their friendship. I asked him where Grace went to high school.

"Exeter."

"That's not where Christopher went, I gather."

"No. Are you trying to compare two Facebook profiles, to see the commonalities? Because that can be done like really easily with code a buddy of mine wrote. I'm a beta tester."

"This sounds infinitely better than asking you to eyeball it."

"Computers were born to do stuff like this. Hold on. For this, I gotta get on my laptop. I'll put you on speaker."

A flurry of clicks and clacks later, he said: "Looks like Dinesh—that's my friend who's worked with me on this—added a whole new functionality since I saw this last. Now this thing even compares if there are any photos where people may appear together through a facial recognition engine. I'm sending you a screen capture of the earliest match."

A few seconds later, Beaker's email buzzed on my phone.

"If I click on this, I won't lose you, right?"

"Of course not," Beaker said, sounding like the exasperated tech-savvy kid that he was.

The photo that came across was not digital, at least not in its initial incarnation; it had the low-quality, washed-out look of a scanned print. Four kids wearing their Sunday best were in the picture, standing in front of an old, gray-bricked church. Seven, eight? Probably about that age. Two on the left, a boy and a girl, were in each other's arms, hugging and smiling: Christopher and Grace, more than a decade ago.

75

Since Christopher had attempted suicide, the chances of me waltzing right in and seeing him probably weren't good. So when the receptionist at the lobby of Athena General asked who I was, I said, "I'm his sister."

"Umm…his *sister*?" she asked.

Perfect. Time for some racial shaming.

"Yes," I said. "Adopted sister." Then I added with the kindest smile, "I was there when he was born."

"Oh. Of course. I'm so sorry."

I handed her my driver's license.

"But your name here is…"

"That's right," I said. "I'm married to a lovely Irish gentleman. I changed my name to Siobhan because my Korean name is Shee-Bong. Sounds kind of like Siobhan, doesn't it?"

Never hurts to throw in a pinch of truth into a stew of lies. The receptionist, tired of being confused and humiliated, told me to go up to the second floor and follow the signs for Room 106.

The hallways here were labyrinthine but well-marked. Christopher's room was located in the new wing, the walls stenciled with inspiring quotes around every corner: Helen Keller, Florence Nightingale, Mother Theresa, Nelson Mandela, the usual suspects. The last one before 106 was by Mahatma Gandhi, who said, "You must be the change you wish to see in the world." How did these people come up with these wise tidbits about life? Did they sit in a room with a notepad with the intention of cranking out a few bon mots, like they scheduled it into their daily planner? Were there terrible ones they bunched up and tossed in the trash? When they got frustrated, did they write down a page full of curse words or doodle rude sketches of anatomical body parts?

Christopher's door was half open, but I knocked anyway. No answer, so I knocked louder. Still nothing. I let myself in. He was asleep. Underneath the white sheets with his hands balled next to his face, he looked even younger than his twenty-one years, especially now that he had shaved off the goatee. There was a closet next to the bathroom, so I peeked; just his t-shirt and pants were hanging in there. I fished his wallet out of his pants pocket and had a look-see. Twenty-two dollars in cash, a Visa card, an ATM card, his driver's license, school ID. The days of finding clues in wallets were long gone. What I should get instead was his phone.

It was on his nightstand, face down against the fake wood. It was PIN-protected, so I opened up my own phone to see some bits of information I'd gathered. His birthday was December 12th, so I punched in 1212 and was not surprised to be let in. I clicked on his phone icon and checked out his recent calls, inbound and outbound. The last call he'd made was to a contact named Grace, made last evening at 7:13 p.m. The call lasted forty-seven seconds, so a brief conversation or a message.

"What are you doing?" Christopher asked.

"What it looks like," I said.

He held out a hand. I gave him his phone.

"How did you find me?"

"I told you," I said. "I'm a detective. This is my job. I actually get paid for this."

"Beaker," he said.

"Well yeah," I said, "that too."

This is all that I'd said to him, but he was already crying. Not hard, but wow, did tears ever fall easily for this guy. I picked up the box of Kleenex sitting next to him and pulled off a few to get him started.

"You know, he's like the best friend I have."

"Maybe that's why he called me, because he cares about you and thinks that I can help."

This made him cry in earnest. Was I going to have to start telling jokes or something? I didn't quite know what to do with my hands. Throw them up in the air? Punch him in the face? Punch myself in the face? All of these alternatives seemed better than what I was doing now, which was nothing.

"I've been looking for you ever since you left Krishna," I said.

"I understand," he said.

A nurse knocked on the door and entered, a slim black woman with a sunny smile.

"Good morning, Christopher," she said. She had a Caribbean accent.

"Hello, Elsie."

She looked over his chart. "How nice for you to have a visitor already."

"I'm Siobhan, Chris's sister," I said.

Elsie placed the chart back in its slot and came over to shake my hand. "I didn't know you had a sister who lived nearby."

If Christopher wanted to get rid of me, it'd be easy. All he'd have to do was tell Elsie the truth. But he said nothing and stared out the window instead, his eyes on the giant weeping willow in the distance, watching its wispy branches sway in the breeze.

"Thank you for taking such good care of him," I said.

"Of course. Breakfast will be arriving soon, and I'll be by later to check in, love."

Christopher remained silent after she was gone. I took out my phone and brought up the Facebook photo Beaker had sent me.

He glanced at it, and of course, it made him weep. I waited. He blew his nose again, then sat up in bed and propped his pillows against his back.

"Okay," Christopher said. "That's enough tears for one day."

I patted him on the shoulder. "Why did you try to kill yourself last night?"

He cleared his throat. We locked eyes. Can you guess what happened next?

I waited until he stopped crying.

"I'm afraid something terrible has happened to Penny, and it's all my fault. All my doing."

"What did you do?"

"I got her pregnant."

I remembered that short story of Penny's that Hajira related to me had some seriously deranged parts with a baby.

"It happens," I said.

"No, I *made* it happen. I poked holes in the condoms every time we had sex, and we had sex a lot. Until she got knocked up."

I stared at Christopher for a good five seconds. Had I underestimated him, what he's capable of?

"It was your idea?"

"Grace's. But I still did it."

"You don't seem like a guy…"

"…who could do something so terrible?"

I nodded.

Christopher looked like he was about to burst into tears again, so I asked before I'd lose him to another deluge, "This has to do with your parents, doesn't it? Their financial involvement with Llewellyn and Krishna."

Something clicked loose in him. I've seen this behavior before from people harboring secrets who are ready to let it go: a profound sense of relief.

"You know, when I think back to how this started, I almost want to laugh, because it doesn't make any sense. How could something as simple as my father asking me about my childhood friend Grace end up *here*?"

That's exactly how it began, according to Christopher. His parents made a terrible bet with some risky investments, and when the losses in Llewellyn's endowment got heavy, they made the even bigger mistake of using their own assets to try to recover. When Christopher's dad realized that Grace was going to be attending Llewellyn, he desperately hoped it was a way for him to make contact with the Parks for a possible cash infusion.

"I hadn't talked to Grace for years, but we'd always gotten along and it shocked and saddened me to see the person she had become, mostly because of her mother. And father, too, by his absence. He's never been there for her, so all she's got is her mother, but not really. Grace was depressed, away from home, and I was there for her…and when I told Grace that my family's got money issues, she comes up with this crazy idea that's going to solve both of our problems. Of course we were drunk off our asses when she proposed her plan, laughing ourselves sick, but then the more we talked about it later…the less outlandish it seemed. You have to understand, her mom Cleo is a master manipulator, and there's no one she manipulates better than her own daughter. That woman isn't capable of giving love. The only person she loves is herself."

"I get that but what I don't understand…*Grace* wanted to you to get Penny pregnant…for *Cleo*? Why would *Penny* getting pregnant help Grace with her mother?"

Christopher closed his eyes and sank deeper into his pillow. He probably wished he would fall in and disappear altogether.

I held the test tube I'd found in his room for him to see.

"Was this part of it?"

I put it in his palm. He pinched it between his thumb and index finger and gazed at it.

"Trace amounts of semen were found in there," I said.

"Mine. Grace wanted to make sure I was healthy, that I wasn't shooting blanks, or something. She was so scared—she'd told her mother already, and if this didn't work, if I couldn't get Penny pregnant…"

I held his gaze and held my silence, willing him to go on.

"I didn't know. You have to understand that I didn't know, not until later. That Cleo wanted…what remained."

"Remained after what?"

"The abortion," Christopher said.

I pulled the chair by his bed and sat down.

"Let me get this straight. You're telling me that Cleopatra Park wanted the *fetus*? For what?"

"I don't know! I didn't ask, okay? I didn't want to know, I just wanted to help Grace."

"And why would a doctor…"

"The doctor who performed her abortion was someone President Wheeler knew. I think he also worked for Park Industries."

Wheeler. Of course she was involved; she had to be. She must've known her school was running out of money. I thought she was a little nuts, but it looked like I'd vastly underestimated her nuttiness.

"Why Penny?" I asked. "Why did you choose her?"

"Korean blood. That's what Grace's mother told her, that she wanted Korean blood. Penny and Grace were the only two Korean freshpersons this year. And since there is no way she'd let Grace get pregnant…"

I didn't know what to say. All of this sounded so ludicrous, and yet here we were.

"It's all fucked anyway. The bank foreclosed our house last week."

Helping Christopher's parents so they could stay, Grace had said when I'd trapped her in the hospital bathroom.

"How did Penny find out about all this?"

"The doctor told her exactly what was going on with, you know, the remains."

"Why would he do that?"

"The only explanation Grace and I came up with is that Wheeler told the doctor this was all on the up and up, that Penny was being paid. I don't know, there was so much screaming and shouting at that point. I tried to calm her down by coming clean and telling her everything, and goodness, was that ever the wrong thing to do. As far as she was concerned, I was a part of the whole plan, and you know what? She's right. I fucked her and I fucked her over. I'm a horrible, terrible human being."

"Excuse me," Elsie said. She was standing by the door, holding a cafeteria tray.

I rose from the bedside. "Hello, Elsie."

"Are you okay, Christopher?"

He turned away and wept into his pillow.

"He's just going through some stuff," I said.

"His attending physician will be coming in shortly," she said. She put the tray down on the nightstand then left the room.

"Thank you," I told Christopher. "It wasn't easy, what you just said."

"I'm so ashamed."

"Just a few more questions. Are you okay to answer?"

"I'll try."

"How did you know Penny was taken to Krishna?"

"I have a friend there, Dido…"

"…blue hair, we've met. What happened to Penny after you arrived at Krishna to settle her down? Where did she go?"

He shrugged. "I wish I knew. She was already gone."

We both turned to the knocking sound against his door. Stethoscope around the neck, a white coat, a serious face: the doctor.

"I'll let you know when I find her."

Christopher nodded. I left.

76

In the hospital parking lot, I sat in my Accord and watched the comings and goings of cars. A waifish man, looking young enough to have just received his license, got into the black sedan sitting opposite me. He closed his eyes and looked utterly spent, and when he opened them again, he saw me staring at him. He averted his gaze immediately, perhaps embarrassed at me catching him at a vulnerable moment. He pulled out.

A white SUV took his place. The husband got out and hurried over to help his wife, who looked super pregnant. But she still insisted on carrying her purse, much to the chagrin of her husband. I could see this was an argument they had often, and not even an argument at this point, more like an inside joke. They made their way to the hospital entrance, holding hands.

Every car in this parking lot was owned by a person, and each person possessed their own personal history. This was life, and it was exhausting. Or maybe it was just me who was exhausted, running short on sleep and overwhelmed by what Christopher had just told me.

Poor Penny. Getting pregnant, having an abortion, and then finding out your best friend and your boyfriend were not who you thought they were. No wonder she went bonkers—a lot of people would.

Now that I was armed with Penny's unfortunate story, what next? As much as I wanted to confront Wheeler, I wasn't going to get anywhere with her. After spending time in Krishna, the weak link in the chain seemed obvious: fragile Dr. Christine Collins, Assistant Professor of Chemistry at Llewellyn and Wheeler's lackey.

I opened up the Llewellyn app on my phone. I remembered seeing two addresses for some of the faculty, and it was the case with Collins. Underneath her school office was her home address, right in the town of Selene. Because it was Monday, the chances of her being back from Krishna were high. The app, in its all-knowingness, made it super simple to see her classes and office hours. She taught her first class at 4 p.m., so it made more sense to go to her house first.

I punched Collins's address into my GPS and drove north on Route 90 under the steel-wool gray skies that threatened rain then made good on its promise. Halfway there, an apocalyptic deluge of a shower pelted my windshield and roof, and it was good to hear that drumming around me. The world could use a little washing now and then.

By the time I got to Selene, the rain had petered out to a mist. I parked off-street and walked up the red-bricked path to Collins's yellow house with black shutters, a modest bungalow with a front porch complete with a hammock. I rang the doorbell.

The front door didn't have any windows, but there were two long translucent pieces of stained glass flanking it, and behind the flowery designs I made out a figure methodically making her way toward the door.

"I know you're there, Christine," I blurted out.

Like a deer caught in headlights, frozen, not a sound.

"You've got a class to teach at four. I'll just get in the hammock and be all nice and relaxed by the time you come out. Is that what you want?"

"I'll call the police," she squeaked.

"What, because I'm trespassing? Fine. I'll go back to my car on the street and wait there."

Her silence telegraphed her mulling it over. She opened the door, but just a crack.

"What do you want?"

"A chat."

"I have nothing to say. If you have any questions, you can contact Llewellyn's Media Relations department."

"Oh, I see. So if I were to call up Media Relations and ask about the missing student at Llewellyn who got knocked up and had an abortion performed by an alumnus doctor, who then took that aborted fetus and…"

The door swung wide open. Collins leaned against the frame for support. She was a pale person to begin with, but now she looked positively ashen.

"Thank you," I said, and strode through.

As soon as I got into her house, I regretted it immediately.

If it was possible for a person to explode, Collins would've gone off like a geyser. She resembled a desperate tweaker right now, her eyes darting back and forth, her fingers strumming an invisible instrument. Not great. In fact, possibly dangerous. Collins slammed the door closed and threw the deadbolt. My mind sped through an inventory of my purse. My mace. I've never used it, and never did I think someone smaller in stature than I would be my first victim, but here we were, two small women facing each other in the foyer with its umbrella can and an embroidered Home Sweet Home sign hanging in a frame.

"It's not right," Collins said. "What you're doing is not right."

"I'm not doing anything," I said. "I'm just telling you what I know."

In her right hand I caught a flash of metal.

77

The knife was the thin filleting kind for gutting fish. It probably did a fine job of gutting humans, too.

Collins took a step towards me, and I took an involuntary step back. This was her house; she knew it inside out, so I was already at a disadvantage. To the left of me was a set of stairs, and to the right was the living room, but this foyer was a cramped space and Collins, in her current unstable disposition, was a jungle cat ready to pounce.

"Are you really going to stab me?" I asked. "Really?"

"I don't know," Collins said. "It's possible. Anything is possible because nothing is possible for me anymore. My life is…my life is over."

I felt something soft behind me—a cushion. I tried to remember what was back there, I didn't dare turn my head because the second I did, I imagined her coming at me like Norman Bates in the shower. A built-in bench, that's what it was, so this must be a seat cushion. Not much of a shield for a knife attack, but better than nothing.

"Christine…please—"

"I'm a chemist, not a zoologist. What the hell do I know about pigs?"

Pigs?

She stared at her knife. "I butchered it. I took it apart. And you, you're making me see it all over again."

I didn't know what she was talking about, but I felt the hairs on my arms standing on end. I had to get her to talk rationally here, or else she really was going to cut me. Think fast, Siobhan. She's a woman of science.

"What was the medical basis for your actions?" I asked.

Maybe it was just the weirdness of the question itself, but it did take Collins out of whatever violent spell she was under. "I suppose it sounded convincing enough, going beyond the placenta or the amniotic fluid, which we were already researching to create serums and creams…"

"So on a scientific level…"

And that was all the time I was gonna be able to buy, because Collins slapped her empty hand against her thigh. "No, no, no! I was weak, I was scared, I don't know what's right or wrong anymore. And I don't care. I don't care what the fuck —"

Ding-dong!

Collins fell to immediate silence when the doorbell rang. We stared at each other. I slowly shook my head and shrugged, letting her know this was not what I'd expected, either.

Ding-dong!

And now there was a different noise, something metallic and mechanical at the door. We both watched as the deadbolt was thrown back into its unlocked position. The door opened. White turtleneck, black slacks: Brent Kim.

"Good morning," he said.

"Good morning," we both echoed.

He moved like a dancer, as he always did, gliding across the foyer in a relaxed, easy fashion. Collins, remembering that she had the knife, raised it up to her chest, like a boxer ready for a fight.

Kim held out his right hand, an open palm. "Christine, your knife. Please."

He could've said, "Twinkle twinkle little star," and Collins would've relinquished her knife just the same. Shorn of her blade, Collins fell to the floor and sobbed. I helped her up to the bench because, well, she looked so pathetic down there. I placed the cushion, the one I'd considered using to parry her shivving a minute ago, behind her back. Collins took the other cushion and hugged it like a stuffed animal. She closed her eyes and rocked back and forth.

"I don't know what that was about," Kim said, "so let's move on."

"How did you find me?" I asked.

"One of my associates captured your license plate last night. You're quite a runner from what they tell me."

"You weren't there at Ondaga Plain?"

"No," he said. "I would've caught you." He wasn't jesting or boasting, it was just a fact to him, and he was probably right.

"So what are you doing here?"

"I'm here to ask you to stop all that you're doing, Ms. O'Brien."

"You're *asking*," I said.

"Yes. Asking for your cooperation. We are aware you are being paid for your services by Ms. Josephine Amber Sykes. We will remunerate you double what she's paying to mitigate any loss of revenue on your part. We understand you are a detective and you wish to resolve your case, but that will no longer be a possibility."

As before, his hyper-civility grated on my nerves. "And if I don't comply?"

Kim clasped his hands together. "I wouldn't recommend it. This comes directly from Mr. Park, and he is not a man you want to refuse."

"So Mr. Park is perfectly fine with a missing sick girl and his wife using unborn babies for her makeovers?"

I knew I was taking a chance here, but it was worth it. I never thought I'd see it, but here it was: the splintering of the Brent Kim façade. For a moment, his glassy, robotic face registered emotion.

"Excuse me?" he said.

"Your turn," I said to Collins.

"Please," she said. "Please just leave me alone."

"Is there any truth to what Ms. O'Brien just said?" Kim said.

The edge in his voice straightened Collins right out. "Not human babies, no. We used pig embryos, oral porcine placental extracts. But we told Cleo they were…"

"*We?*" Kim asked.

"Vera Wheeler and myself." Collins shook her head. "It's all madness. There's no rhyme or reason to anything that was asked of me. The only thing I could have done—should have done—was to say no. But I didn't. I can't lose this job, not after my last..." She didn't say more, but I could infer the rest. Slept with a student, made up some bogus bits on her CV, academic faux pas that derails your career.

"You did all this...to save your job?" I said. "Really?"

"You don't understand," Collins said. "It's incremental, what Vera forced me to do. Cross one line, and the next line becomes easier. Our college is about to go under, it's more than just me, hundreds of people are going to lose their jobs, their healthcare, even their retirement. Vera gave Cleo what she wanted..."

"Not really, though, right? I mean you didn't actually deliver the human fetus."

"No. I guess if there's one thing we did do right, it was that. Cleo had a Park Industries doctor perform the abortion to make sure it was done, but the anti-aging serum that Vera offered her was our proprietary technology, for our eyes only."

"You know that your boss's wife is nuts, right?" I said to Kim. "I mean Wheeler is nuts, too, but it all starts with Cleo."

Kim's robot face was back, but there were now cracks in that emotionless glaze. "That's neither your concern nor mine."

Fatigue. That's what it was. Brent Kim, as close to a Terminator T-1000 as a man can get, was tired. And I just realized why. "Why weren't you at Ondaga Plain last night?"

Breaking of the Kim façade, the sequel. He said nothing, but I felt plenty in that silence. I brought out my phone and queued up the freaky video I'd taken of the amrita ceremony between a meditating Krishvananda and a naked Cleo.

"Why would you, the captain of the bodyguards, the one responsible for the safety and well-being of his boss's wife, choose not to be by her side?" I clicked on the "play" button and turned the volume all the way up. The eerie female chanting turned into a grating metallic cacophony of sound.

"Turn it off," Kim said.

"Maybe because you'd already seen enough of her madness and couldn't subject yourself to one more nutjob outing?"

Instead of grabbing my phone out of my hand and hurling it across the room, which I could feel was what he'd wanted to do, Kim held it and made himself watch the festivities. His eyes never blinked.

He returned my phone. "I assume you're smart enough to share this video with no one."

"It's synced up in the cloud, as is anything that's on my phone," I said. "But no, I didn't email it to TMZ."

"That's not funny," Kim said. "They would pay for this."

"All I care about, Mr. Brent Kim, is finding my client's daughter, who may be in significant physical distress at this point. Everything else is a distraction. The only reason why I'm still pursing all this fucked-up shit is because there's a connection here between this mess and my case. Understand?"

Kim turned away from me and took out his own phone, a white slab encased in a black plastic case. He spoke quietly in Korean, which I knew enough to recognize but not enough to understand. Every time I hear that language, it slathers on a coat of guilt—and I'm not even sure what that guilt is about. A shrink would probably say it goes way deep, all the way to my abandonment by my birth mother. Probably does, but so what? How does recognizing the origin of a certain negative emotion help to alleviate it in the future? The point, the therapist would say, is not to alleviate it but let it pass through you.

Before this could turn out into a full-blown psychoanalysis in my mind, Kim got off the phone.

"Mr. Park would like to see you both," he said. "I will drive you. It's a three-hour trip."

"Doesn't sound like we have a choice," I said.

"You do not," Kim said.

"But I have to teach my class this afternoon," Collins said.

He glanced at his watch, white face and black straps. "You'll be back in time."

"But it's after ten. If it's going to take three hours there and three hours back, how can you say…"

"You have my word that you'll be back in time," Kim said, and that was that. Collins led the way. I followed. We got in his white Mercedes with black seats. What else.

78

Much to Collins' chagrin, we made a pit stop at my office. She and Kim waited in the car while I picked up the financial statements I'd left for Stacy. I was surprised and happy to see Craig, there, too.

"How did your patent hearing go in Albany?" I asked.

"Good, but never mind me and my boring work," he said. "Seems like you made some massive progress since I left you."

"Less skill and more luck, but I'll take it."

Craig pointed out the window at Kim and Collins, who were now standing outside the car, taking in the late morning Athena air.

"I recognize that guy from Krishna," Craig said. "He's very polite."

"He could be the new Ms. Manners. The woman is Christine Collins, a professor at Llewellyn who's had better days than this."

"So you are being chauffeured to…"

"…New York City. Off to meet Won Ho Park, the head honcho of Park Industries. Can't hurt to have hard evidence on hand. So is it indeed fishy, this special relationship between Llewellyn and Krishna?"

"They've been moving liquid assets back and forth for the last two years," Stacy said. "Imagine you have credit card debt between a Visa and a MasterCard and you use those blank checks they send you to alternately pay off the cards each month. The loan never goes away but you still have to pay interest, which still compounds and accrues. Krishna moved their fiscal year-end to the opposite of Llewellyn's, which gave them six months to break apart the transactions. It's actually kind of ingenious."

"And illegal?" I asked Craig.

"Not outright thievery, but both institutions can be held accountable for a number of good faith violations. This will also trigger an IRS investigation for both parties since they are both non-profit entities, and the feds are certain to find even more issues. Stacy and I summarized our findings down to two pages with bullet points. If you give that to anyone who knows anything about financials, they'll get a good read of the situation."

"Vachess Holdings?" I asked.

"The architects of the scheme," Stacy said. "Their fingerprints are everywhere."

"Brandon and Sabine Vachess. A lien was just placed against their business by their bank," Craig said.

"I love you guys," I said.

Stacy opened her arms for a team hug. "Now go get 'em, tiger."

79

Brent Kim drove like the car didn't exist. Or maybe more accurately, I couldn't feel I was in a car. The Mercedes deserved some credit, as its all-leather seats were super plush, plus there was virtually no road noise, and the woody dashboard was a throwback of old tech via high tech, a touchscreen panel that wrapped around the entire length of the dash and simulated analog gauges with such startling clarity that I'd initially thought they were real.

"Nice wheels, Brent," I said.

"Thank you," he said. Not much for conversation. Collins, depressed and tired after trying to kill me, lay on the backseat with her feet drawn in close to her body.

We hit a hundred miles an hour on the New York Thruway at times. After the clock struck noon, Kim took the next service exit and drove up to the McDonald's drive-thru window.

"I will purchase six burgers, three with cheese and three without, plus three small fries and three small Coca-Cola beverages," he spoke into the microphone.

"But I wanted the Chicken McNuggets," I said.

"And a small Chicken McNuggets," he added.

"That was a joke," I said, but he let the order stand.

"I'll eat it if you don't want it," Collins said, rising from her sad slumber. "I like McNuggets."

"Please distribute the meals to yourself and Ms. Collins," Kim said after he picked it up from the window. "Leave one cheeseburger, one hamburger, and one small fry for me."

"Sure, Dad," I said.

It was like the most un-fun road trip ever, but there were few scents more irresistible than fast food from McDonald's. All of us eagerly devoured our burgers and fries.

"You don't look like the type who'd frequent McDonald's," I said to Kim.

"You are correct."

"Pretty good, isn't it?"

"Delicious to a fault," Kim said.

An hour later, we crossed the Hudson River on the brand-new Tappan Zee Bridge—the Mario Cuomo Bridge, actually, but no one will ever call it that, ever—whooshing by the massive metal girders. Kim got on the West Side Highway heading north and we passed the piers off the Hudson River on our right. When he turned right on 57th Street, I glimpsed the green of Central Park peeking through the spaces between buildings. It'd been a few years since I'd been to the Big Apple, and its sheer density never failed to surprise me.

Up ahead was a polished sliver of a skyscraper so tall that I could barely see its top.

"That's where Mr. Park lives?" I asked.

"Central Park Tower," Kim said. "The tallest residential building in the world."

We pulled into an underground garage. As soon as we were out, a valet came scampering from his glass cube to park the car. So this was how the one percent of one percent lived.

Kim led us to the bank of elevators. He hovered a key fob near the panel and it automatically selected P. The one before that was 94, so the penthouse was on the 95h floor.

The double-height foyer featured a wooden staircase that curved up and to the right in an angle imbued with craftsmanship and elegance. Behind the staircase was a window that ran up the length of both floors, the glass revealing the blue and white of the sky. As we ascended the staircase, it was like we were walking up air, like the god who lived in this urban palace.

"Mr. Park is in the Entertainment Room," Kim said. "It's faster to take the elevator."

The doors were gold, and it was all mirrors and gold inside, too.

"Nice digs," I said.

"The fruits of success," Kim said.

"I knew people lived in places like this," Collins said, "but seeing it myself doesn't make it any more real."

At the Entertainment Room, the city fully came into view through floor-to-ceiling windows, the autumnal sprawl of the Central Park trees serving as a base to the jagged skyscrapers beyond. There were six sofas, all white, all leather, and tucked in corners were more sitting areas, square white leather cushions that looked like fat marshmallows stuck together. It was a space large enough to comfortably hold a wedding, but right now, there was only one person, Won Ho Park, who sat on the sofa in the middle of the room wearing a black shirt and white pants, the opposite color scheme of his bodyguards.

Park sat in front of a wooden TV tray table, sipping a glass of red wine.

It was comical to see such an ordinary piece of furniture in a place so extraordinary, especially amid such an impressive collection of artwork. Interspersed throughout the room were sculptures on white pedestals and a few full-sized statues, too. On the opposite side of the wall of windows were paintings by masters like van Gogh and Picasso, originals, no doubt.

Fifteen paintings spanned across the length of the wall. In the center was a Chuck Close, one of his massive black and white photo-realistic headshot paintings from the late 1960's, this one of a hippie girl with straight hair and vacant eyes. Standing here, it was too much to take in—the view, the art, the space. Did Park even see the beauty that surrounded him? My guess was no. After a while, everything falls into the background, even the astonishing.

"Thank you for coming," Park said, rising. The man was as short as I was, but he possessed the voice of a giant, deep and resonant.

"Impressive place you got here," I said.

"If money cannot buy impressive things, it is failing to serve its purpose."

He spoke with a heavy accent, but his English was excellent.

From the handful of photos I'd seen of Park when I was researching Cleo, I knew he was a supremely confident man, but what those photos hadn't picked up was his pervasive intelligence. It was in his eyes, peering at me as if I were an engine to be taken apart and then reassembled, to see how I worked. His cold gaze unnerved me. With his money and power, he could make all of this mess disappear. He could make me and Christine disappear. All the more reasons for me to stay as cool as possible.

"So," I said, then paused for dramatic effect, or at least what I'd hoped was one. "Care to share why you wanted to see us in person?"

"I gauge best when I see people face to face," Park said. "Brent told me you have a video in your possession. I would like to see it."

"Did he also mention this video is backed up on my cloud account?"

"I know you are frightened, Ms. O'Brien," Park said. "You are doing your best to mask it, and I applaud your effort, but the video. Now."

So much for my tough-gal act. I queued it up and handed it to him. Because there was no fabric at all in this room (no curtains, leather couches), the tiny speaker on my phone filled the cavernous space with the chants of last night's participants. Park took a seat and watched from start to finish. If he had a reaction, I wasn't seeing it. Was it because his wife Cleo pulled crap like this in the past and none of this was noteworthy? Or was it because Park was such a disciplined sociopath that nothing bothered him? Either way, I felt uneasy.

"Thank you," Park said, handing back my phone. "Now you, Dr. Collins. You are a professor at Llewellyn College?"

"Yes," Collins said, her voice barely audible. "Assistant Professor."

"Of Chemistry. And Brent tells me you were asked to dissect a porcine fetus, though the organs and such were presented as that of a human. This is true?"

"Yes," Collins said. I didn't think it was possible for her to sound even quieter, but she did.

"And you believe it is my wife who was the cause of this action?"

Collins looked to me, then Brent, then back to Park. If there was a hole, she would've stuck her head in it. But there was no hole.

"I don't know," she said.

Park slowly turned his gaze to Kim, and even though that look wasn't leveled against me, my stomach lurched a little on his behalf.

"I'm sorry, Mr. Park," Brent said. "But she said differently a few hours ago."

Since he did save my life, I chimed in my support. "I heard her, too."

Park pushed his TV tray table aside, rose, and walked over to the windows. The sun slid behind a pocket of clouds and the city turned darker for a moment.

"Dr. Collins, do you know why my wife wanted you to dissect the creature on her behalf?"

"No," Collins said.

"Would you care to make a guess?"

Collins looked like she might pee her pants.

"Because she wants to be young," I said.

Park turned around.

"Time," he said. "The most treasured resource. I may have more money than most people on this planet, but my clock ticks down just the same as everyone else's. As you can see from my home, I value beauty. And beauty is youth. Not entirely, but youth is an automatic kind of beauty, an effortless beauty, and even though my dear Cleopatra has taken to extremes here, I cannot fault her desire to be beautiful. No doubt her actions to achieve that elusive goal are misguided, but she is a living work of art, *my* living work of art. However, her ambition has caused grief to others, which shames me. This Vera Wheeler— even though my daughter is attending Llewellyn, I have never been to the school and have never met its leader. She seems to have made a particular friendship with my wife."

"Her friendship might be with your money," I said. "According to these financial statements, you made a donation to Llewellyn last year?"

"It is possible. I make donations to many charitable and educational causes. If one was made to Llewellyn, most likely it was initiated by my wife."

I located the bullet point Stacy had made for me on the financial statements. "It was for 1.5 million dollars."

"Unless it exceeds a hundred, I do not participate," Park said.

A man's got to have standards, I guess.

"Llewellyn is a debt-ridden institution of higher learning that's being propped up through financial shenanigans with the Krishna Center for Yoga and Wellness. I don't know how much Brent told you about why I'm involved."

"A girl is missing, the daughter of your friend. Brent told me you were causing a fuss, making my wife and my daughter uncomfortable, which is why I wanted you to stop. But I can see you have just cause for your actions, and I am also appreciative that you kept this video to yourself."

Park clapped his hands twice, and through the hallway on the left, another man in the Brent Kim mold appeared. Park spoke in Korean, and the man nodded.

"Will you get the helicopter ready for us, Brent?" Park asked.

Kim nodded and left.

"Helicopter?" Collins asked.

"Brent told me you needed to be back at Llewellyn by 4 p.m. This way, I estimate you will be an hour early. I feel it is time that we reached the bottom of this issue, because this has already been a spectacular waste of my time. It shall take another fifteen minutes for Brent to get the copter ready, so please, look around and enjoy the art."

"Is it okay if I just sit here and wait?" Collins asked.

"You are the driver of your own destiny," Park said.

A Manhattan palace, a helicopter, a man with a $100 million minimum to take action. A woman using pig embryos to stay young.

What world was I in? I couldn't help but laugh.

"What do you find humorous?" Park asked.

"Oh, just life," I said.

"You are Korean, I believe," he said.

"I was adopted," I said. "Back in the old country, I would've been called Shee-Bong."

"Brent tells me you have not been a detective for long."

"I was assisting my boss, the actual detective, but he passed away."

"I am sorry to hear that. But I must correct you, Shee-Bong. You are every bit an actual detective as any I have encountered."

His words touched me more than I thought they would.

"Thank you," I told him.

Kim returned with a black sport coat for Park and told us that the helicopter was ready. He lead us to the elevator, and the four of us rode it up.

I'd seen enough movies to know that helicopters kicked up quite a bit of wind, but goodness, it was like being in a cyclone. It was a huge red, white, and blue thing, with "AW189" embossed on its side. The noise was deafening as we neared the spinning blades. I shielded my eyes to keep the debris away.

I got in. The seats, arranged in an inviting circle, looked like La-Z-Boys and felt likewise. Kim strapped me in. The doors closed. The helicopter lifted away from the concrete pad atop the building, and we were up in the air, the island of Manhattan growing ever smaller. This was turning out to be a very long day, and ensconced in the luxurious softness of this utmost first class seat, I felt an overwhelming need to nap. I slept. Boy, did I sleep.

Flying into Athena on a helicopter was something that everyone should experience. Seeing Athena Falls from above, I realized I'd never seen it from the top, the foamy water falling over the edge as if to say, "I give up." The gorges were even more gorgeous, the cavernous gap between two monolithic cliffs that became Autumn Creek written on the earth like a signature.

We flew past the city and headed northwest, above an endless array of brown fields. Whatever crops that had grown were now wrapped into enormous cylindrical bales, stacked into triads. A few minutes later, Lake Selene came into view to the left and Llewellyn College on the right.

We descended onto the athletic field. There were a few students running around the track, but they were quickly shooed away by Park's guards. By the time we landed, four of his men were on the grass, surrounding the helicopter.

Park tapped his gold Rolex. "3:04 p.m., Ms. Collins. Plenty of time for your class."

"I can go?" she asked.

Park nodded.

She unstrapped herself from the seat and jumped down from the open door like a rat let out of a trap. She looked back twice, as if afraid of being followed. Poor woman.

"I hope we will not have to involve her going forward," Park said.

"Because she's suffered enough," I said.

"Because I find her diffidence exhausting."

"Mr. Park," Kim said, getting off his phone. "Vera Wheeler is at the Selene Police Station."

"Good. And where is Cleopatra?"

Kim got back on his phone and texted, then waited for a response. "She's on her way back to Manhattan from Krishna."

"And my daughter?"

"She's in class."

"I would like to see Grace first. Please make sure Wheeler stays at the police station so we do not waste time locating her."

"Yes, sir," Kim said.

Park rose from his seat, so I did likewise. As we made our way out of the helicopter, he said, "Brent told me the girl who had the abortion was Penny Sykes, who was at one point living with my daughter at her dorm."

"That's correct," I said.

"So my daughter is involved as well."

"She and a male friend engineered the pregnancy at Cleo's request. They were childhood friends—Christopher Vachess?"

Park shook his head. "Running a multinational conglomerate is a time-consuming affair."

As we left the field and entered the parking lot, a car identical to the one Kim drove Collins and me to New York City pulled up, a white Mercedes with black seats. Couldn't be the same car since that one was sitting in the garage in New York City. Kim was once again behind the wheel.

"Did you guys get a bulk discount from the dealership?" I asked him after getting in the back seat with Park.

Kim ignored me. "Grace is in an English seminar taught by a Professor Lawrence Marks."

"I know Marks," I said.

"Good," Park said. "Then you can remove her from her classroom so I can talk with her."

It was an overcast day at Selene, yet again. Kim drove us down the hill and made a left onto the main campus. Park took in the scenery, which had turned browner, more desolate, since I was here a few days ago. The Llewellyn clock tower rang its half-hour rueful resonation.

"It is very quiet here," he said.

"Even with the addition of male students, it's still a very small school," I said.

"I have not been an active participant in Grace's upbringing. I've left that to my wife. Perhaps that was a mistake."

I recalled what Craig had told me about Park Industries, how it exerted its powerful financial muscle to get what it wanted. Park was serious man, a frightening man, but still, a man—with a wife and daughter he could not control.

"I was adopted by an Irish father and a Swedish mother, so I had some emotional bumps and bruises growing up. It probably would've been even more challenging if I only had the guidance of a single parent."

Park nodded to himself and kept staring out the window.

Kim pulled up at the entrance of Grover Hall. Park and I got out and climbed the twenty or so steps that led to the building's entrance.

"I find the architecture attractive," Park said. "Such as that gargoyle above."

I hadn't noticed it until he pointed it out, the stone statue shadowed by the tall elm that stood above it.

"It's a nice campus," I said.

At the top of the steps, he turned back. From here, under steely clouds, Lake Selene was like a sheet of gray ice, absolutely still. "Quite pleasing to the eye," he said

Like the class I'd attended earlier—or not attended, I did leave before it started in earnest— Professor Marks was in 107, which still resembled a large dining room. Marks sat at the head of the table nearest to the door, and there was Grace, on the opposite end of the table. When I turned to Park, I noticed he wasn't anywhere close to me. He was on the other side of the hallway, motioning for me to get her. Was it my imagination or did he seem…nervous?

I knocked and then entered.

"Well, well, well," Marks said. "Are you making your triumphant return to my classroom, Detective?"

"Not so much," I said. "I need to borrow Grace for a minute." Grace wasn't fond of seeing me, but tough tarts. I whispered into her ear. "Your father is here."

Grace, her hair tied in a tight bun, initially looked at me with suspicion, but that gave way to a smile that echoed her father's words in my brain: *youth is an automatic kind of beauty, an effortless beauty*. Unadulterated joy bloomed across her face.

"Really?" she asked.

"See for yourself," I said.

As soon as I opened the door to the hallway, she threw her arms out and ran toward him.

"Daddy!" she squealed.

"Hello, my precious gongju," he said. Korean for princess. From where I was standing, I had a good view of Park's face as his daughter sank herself into him, and the softening of his expression, of his whole body, really. It explained a lot. I wondered if his reaction to his wife would be any different.

"I can't believe you're actually here! You missed Parents' Weekend last month…you said you'd be there…"

"I was in Shanghai, unfortunately."

"You're busy, I know."

"Going forward, I promise to be present for you."

"You mean it? Really?"

"I give you my word," he said.

"Why is *she* here?" Grace asked, throwing me the evil eye.

"Ms. O'Brien is here to perform her duties. She told me about…"

He looked at me, paused, then focused back on his daughter.

"...actually, there's nothing for you to worry about."

"I wish she'd go away," Grace said.

"Today will be the last day you will see her," Park said.

"Goodie. Will you stay for dinner?"

Park cupped her face with his hands and kissed her forehead.

"Of course."

After another hug, Grace ducked back into her classroom. Park straightened his shirt and retraced his steps back to the entrance of Grover Hall.

"You look like you want to say something to me, Ms. O'Brien."

"Do I?"

"I am aware you do not have children of your own. If you did, you might understand."

"I may not have kids, but I was a kid once. And if my parents had not called me out on my screw-ups, then I would've become a different person."

"She is my only child," Park said. "And this discussion is over."

We descended the stairs outside in silence. Brent Kim was waiting for us. He opened the door for Park then entered the driver's seat.

"Whatever happened to ladies first?" I said.

"Would you rather walk to the police station?" Kim asked.

I ran around the car and got in.

82

The three cruisers in front of the Selene Police Station were all blocked in by a trio of double-parked white Mercedes sedans. A fourth car, a black BMW, was not. I recognized this one: it was Vera Wheeler's.

As we made our way to the entrance, Kim barked into his phone in short, clipped sentences. The glass door swung open and was held there by one of his guards. The precinct was like every other two-bit small-town station I'd been in, a reception desk in front, two large desks in the middle, beige filing cabinets against the far wall, and an office with a window in the back. It could've been a bank.

All four chairs were presently occupied, three of them by Selene officers, one of them by Wheeler, who was her usual coiffed self in a white silk blouse and snug white skirt. Her blonde hair was pulled back in a bun, giving her that Sharon Stone *Basic Instinct* vibe. Hovering over them were four of Park's men. The cops did not look happy. The only logical explanation was that they were all being held there by the guards, as per Park's instructions to make sure Wheeler didn't leave. I guess for some reason, the command was extended to the police force as well.

"Brent, what is this? You're holding me, and this entire police station, hostage?" Wheeler asked. Then she saw me and her exasperation turned to disgust. "Oh my god, will you please get a fucking life and leave me alone?" Her attention then went to Park, and I could see she was struggling to place him. And when she did, her entire demeanor changed. It was kind of comical, seeing her run the gamut of her emotions in such a short amount of time. Her voice turned silky smooth. "Mr. Won Ho Park?"

"That is correct."

She rose and offered her hand. He shook it.

"It's an honor to meet you. I'm not sure how much Cleo has told you about myself and Llewellyn…"

"Not much at all," Park said, "and that is my preference."

Wheeler was trying to figure out just why Park was here. She opened her mouth to say something, then stopped. That might have been the smartest move she'd made all day.

The front door opened again and in came my old friend, Officer David Girard.

"What the fuck?" he said.

"We're here to escort Ms. Vera Wheeler back to campus," Brent Kim said. "My apologies. It seems like my men may have gone beyond their call of duty."

The veins in Girard's neck stood out like cables. "You guys think you run this town, but we are the law. You understand? We're the U.S. fucking government."

"Your officers were not…"

In the time that it took for Girard's right hand to slide to his holster, which was maybe half a second, Kim picked up the stapler and flung it from where he was standing. The stapler smacked right into Girard's hand. And before he could scream out in pain, Kim had blazed past me and had Girard in an arm lock that looked like the one he'd used on Beaker back at Llewellyn's gymnasium during the basketball game. The stapler throw, the dash, the arm lock —one action flowed into one another, as if they were part of some violent modern dance.

"Ms. Wheeler," Park said. Her attention was on Girard, who was grunting under Kim's grip. "Ms. Wheeler," Park said again.

Wheeler, like everyone else, had been frozen by the furious action. "I'm sorry. Yes?"

Park handed her the sheaf of financial papers I'd brought for him to see. "Your college is experiencing cash flow issues."

She only had to look at the first few pages to know what it was. Despite the redness creeping into her cheeks, she put on her best smile. "Where did you get this?"

"Does it matter?"

Wheeler considered her response. "I suppose not."

Kim handcuffed Officer Girard and left him on the floor.

"This is not the way I'd envisioned this meeting," Wheeler said. She stood up straighter, drew in a substantial breath, and expelled it with vigor. "But it is what it is. When the world gives you lemons, you make lemonade. Mr. Park. May I please have your attention?"

Park leaned against a desk and crossed his arms. "In this analogy, I am the lemon?"

"I like your sense of humor."

"And I like your sense of flattery."

She was a stunning woman when she wanted to be. When she exuded confidence like she did now behind that playful smirk, she was that eighteen-year-old blonde runway model again.

"Your men here, when they were preventing me from leaving the station, they told me their boss was visiting the college. I didn't understand what they'd meant, but I do now. You were visiting Grace."

"I spoke with her, yes."

"And I hope you got a chance to see the campus."

"From the top step of Grover Hall, I found the view visually arresting."

Wheeler placed a hand against her heart. "That is one of my favorite spots. As lovely as that view is, you should see the one on the north side of the building. It faces the quad and in springtime, the magnolias are in bloom and they are a sight to behold."

"You paint a lovely picture," Park said.

"Your wife is one of the most beautiful women in the world. Last year *Architectural Digest* featured your Manhattan penthouse. I've read about your art collection—that Chuck Close you own is a real find, the only one from his early period that features a model who could be an actual model."

"Not many people recognize that about *Jane II*," Park said.

"I do. Because like you, I'm a believer of beauty, as a commodity, as a currency. The work we're doing in Travers Hall is just the beginning. I want to empower Llewellyn women through beauty, and the only way to achieve that is to transform the subjective aesthetic into an objective science. I know you understand, Mr. Park. The last thing I wanted was to share my ideas to you in a police station. I've been working on a multimedia presentation for over a year, one that I hope you will still let me show you."

Everything clicked, and it pissed me off.

"So instead of helping Penny," I said, "you took advantage of a terrible situation—Grace's desperate desire to appease her mother—so you could lure Cleo Park. But she wasn't your endgame because you needed more than a couple million to save your sad little beauty school. Only her husband could supply you with a bigger hoard of cash."

"Call it whatever you want," Wheeler said. "But for me, it's a cause. It's bigger than me, it's bigger than all of us. We're talking about a revolution, a paradigm shift in the way we consider the true value of beauty. You see that, don't you, Mr. Park?"

Park betrayed no emotion. But behind those dark eyes was the cold analyst, taking her words apart, weighing them on the scale of his mind.

The door to the station opened once again, and a tall man with short gray hair who looked like he was born wearing a uniform entered. Barrel-chested and military, I'd seen this guy before but couldn't remember his name.

"Chief," Officer Girard said. "You wouldn't believe what's been going…"

"Shut it," he said. Sumner, that was it, Selene's chief of police. He walked up to Park and shook his hand.

"Mr. Park," he said. "Commissioner Quirk called me directly, and he doesn't do that often. I'm Everett Sumner."

Sumner told all of his officers to take a walk except for Girard.

"Is it true a Llewellyn student is missing?" Sumner asked Girard. "Penelope Sykes?"

Girard looked to Wheeler, who rolled her eyes.

"She's fine," Wheeler said. "Causing way too many problems, not to mention that she was a danger to her own well-being."

"That's called kidnapping," Sumner said. "A felony."

"Not if it's what she wanted. Not if she signed all the proper, legal waivers to secure personal privacy as an eighteen-year-old adult."

"So she wouldn't cause any more ruckus to interrupt the Cleo Park dog-and-pony show you were putting on," I said. "You know she's got Graves' Disease? That her medication has run out, and without it, she could die?"

From the look on her face, it was obvious this was news to Wheeler, but she wasn't about to be denied now. She stood up straighter and said, "Penny's fine. Nobody's reported that she's ill."

"You actually call yourself an educator," I said. "You're sick in the head. Where the hell are you keeping Penny?"

"Well?" Wheeler said to Park. "Do I have your interest, Mr. Park?"

Park walked right up to her. In her heels, Wheeler stood a good foot taller, but it was she who seemed tiny next to Park.

"It feels as if you are using a human being as a bargaining chip."

And here it was Wheeler who surprised me.

"Whatever it takes."

Park smiled, then laughed.

"You are an interesting woman, Ms. Wheeler," Park said.

"Will you help my school?"

Either Wheeler was a few beers short of a six-pack or she had balls of steel. Maybe they were one and the same.

Park stared at her for a good few seconds. Uncomfortable seconds. Then he nodded assuredly, as if he had verified an internal calculus.

"I will help your school."

"Penny Sykes is in the basement of Travers Hall," Wheeler said. "She might be a little sedated, but again, it's what she wanted. My plan is to have a sleep lab there. A good night's sleep is the key to health, which of course goes hand in hand with beauty."

"Assist Ms. O'Brien," Park said to Kim.

While Wheeler was expounding upon the salubrious benefits of slumber, I was already on my way out the door while bringing up Josie's name in my phone's contact list.

"Let me drive you," Kim said.

"Thank you," I said.

At the station's exit, I heard Park's voice behind me.

"I will purchase Llewellyn, Ms. Wheeler. And you will no longer serve as president."

"I don't understand," Wheeler said. "You said…"

"…that I would help your school. Not *you*, Ms. Wheeler, but your school. To reiterate your own words, this is bigger than all of us. Oh no, please, think positive thoughts. Right now, the contorted frown on your face, it is highly unattractive. You owe yourself, and your movement, more than that."

Like a proper gentleman, Kim held the door open for me, and I walked through, laughing.

83

As it happened, Josie was in Auburn for work, which meant she was twenty miles away. Still, she must've driven like Jeff Gordon, because she arrived not even five minutes after we got to Travers. There was a quarter-sized mustard stain on her white blouse and her hairclip had failed to rein in her hair, but for the first time in a long, long time, she looked happy. Before I even said hello, she ran to me and gave me a bone-crushing hug.

"You found her," she said. "You found my baby."

"We're almost there," I said.

"She's in the basement? What, like in a dungeon or something?"

"I don't know. It didn't sound like it, but I have no idea what we'll see down there."

"And is this your partner?" Josie asked, gesturing to Kim.

"A pleasure to make your acquaintance, Ms. Sykes. My name is Brent Kim, and I am providing support to Ms. O'Brien at this particular moment, but we are not partners in any capacity."

"Okay," Josie said. "'No,' would've worked, too."

"I like to be as clear as possible. Shall we proceed?"

Kim led the way and we followed him to the entrance of Travers. The building looked no different than the last time I was here, the windows obscured by white paper, red and green LEDs blinking off the numerical keypad lock by the doors.

"He's very polite," Josie murmured.

"He's also got some moves," I said, feigning a punch and a kick.

"Looks the part."

To our surprise, the door swung open from the inside. Perhaps since my breaking and entering, Wheeler had increased the security,

313

because in front of us was an imposing figure in a Selene police uniform, whose arms were as large as my thighs.

"This is a restricted area," he said.

In Kim's hand was a gun, and the gun was pointed at the guard's head.

"Please take out your handcuffs and get on the ground, face first," he said.

The guard did as he was told.

"I thought you said he could do karate," Josie whispered to me.

"We were told that your daughter's health may be compromised, so time is of the essence," Kim said, apparently also gifted with amazing hearing. He cuffed the guard behind his back and around the wrought-iron bench. Then he told the guard, "My apologies. You can talk to Chief Sumner after we are through; he's aware of us and our actions. We need to enter the basement of Travers Hall to extricate a sequestered student. Can you please help us?"

The guard snorted a laugh and said nothing. Kim took one hand and put it against the guard's mouth while running his fingers up the guard's trunk-like right forearm and pressed his thumb into a spot. The guard's eyes filled with tears and his groin darkened while Kim muffled his scream. Kim took his thumb off and the guard looked drugged.

"Can you please help us?" Kim asked again.

"Room L-02. There's another guard down there."

"Thank you," Kim said.

We entered the lobby, which still looked as if somebody had taken a bucket of black paint and dumped it everywhere. The only difference was that there were more lights now, making it easier to see where we were going.

"I was here not too long ago," I said. "I can lead us down there."

We took the staircase down. As soon as Kim opened the metal door that led to the basement, we heard a voice.

"Taylor? Our shift ain't over for another hour."

The gun, the cuffs, the same. Except unlike Officer Taylor, this guy wouldn't have to change his underwear because he complied quite nicely.

"Two doors down," he said. "I gave her lunch today."

"Is she okay?" I asked.

He shrugged. "Didn't see her, but the tray from dinner last night was empty. Code is 13026. Same for the other girl."

"What other girl?" I asked.

"There's another one in L-01."

L-02 wasn't far, just two doors down. Josie grabbed my hand and squeezed it as Kim entered the code. The electronic lock buzzed and he opened the door.

"Penny?" Josie said.

The space wasn't much bigger than a college dorm room, a bed, a dresser, and a door that must've led to the bathroom. It didn't smell great, sweaty like a locker room, musty like an attic. The walls were painted gray and all the furniture was clinical white.

"Mom?" said a tiny voice.

That's all that Josie needed to hear. She ran in and found her daughter in bed. Her hair was matted and her eyes were red and bloodshot, but it was the same girl in the photograph I'd been carrying on my phone for the last month. Thinner, definitely, but not dangerously so. Josie enveloped Penny into her arms, into her body, into herself.

My baby, my baby, Josie said over and over again through tears, while her daughter repeated, *I'm sorry, I'm sorry.* Their words were becoming fused, incantatory, an intermingling of joy and relief. A white woman and an Asian girl, looking nothing alike, and yet they were undeniably mother and child. They had their work cut out for them, but right now, they were together, and that was enough. Watching their reunion, my mind drifted to two people who were no longer around, Marlene and Ed. I hoped both my old friend and my old boss were up there somewhere, resting a little bit easier now.

I turned to Kim to thank him, but he was already gone.

I left Josie and Penny to their own devices and proceeded to L-01. Was this girl a backup in case Penny didn't pan out?

L-01 looked no different than L-02 but smelled less rank, probably because whoever was here hadn't been cooped up for as long as Penny had been.

"Anybody home?" I said.

A young Asian woman was in bed. As I approached her, she opened her eyes.

"Hello," she said. "Is it already time for dinner?" She spoke, surprisingly, with a Spanish accent.

"No," I said. "Do you know where you are?"

She looked at me but wasn't really looking.

A vacant smile. Whatever she was on, it was more than what Penny had gotten. What emotional turmoil had brought this poor girl to this mess? I didn't know, but one thing for sure: she wasn't going to find any answers here.

84

"Hello…Carson?" I said to the spiky-haired blonde girl at the front desk of Tender Llewellyn Care.

"Katie," she said.

"One of these days, I'll get it right."

She buzzed me in. A week after finding Penny, I'd gotten a phone call from Faith saying she wanted to thank me in person. I was on my way back from Rochester to look up an old house survey for one of Ed's clients, so this late fall afternoon was as good a time as any to stop by.

"Siobhan!"

Before I knew what was happening, her arms were around me.

"You know, it wasn't so long ago that you trapped me in the basement of Fordham Hall with the lights out," I said.

She laughed and let me go. Her green hair was hidden under a strikingly red bandanna, but there was something else different about her.

"You look so…happy, Faith."

"That's because I am," she said, "and you're the reason why."

I followed her down the main hallway, and when her footsteps became slow and careful, mine did likewise. In one of the dorm rooms was Christopher, sound asleep. I didn't get a good look at him as Faith just wanted me to have a quick peek, but he was snoring lightly.

We backed out as quietly as we had entered. I followed Faith to her room, located across the hallway. Her room, which had been a pigsty the last time I was here, was still a pigsty. I leaned against the door frame as Faith excavated a seat on her bed.

"There he is," she said, "my Christopher."

"You like him."

"I *love* him."

"That's good," I said, not knowing what else to say, really. I was glad he was in a better place, but he'd also been a huge pain in the ass not that long ago.

"It's more than good, Siobhan. Not only did you save Penny, but you saved Christopher, too. When he confessed to you about what he did to Penny, that was his rock bottom, and now with all that horror behind him, he can be a person again here in TLC."

"He transferred out of Lenrock?"

"Christopher's not going to get the personal attention he needs from that indifferent behemoth of a school. It was one of the stipulations of his release from the hospital after his suicide attempt, that he got the best psychological care possible while still pursuing his undergraduate education."

Looking at Faith, I thought about Kathy Bates in *Misery*, playing the crazy nurse who'd kept James Caan captive. Maybe that's a little harsh, because Faith had a good heart and wasn't insane, but nonetheless, there was something desperate here.

"How are things here, without your mother?"

"You mean without our president."

"Sure."

"Like Christopher, Llewellyn, too, has hit her rock bottom. Now that President Wheeler is gone, we can begin the process of healing."

Could two broken people mend each other? Maybe. I wished Faith and Christopher the best of luck and left for the lobby.

"Goodbye, Katie," I said to the girl at the desk.

"It's Carson. Katie's shift ended five minutes ago."

85

"It's really happening," Craig said.

I'd just sat down at Elkwood when he handed me his phone. It was Friday night, all the diners grateful to put another workweek to bed. A couple next to us were already chomping down their meal, both digging into the tempeh and grits special.

The headline from *The Binghamton Bulletin*:

Park's Purchase of Llewellyn College Unanimously Approved by Trustees

I scanned the article and saw that Vera Wheeler would no longer serve as president of Llewellyn but rather as Chief Educating Officer of the Park Educational Institute: "I'm very excited about this new opportunity that will arise from having strong financial support for Llewellyn College. The future has never been more enthralling."

"I'm surprised Wheeler's still involved, after what you told me about the police station encounter with her and Park," Craig said.

I handed the phone back to Craig. "Park said he was a man of his word; I'm glad to see it's true. Before I left Llewellyn after recovering Penny, he told me what happened in the basement of Travers would never happen again, and that he would personally make sure Wheeler is held accountable for her actions."

"So he makes her Chief Educating Officer?"

"It's a made-up title. She's not in actual jail, but this'll have to be close enough." I tapped on the photo on the newspaper story, a shot of Broadhurst Hall. "Can somebody just buy a college?"

"It's not something you see every day, but yeah, it's a thing. It even happens to state entities, like when New York's Regents College became Excelsior a while back. Higher education is, like everything else in our capitalistic world, a business, and if investors think they can make money..."

"I wonder if that's why Park bought it. They've excavated another huge hole on the south side of campus. To match the one in the north, I guess. I don't know what his plan is, but the man's got one. Anyway, one interesting bit of news deserves another." While I fished out my folder from my backpack, the waitress came over to take our drinks order. A no-brainer, as the Moscow Mule was the five-dollar drink of the day.

I pushed two pieces of paper toward Craig.

"You must've done some good old-fashioned digging through public records."

"Wasn't easy, as they'd both changed their names twice through two marriages, not to mention they were foreign ones, South Korea and Ukraine."

"I was about to say there isn't much I can understand here outside of numbers."

"That's right," I said, and smiled. "But that's all you need."

Craig scrutinized the two birth certificates, Ahn Ga In on the left, Vera Breznova on the right, Cleo Park and Vera Wheeler as they were born. Craig chuckled.

"So it wasn't plastic surgery or Botox or voodoo that kept these two ladies looking so young. They just turned forty!"

"Wheeler lied about her age because she'd developed quickly and wanted to model when she turned eleven. Not sure why Cleo pretended to be older—it's weird as women are known to do the opposite."

"Weird does fit her profile."

"I can't imagine Park doesn't know, so there must be a reason."

Our drinks came, a pair of copper cups with a lime garnish. Like our neighbors, we both ordered the special.

"May I propose a toast?" Craig said.

"Of course."

"To you solving your first case, and for me for my first week of cognitive behavior therapy."

We clanged. We drank. Ginger beer, vodka, and simple syrup: sweetness with a kick.

"That's great, Craig. But…"

"But what?"

"You and me…we get along, but…I just don't want you to be doing this because you think you and I are going to…oh jeez, I should just shut up."

Craig reached over and held my hand. "You're just being you, low expectations. And I'm just being me, ever the optimist. It's okay, Siobhan, I understand. Maybe you and I won't work out. But then again, maybe we will. All I know is that in order for me to move forward, I have to do this work, and it's good. It's hard, but it's good. But enough about me and my complexes, what about you? Are you still on the fence?"

"About what?"

"Well, not too long ago, when I'd looked over your paperwork to take over the agency, you weren't sure."

I took another sip. "Let's just say I'm surer than before."

"Your email from this morning mentioned the Krishna folks got in touch with you," Craig said.

"That was an easy one. I showed excerpts of the amrita video to Dharma, who communicated it with the rest of the Krishna Roots, the old-timers. As much as they still love their guru, they realized it wasn't going to work with him. So for the first time, the two factions are working together, old Krishna and corporate Krishna, which is good because although they aren't as financially strapped as Llewellyn was, after the firing of Michelle West and her cohorts, they desperately need new leadership."

"Do we dare hope better days for them?"

"Hope is free," I said, and we toasted for a second time. "I'm sorry I kept you waiting, by the way."

"I got your text, so no worries. How are Penny and Josie doing?"

"Better after signing for their UPS delivery. They got the check from Park Industries for two million dollars."

"Right on schedule."

"Which reminds me, they wanted me to thank you for looking over their non-disclosure agreement."

"Thankful enough to give me 5%?"

"Probably not."

"Damn," Craig said, feigning disappointment. "And what about Maria, the other gal you found in the basement of Travers Hall?"

"The Korean girl born on Mallorca of all places—she's on a plane back home as we speak. Her exchange program with Lenrock is, shall we say, over."

"I still don't understand how Wheeler convinced her that being drugged in a windowless room would help her."

"Her fiancé broke up with her…via text."

"Yikes."

"They were supposed to get married this summer."

"I can see why she might have been depressed."

As soon as I drained the rest of my drink, my purse rang. On my phone, the caller read as BRENT KIM. I couldn't remember him ever calling me, and I definitely did not have him as a contact.

"Take it, but don't be too long because here comes our food."

The waitress, balancing one dish on her forearm and another on her right hand while carrying a pitcher of water with her left, set our dishes in front of us.

"Brent?"

"Hello, Ms. O'Brien. Apologies for interrupting your evening."

"That's okay. I don't remember adding you into my phonebook."

"You did not. Park Industries owns and operates your cell tower, so we can push certain notifications through the carrier."

"Is that, like, legal?"

"It's in your end-user agreement, the finest of fine prints. Regardless, Mr. Park would like to talk to you."

"What about?"

"It regards a friend's son. And since Mr. Park believes you to be a competent investigator, he'd like to recommend you. Can you be available tomorrow morning at nine?"

I told him yes and hung up.

"What was that?" Craig asked.

"I think," I said, "that's my next job."

Acknowledgments

A heartfelt thanks goes out to my early readers, who suffered at the hands of my clumsy prose and dead-end plotting: Dawn S. White, Ava Sloane, E.A. Durden, Michael Bahler, and Stewart O'Nan. You're all aces.

I'm especially grateful to Madison Smartt Bell, who not only offered editorial guidance but lead me to my incredible editor, Chantelle Aimée Osman, and the rest of the team at Agora/Polis Books. Thank you to Chantelle and Jason Pinter for taking a chance on this "literary" writer's first mystery novel.

Lastly, words can't do justice to the dedication of my agent, Priya Doraswamy, who continued to believe in this book when even I lost faith.

And actually, one more thing, and maybe the most important thing. I believe creativity to be fragile, and I don't mean in some precious, I-need-my-perfect-cup-of-tea type of way. I may have written all the words to this novel, but they only got written because I have a loving wife, a fantastic family, devoted pets, a generous mentor, and an understanding boss. So much has to go right for this book to exist, and I know full well how lucky I am. So thank you Dawn, Mom, Sunny, Bill, Chung, Emeric, Ginny, Lily, Mac, Stew, and Tom Valva, for all your graces.

About the Author

Sung J. Woo's short stories and essays have appeared in *The New York Times*, PEN/Guernica, and *Vox*. He has written two novels, *Love Love* and *Everything Asian*, which won the 2010 Asian Pacific American Librarians Association Literature Award (Youth category).

He lives in Washington, New Jersey.

Follow him at @SJWoo.

CPSIA information can be obtained
at www.ICGtesting.com
Printed in the USA
LVHW021000300620
659313LV00001B/40